LESS THAN
CHARMING

LESS THAN
CHARMING

REBECCA A. DEMAREST

Parkhurst Brothers Publishers

MARION, MICHIGAN

www.parkhurstbrothers.com

Parkhurst Brothers books are distributed to the trade through the Chicago Distribution Center, and may be ordered through Ingram Book Company, Baker & Taylor, Follett Library Resources, and other book industry wholesalers. To order from Chicago Distribution Center, phone 1-800-621-2736 or send a fax to 800-621-8476. Copies of this and other Parkhurst Brothers Inc., Publishers titles are available to organizations and corporations for purchase in quantity by contacting Special Sales Department at our home office location, listed on our web site. Manuscript submission guidelines for this publishing company are available at our web site.

Printed in the United States of America

First Edition, 2016

2016 2017 2018 2019 2020   16 15 14 13 12 11 10 9 8 7 6 5 4 3 2 1

Library of Congress Cataloging in Publication Data: [Pending]

ISBN: Hardback 978-1-62491-070-8

ISBN: e-book   978-1-62491-071-5

Parkhurst Brothers Publishers believes that the free and open exchange of ideas is essential for the maintenance of our freedoms. We support the First Amendment of the United States Constitution and encourage all citizens to study all sides of public policy questions, making up their own minds. Closed minds cost a society dearly.

Cover and interior design by Rebecca A. Demarest

Proofread by Linda Parkhurst

Acquired for Parkhurst Brothers Inc., Publishers and edited by Ted Parkhurst

062016

For my husband, Jason;
with bacon or without.

TABLE OF CONTENTS

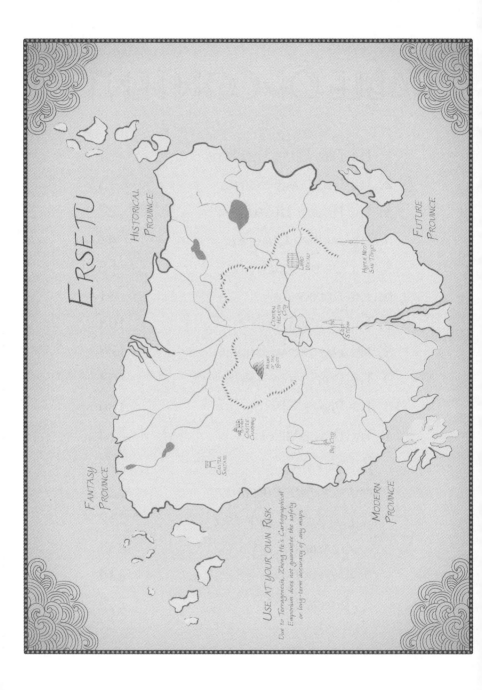

ERSETU

HISTORICAL PROVINCE

FUTURE PROVINCE

FANTASY PROVINCE

MODERN PROVINCE

USE AT YOUR OWN RISK

Due to Terragnosis, Zhang He's Cartographical
Emporium does not guarantee the safety
or long-term accuracy of any maps.

THE FREE PRESS TWO STEP

I had spent all day crafting my plan of attack. Flowcharts of possible strategies for the confrontation and pre-planned arguments for any form of defense my opponent could offer me were scattered across my desk. I thought I was ready, but I was not prepared for the vehemence and determination of my opponent.

"Because it's too dangerous, Sophia, that's why, and I wouldn't be able to live with it if you were hurt, again, pursuing a story for *The Daily Scribe!* Remember the pumpkin doping scandal and the hot water that got you in?" Geppetto sat on the edge of his desk with a sigh. "We almost lost you to the fertilizer smugglers from the advanced sciences division."

I leaned forward in my chair, bracing my arms on my knees, trying to figure out a better way to combat the toymaker's argument. "But I was fine in the end, and this is different. A little white-collar crime investigation about possible fraud in the finances for the big anniversary celebration. Nobody can spend such an exorbitant amount of money in such a short time. The worst I can expect are some paper cuts and a shoving match with an overly protective secretary. You know I can handle those."

"The Charmings can spend that much money at once, and frequently have in the past. You should see the list of parties they are preparing; the menus alone..." Geppetto got a dreamy look in his eye before returning to reality. "No, I won't sanction an investigation. Besides, there's a ballroom dancing competition coming up next week, and you're our foremost expert."

What my boss was obliquely referring to was the decades I had spent dancing the night away with my eleven sisters at a magical party hosted by twelve enchanted princes at the end of a dank, underground passageway. It had driven our poor father to madness as he tried to figure out how our shoes got danced to pieces every night. It didn't matter that I hadn't *been* dancing in a century, everyone still assumed I was a dancing princess at heart, so I got stuck with every dratted dancing and shoe-related assignment to cross Geppetto's desk.

I tried to think of a way around his objections to my proposed story idea, but his mind was obviously made up. It wasn't fair. Geppetto didn't treat any of his male reporters this way, except perhaps Pinocchio, who couldn't even be trusted to run the printing press without screwing something up.

Sure enough, there was a loud ker-thunk, followed by a twanging sound, and the boy's high reedy voice calling, "Sophia! Um...help?"

I sighed again and shook out my skirts as I stood. "Don't think I'm done trying to convince you."

"Maybe once the big celebration is over and it won't be such an embarrassment to the Charmings to have you poking about in things. We will revisit the issue then. But for now—" Geppetto ripped the top page off his yellow legal pad and handed it to me. "The dancing competition in the 1940s district in the Modern Province. Go."

I saluted my mentor, throwing as much irony into the motion as possible, then went to bail out the previously wooden boy. Days like this only served to remind us that his agility hadn't improved much despite the cosmetic changes to his dovetail joints and spring-mounted eyes. They also reinforced my wish for Geppetto to give in and buy a digital printing press from one of the more modern story provinces. The jammed block of type Pinocchio had managed to wedge into the Gutenberg-style press was thoroughly stuck, and it took quite a bit of delicate prying with a shim to get under it. As it popped loose, I nearly took off a piece of my finger along with the recalcitrant metal. I dropped the pieces in their respective slots on the tray of type and handed the shim back to Pinocchio to finish clearing the tray as I worked to get the ink off my hands.

His childlike fingers danced across the trays, lining up the type for their next headline, *Hansel Wins with 40 Pound Pumpkin.* "You're a miracle worker, Sophia."

I patted him on the shoulder before heading back out to my desk in the bullpen. It was one of several in the crowded workspace, jammed together to take as much advantage of the space as possible. "No, just clever. Say, hun, who's got the assignment to cover the anniversary celebration in Central Hearth City?"

"I think Father gave it to Aurora, why?"

I tried to hide the small smile of victory I could feel curling around my lips. "Simple curiosity. I could use some backup on this dancing competition crap, and I needed to know who would still be in town."

While *The Daily Scribe* was a popular paper here in the Fairy Tale Province, it hardly ever printed what I would consider to be real news. Over in the Modern Province, you got the news stories from the Human World since new characters with knowledge of modern events were constantly being written. It was interesting and eventful. But all of our stories centered around who grew the biggest crops at the fair, which prince was sleeping with which princess, and the occasional story about some tragic accident. What we didn't report on was all of the juicy tidbits about how some of the ex-royalty managed to support themselves in the style they were accustomed to. Aurora had some particularly salacious tendencies that were going to work in my favor today.

I found the fair-haired beauty at her desk, chewing on a recycled paper pencil and scowling at the yellow sheet of legal paper in front of her. I plopped down on the edge of her desk. "Well if it isn't my favorite narcoleptic! How's it spinning, sleepy?"

"That gets funnier every time, Sophia." She grimaced and worked a folder out from under my embroidered skirts.

"I know, but I can't resist. You make the best faces." She stuck her tongue out at me, but I ignored it. "I wanted to come see how you were getting on in preparation for your story in Central Hearth City."

She broke out in a grin and leaned back in her chair, crossing her hands behind her head in a most un-princess-like gloat. "That's right, didn't you want this assignment? Terribly sorry, someone must have let slip to Geppetto about your plans to ambush the financiers. I guess I'll have to suffer through covering the largest party of the century — strike that — in the last five centuries. It isn't every day you get the 500 year anniversary of the Nursery down at the Hearth, now is it?"

"I know, but it's such a shame. I've got a lovely piece here that's right up your alley, a dancing competition. No chance of spindles or anything." I waved my sheet at her, and she laughed.

"Why would I want to trade assignments with you? I will be spending a week in the largest and most metropolitan city in our world, getting dolled up and going to all the parties, while you sit on some hard bench and watch bumpkins pretend they can dance."

"I don't know. I guess I'm afraid that while you're gone, someone might clue in your dear Prince Philip to your moonlighting over in New Hollywood." I smiled as all the color drained from her face. Everyone knew that Prince Philip was a true traditionalist, eschewing anything technological from after his original creation. However, Sleeping

Beauty had a prime opportunity to contract out as a dead body in the film and TV program reproductions our world produced. All her practice of playing dead, courtesy of her origin story, made her a surprisingly life-like corpse on screen, and it paid well enough to keep her in the fancy dresses she so adored, but was terrified to make for herself. If Philip ever found out she was playing with film...

"You wouldn't dare."

"I can't talk if I'm out of town." I held out my assignment detail sheet to her, and waited for her to make up her mind. It didn't take long.

"You are the worst princess, you know that, Sophia?"

I shrugged, grinning. "What can you expect from the unnamed 12th princess? I've got to make do."

I took Aurora's sheet and scanned the list of suggested interviewees, noting that Geppetto had already sent a letter ahead requesting an interview with the First Mother. "This should do me. And he shouldn't even notice until I'm well back. Unless someone should happen to squeal..." I raised an eyebrow at Aurora.

She scowled, but made the motion of zipping her lips. She slouched into her chair and started ignoring me, which I took as good a cue as any to leave. My battle was won, the prize acquired. I know better than to kick an opponent when they're down. It'll only make them that much more gleeful about kicking you back when it's their turn.

I folded the paper and tucked it into my handbag before heading for the door. This is what I lived for: the excitement of new adventure. When I'd grown bored with sitting around my father's castle all day and going dancing with my sisters night after night, I had gone looking for something more to excite me. I'd heard a travelling storyteller tell a story from Big City in the Modern Province about an investigative journalist and had become enamored with the concept. A beautiful woman turning over the rocks and shining a light on the scum that was under them, fighting against injustice and crime with her wits and her words—I was smitten. Unfortunately, most, if not all, of our scum were safely tucked away in various institutions for the criminally or unstably written. They were never given the opportunity to join the general population after they came out of the hearthfires.

The lack of intrigue, mystery, and mayhem hadn't stopped Geppetto from hiring me, however. He had started the first newspaper in our Province because he had gotten tired of spending day after day carving toys. He'd always loved gossip, and the moveable type presses that had started to become popular made it easier than ever for him to spread the word. He needed a writer or two to help him cover all the big balls and events and he took me under his wing. For the last hundred years or so, that was all I wrote about: dancing, dining, and who was trying on whose glass slipper, if you know what I mean.

The best part about this assignment was that I would get to travel. I hadn't been back to Central City since they dedicated the new incubation wing, almost 200 years ago. I had to hurry home and pack since it would take me more than a day to get to the city by coach, and my first appointment was a little too soon for comfort.

There was a clatter and yelp from the press room as I went out the front door, and a faint "I'm okay!" rang out. Geppetto's remonstrations thundered behind me as I went forth to do deadly battle with the social elite.

👑

It took me a little while to decide whether my regal travel dresses or my more practical trousers would be better suited for the interviews coming up. I finally went with the trousers since I would be at the First Hearth—there was a large enough mix of people of every genre there that it didn't much matter what you wore. There were women in virtually nothing who hailed from the earliest—and, to be honest, the latest—stories, as well as prim women from the Islamic Revolution who looked down on any woman who wasn't covered head to toe, front and back. Then there were the non-human characters whose biology was so foreign, there was no way to tell if they were underdressed or not.

So I packed one princessey dress full of ruffles and beading, a beige linen suit and a couple business blouses along with my low patent leather pumps, donned my travel leathers for the trip, and was done just in time to catch the afternoon coach to Hearth Center. Thankfully, it was still warm enough that they were running the open-air cabs, so the pungent and earthy smell of the four dwarves headed into the capital with me wasn't too overwhelming. They ignored me for the most part, arguing over how they were going to present their case on a mining dispute with a neighboring clan over who bore responsibility for the wastewater contaminating their border river.

Before nightfall, we pulled off the road at a small inn that had decided that modern convenience was a grand thing. It had hot and cold running taps in all the rooms, for which I was grateful after the dusty ride. I had tried to convince my father to hire someone to put a shower in my suite at the castle, but no. I relished the thought that I was going to be spending a week in the most up-to-date city in all of the provinces and entertained myself through dinner making a list of things I wanted to buy to bring home with me—some of the new high-yield solar-powered charging stations, a cell phone, and, if the price had come down, a satellite uplink for Internet since the Fairy Tale District was not wired for high-speed access.

After freshening up, I settled in at a table in the dining room between a group of elves and a trough for a manticore, to eavesdrop on the local characters while partaking of the leftover-bits-from-yesterday stew the innkeep had provided. The main door to the inn swung open and the figure of a storyteller in her multicolored cloak took in the room before moving her staff, carved to look like a scroll, and letting the door close behind her. The room quieted as we watched her walk to the barkeep and bend down low enough to whisper in the imp's ear. He nodded, hopped down from his stool behind the bar and arranged a chair next to the hearth at the front of the room. The storyteller settled herself and several of us raised our hand to the bar, signaling our willingness to keep the teller's drink of choice flowing for the evening as we shuffled our chairs to a better position for listening.

After a moment of staring into the hearthfire, the storyteller threw off her cloak and turned to the room. "May your story fall on listening ears."

"And may those ears hear," we responded, dutifully. I was eager to hear what this teller had in mind for the evening. Ever since I was written, I had adored listening to the storytellers, characters that had dedicated their lives to the Storyteller. Regardless of what faiths we had been written with, the Storyteller held the loyalty and love of most characters and his emissaries among us were treated with reverence.

She settled into the chair at the hearth and waited for the rustles in the room to subside. "I am Kith, teller of stories, and I bring to you tonight a *Tale of Beginnings.*" A murmur ran through the room at her unorthodox choice but we quieted quickly under her glare. Her opening had been standard but her choice, the *Tale of Beginnings*, was usually reserved for induction of new characters into their provinces, after they had gone through the retraining program to get them used to the fact that their life wasn't scripted anymore, and, oh yeah, by the way, none of their magic or futuristic techno-info was going to do them a lick of good here. It was a story that was reserved for what passed as children among us and her choice of it this evening was out of character.

"Before there was imagination, before there was story, there was Man. Before teller and character, there was Woman. Man and Woman lived and hunted in a desolate world, devoid of the beauty of imagination. Their lives moved forward, without meaning, without purpose but to eat and be warm and mate. There was nothing in their minds concerning beauty or enlightenment. They spent every night around their fire to stay warm, but their minds were silent. And then Man spoke. 'Would it not be good,' Man said, 'If we were to kill a beast big enough to eat for a moon cycle?' Woman thought about it for a moment, and replied, 'To kill a beast so large would require a great hunter. We have no such hunter among us.' For the first time, Man and Woman speculated. They wondered what would happen...if.

"'What if,' Man said, 'We were to have a daughter, a daughter so strong she could pull down the trees to make her spear? What if she could throw so hard as to pierce the very heart of the greatest beast? She would never be hungry for she would never miss.' And from the imagination of Man and Woman, the First Character was born. From the sparks of the First Fire and the lips of humans she was born. Their imagination twined through the embers and flames and found a spark to carry their thoughts here and from it, the First Character grew.

"She was not alone long, for as Man and Woman learned the comfort and strength of story, there came about a change in them. A division of Hunter from Teller, a mantle they wore when they sat around the Fire, and from this division was born the Storyteller. he was amassed from many fires and many tellings, with the power of imagination ingrained in his very bones.

"As time passed, Man and Woman learned to stretch and expand their imagination. Characters of all types started to form in the sparks of the First Fire and, together, First Character and Storyteller brought them gently into this world, to live a life created by Man and Woman, welcomed by First Character, and sustained by the voice of the Storyteller."

The teller was silent for a couple of moments, staring at the fire rather than the room. The room stayed utterly still until she whispered, "May your story end well."

"And may the next begin," we replied. There was a scraping of chairs as people returned to whatever it was they had been engaged in before the storyteller entered; I turned back to my shopping list, trying to shake the feeling that the teller had been staring at me the whole time. I rarely needed or attracted attention from tellers, as my story was still told by humans and their imagination sustained me. It was the job of the tellers to tell the stories of characters whose tales had been forgotten by humanity, to keep those characters from fading, even though their support paled in comparison to true, human, tellings. It was at least enough to keep a character alive, if not well.

It was said that the Storyteller, the first storyteller, was capable of keeping a character from fading long after the humans forgot about them with a single recitation of their tale. No one had seen the Teller for several centuries and some of the newer characters treated the stories of the Teller like those of any of the other religions—a polite societal fiction. There was no denying that the storytellers that travelled and manned the Hearths sustained us, but there was little faith left for the Teller, himself. Most assumed the Teller had faded long ago, along with the First Character.

I was pulled out of my reverie by a thump as the teller dropped her staff against the table and sat in the empty chair across from me. "I hope you don't mind, there isn't a lot of room about tonight."

"Of course not, teller, my table is yours. Would you care for some dinner?" I carefully trimmed my quill and put away my list. Tellers were usually solitary people, so I wasn't sure what this one wanted by actively seeking me out. However, it was always best to be polite since you never knew when you would need your story to be reinforced. That awful Barbie movie a few years ago had done wonders to boost my overall presence, but my story wasn't exactly popular anymore.

"That would be lovely, thank you. I've been on the road all day, journeying to Central City. I am absolutely famished."

I signaled to the barkeep for a second meal and studied the teller in front of me. She seemed young for a teller, not much older than my late adolescent appearance, but that didn't say much considering I was well over 400 years old. The Grimms may have written my story down in 1810, but my sisters and I had been dancing in people's imaginations long before that. This teller, though—there was something about her eyes that made her seem even older than that. Her skin was dark, with the sun-weathered quality you got with characters written into Saharan adventure novels. She blithely ignored my scrutiny and finished adjusting her cape and robes to a comfortable position. After a moment, I couldn't stand her silence.

"Was there a particular reason you wished to sit with me tonight, Teller Kith?"

"Oh, no, Sophia, you just seemed a friendly face in this crowd of ruffians. Besides, I wouldn't want to have one of these poor farmers offering to buy me a meal. They shouldn't have to spend their hard-earned money on me." Her eyes were bright with mirth and subtle calculation, but her smile barely touched her lips.

A small laugh escaped me, and I nodded my head in acquiescence. "Fair enough, teller. Your business is your own and you are always welcome to a meal at my table. I must say though, it was an interesting choice for tonight's tale."

Kith quirked an eyebrow at me. "You mean, why didn't I take the conventional route and tell for someone in the room? I felt that some in here needed to be reminded of a few things, that's all."

I grumbled about that not answering anything and she laughed, a true full laugh that left a smile on her face. Sheepish, I toyed with my bowl of stew until hers was placed before her by a shy young barmaid. "Thank you, Julia." Kith said. "Could I trouble you for a glass of water as well?"

"Of course, miss...teller. I'll be right back." She scampered back to the bar and hastily started wiping down a glass.

I frowned as a thought struck me. It wasn't so unusual for a teller to know the names of the royalty of the lands she passed through, but I wondered if she knew the barmaid. "You've been through here before?"

"No, the last time I walked these roads, there wasn't even an inn." Kith dug into her stew with relish, making a pleased noise at the taste and warmth, despite the unrecognizability of half of the ingredients.

"Do you know Julia from somewhere else then?"

"Heavens, no. It's a teller's responsibility to know her stories, wouldn't you say? Julia's a wonderful shepherd's daughter. Good to her parents." Julia returned with the glass of water and the teller laid a friendly hand on her arm. "Thank you, child. May your story be heard." The girl flushed and stammered out a thank you before rushing back to the bar.

My chair creaked as I leaned back, watching Julia go. There was something definitely off with this teller but I still couldn't put my finger on it. "I have to admit, I've never met a teller that has such an instinctive grasp on character's stories. You're a first."

"Perhaps you need to spend more time with good tellers. But that's beside the point. You're traveling to Central City yourself, are you not?" Her stew was almost half gone at this point, and I wanted to get to the root of who this Kith was before she finished up and turned in for the night.

"Yes, to cover the anniversary. And you? Why are you headed into the Central City?" I didn't particularly care that it was considered rude to ask why the itinerant tellers went where they went. It was widely assumed they followed the Storyteller's will and it was left at that.

Kith was wiping the inside of her bowl with a crust of bread. "I have business there with someone. At the Hearth, as it so happens. Perhaps I'll see you again."

"Speaking of which, there are still a few spaces left in my carriage if you'd rather hitch a ride the rest of the way tomorrow. You'd have to share the space with some litigious dwarves, but they're not all that bad."

The teller's empty glass clanked on the table as she put it down. "Thank you, but I believe I will pass. The walking does me a world of good. Till we meet again, Sophia. May your story end well."

I knew when I was being dismissed for the night, and I allowed myself a small moue of disappointment before standing and giving a bow to the teller as she retired for the evening. "And may your next begin, Teller Kith. Have a pleasant evening."

"I already have, love, I already have." She laid her hand on my arm briefly before making her way carefully through the throng, murmuring greetings to those she passed, blessing characters and clasping hands all the way to the door.

The next morning, my coach left bright and early, all of the dwarves complaining bitterly about the quality of the ale at the inn as it appeared to have left them with sour dispositions and even more sour breath. I couldn't help but laugh to myself at their synchronized moans as we ran over ruts in the road. They soon dropped off back to sleep and I was given a pleasant morning to myself, reading the newest novel by John Grisham. The freshest stories were always widely circulated among the provinces to satisfy our voracious appetites.

There wasn't a character among us who didn't love and crave the narrative word, considering it is the stuff we were made of. When new characters sparked into life, the first thing the caretakers at the Hearth did was gather everyone associated with a new work and ask them for the details of their stories, which were then set down in prose to be shared with the kingdom at large. The distribution of their story to the other characters helped give them an extra boost of stability, and when they were integrated into the society at large, they would find a warm welcome from the people who already knew all about their background, motivation, and deepest darkest corners of their psyche. It made it hard to keep secrets.

Most characters, myself included, carried very small editions of their favorite versions of their own personal stories as a talisman or keepsake. I do love the way the Grimm brothers wrote us, and last Christmas, my father had presented my sisters and I with matching leather-bound books the size of matchbooks, with glorious little illustrations. I wore mine on a chain around my neck, tucked into my bodice. I fiddled with it as I read the Grisham novel, running the chain through my fingers. It wasn't until Central City was coming into view that the dwarves started to wake up.

I put my books away and leaned out the side of the carriage to call up to the driver and ask for permission to sit up front with him to watch the city rise before us. He grudgingly agreed and I swung up to sit beside him. As we came around the last bend of the forest, the city sprawled before us in all its storied glory.

👑

THE OLD FLAME-ENCO

Central Hearth City appeared, if possible, even larger than the last time I had seen it. Admittedly, that had been a very long time ago, before the boom of pulp fiction and self-published authors had swollen our numbers. The city sat at the headwaters of four rivers, with the First Fire itself on the shore at the confluence, and the enormous First Hearth built around it, dominating the skyline.

From there, the city sprawled out in all directions, a hodge-podge of every conceivable generation of architecture and technology. Well, technology of the modern world. If a human can't imagine the mechanics of *how* something works, it doesn't function here. There is no magic, no laser rifles, no intergalactic spaceships, all of which makes things harder for the characters that come from the fantasy and science fiction books. Characters from historical and modern fiction can at least surround themselves with the familiar. I'd heard stories about some powerful magic users who break down completely when they find out that their entire mode of existence no longer functions.

This city supported not only the Hearth and the complex of buildings dedicated to incubating and acclimatizing new characters to our world, but the Market as well. There are markets in every town, but they don't hold a candle to the Central Market. It is a huge bazaar full of street vendors hawking things such as medieval ball gowns in front of eight-story department stores, or iPhone knockoffs out of pushcarts drawn by goats. Every type of shopping experience, every item you could want from any of the provinces, can be found in the Central Market.

⚔

As we entered the outskirts of the city, the buildings around us became denser until, after about 20 minutes, one could comfortably say we were in the city proper. Our carriage shared the streets with 1920s buggies and the latest model of Tesla electric cars. Conversations around us were carried on in various languages, including everything from Japanese and English to Klingon and Elvish. I could understand about half of the conversations—even though I'd been conceived of in a German mind, my story, and therefore I, had been translated so many times that I had lost count. Not into Klingon, thank goodness. That particular language I picked up during a brief romance with a Red Shirt who had wandered through our kingdom years ago. He was boring, as he had been written without any depth and hadn't been around long enough to mature yet. I suppose it had been the promise of modern technology and attitudes that had drawn me to him.

We had entered into the city by way of one of the main axis roads, which bisected the city and met at the First Hearth building. They were the main thoroughfares out of the central land to the various provinces, each based on a particular genre. The time-tested distinction suited most characters, as they were simply more comfortable in environs that were similar to those of their creation. Thus, there were the Fantasy and Futuristic, Historical Fiction, and Modern Fiction Provinces, with many independent counties and cities within those provinces. For instance: the Historical Province was further broken down by areas of time period, the cutoff date for "historical" being the advent of the moveable type press; Fantasy and Futuristic were a web of independent monarchies and city-states, with occasional minor skirmishes breaking out between the various subgenres and cult classics; Modern Fiction broke down along the lines of current world politics, always a fun negotiation.

As we started to approach the rivers at the center of the city, our street merged into the Corridor of Religion. When religiously oriented characters first arrive, they are usually incensed by this street. Places of worship line both sides of the street for every conceivable religion, from Buddhism to Christianity to The Great Flying Spaghetti Monster to The Force. The real kicker is that you can actually meet the prophets and gods of each religion face to face. The conversation always goes something like this:

"But [my personal] religion is real! It isn't made up. I know, because I'm from a realistic fiction book! How come [insert deity's name] is here? He's not some character from a story!"

"Think about it. Even if the original stories of your religion are true, how many times have they been altered? How many authors, sincere adherents or laymen, have altered or made up new sets of stories?"

"That makes a lot of sense. And now I can go ask [deity] some questions that have always bothered me."

"Absolutely, it's encouraged. [Deity's name] is a pretty nice [guy/gal/thing]. I'd stay away from the Klingon temple though. They're a pretty rough crowd if you don't know your way around a Bat'leth."

Usually the character would attend a few worship ceremonies, have a conversation or two with their spiritual leader, and then go on their way thoroughly disillusioned with whatever religion it was they were originally following. There is something about a laid-back man with long hair and sandals completely devoid of the ability to do miracles that can take the wind out of one's religious sails.

After we passed the last of the temples, we reached the Libraries. Right before the Hearth buildings, there is a ring of Libraries (each dedicated to a specific subgenre, with architecture to match) that hold the stories of every character ever conceived. Thus you had a ring of more than 20 buildings in all sorts of styles from ancient Grecian temples to medieval castles to clean-lined buildings Steve Jobs would be proud of, all nestled together in a circle around the Hearth administration buildings. They are our true places of worship. It's where we come to trace our literary lineages, learn about each other, and reinforce our very existences by sharing our stories amongst ourselves.

If any particular story interests you, you can request a copy from the storytellers who mind the library. When I was first told, you had to wait a month or two for a teller to hand-scribe a copy for you, and it would cost you a pretty penny to have it bound. Thankfully, the technology for print-on-demand had taken hold quickly on our side of the fourth wall, and now you could have a copy of almost any book by the end of the day for only a couple dollars.

Once through the ring of book-stuffed buildings, we reached the buildings of the Hearth itself. They were strikingly different from the libraries. Where the genre buildings tended to sprawl, the Hearth buildings were built on vertical lines. They contained administration offices, acclimation centers, and more therapists than I think are strictly necessary. The building that contains the Hearth itself is the tallest building in our world, and is a hybrid of art deco skyscraper sensibilities and slick modern-glass lines. Our carriage pulled onto a side street where a livery had a stablehand ready to take charge of the horses, letting all of the passengers disembark. Only authorized hearth vehicles (all small electric vehicles with little horsepower and silent operation) were allowed further into the mile square complex around the Hearth, so we would go the rest of the way on foot or by pedi-taxi.

I took my leave of the driver, made sure to give him a substantial tip, then patted one of the dwarves on the head with a "I'm sure it'll be a short trial, you're all such impressive litigators," and danced away before he could take a swing at me with his pick. I couldn't help myself; they were so ridiculously stereotypical on the ride down. I had to get at least one jibe in.

Six very different hotels were nestled within the complex at the Hearth, and I made my way to the Boar and Unicorn, a delightful, old-style inn with electricity, clean linens, and hot and cold running water. I'd called ahead from the inn the night before and booked myself a room for a week, to ensure I'd have all the time I needed to interview everyone on my list.

The revolving door at the front of the building was new, but I liked how it had been worked into the traditional open-beam design of the place. The Boar and Unicorn might look as though it had been designed and built in the early 1600s, but it had over 200 rooms and was four stories high. To cater to the clientele who were still uncomfortable with technology, it had no elevators, making higher floors undesirable to most visitors. You had the usual choice of single queen, king, or double queen, but you also had your pick of Medieval, Dated, or Contemporary levels of technology within the rooms themselves. I always chose Contemporary when it was available.

I worked my way through the crowd filling the lobby, which looked like it had stepped out of a Dungeons and Dragons manual, and sidled up to the front desk, waiting for the man behind the counter to finish with the out-of-place woman in a pinstripe suit ahead of me. "The Carlton was all full up with some convention of meta-tastic authors or some such nonsense. Please tell me you have a room with television and a hot shower left?"

"Of course, love, we can accommodate you. A single queen be alright? I have a king available, but it's on the third floor."

"The queen will do fine, thank you." She signed the register and handed over her credit card. After she'd sashayed off to her room, I stepped up to the desk.

"Sophia! It's been, what, 200 years since you last graced us with your presence?" The innkeep was a large, florid man by the name of Gustav, who, if you inspected him with a microscope, would have "innkeeper" written over every cell, as he was the embodiment of every unnamed innkeep ever written. Every time someone wrote an innkeep character but didn't bother to name him, his description and story got added on to Gustav. Thus, he was large, jovial, occasionally short-tempered, watered down his ale (which is why he wasn't allowed to barkeep), and always knew the town gossip. He named himself about 100 years after his first story. It only took him that long, he said, because he needed to find the perfect name to reflect the many, many large jolly men he was representing. Naming yourself wasn't unheard of, especially among the older characters. Once you'd been around for a while, you got tired of being called *hey you, youngest princess,* or *Private Smith.*

I smiled and happily returned the proffered hug. "Gustav, you marvelous man, you. How's the inn holding up?"

"Couldn't be happier! It's always bustling. I've got the usual stream of newbs coming through on their work-study jobs, but no one's bungled anything for years. They're getting better at catching the unstable ones over at the Hearth before they hit the general population, that's for sure." He scratched at his beard and narrowed his eyes. "Actually, it's been a bit dull. Wonder if they'd let one slip through if I asked real nice, with a keg or two..."

"Gustav," I laughed, "You never change, do you?"

"Only with the telling, missy." He clapped his hands together and was back to business. "I've got you in your usual room, top of the house, last on the end facing the libraries. Will you be needing anything special while you're here?"

"Nothing major, I promise. Except, maybe don't let Geppetto know I'm here if he calls?" I thought back to the last time when I'd begged and pleaded with Gustav not to tell anyone I was there. I had decided I needed to run away from the family for a while and he was more than accommodating. "I plan on doing some shopping. You wouldn't mind if I had the packages sent over, do you?"

"I understand perfectly, and I'll even have one of the porters put them in your room for you, how's that?"

"Perfect, as always. You're a dear." I stood on tiptoe to peck his cheek, and then took the proffered key. Gustav gestured at one of the young men hanging around the end of the main counter.

The youngest one snagged my luggage and started to lead me off down the hall. "Room 413, is it, miss?"

"Yes, thank you. What's your name?"

"Edward." He didn't seem to be struggling at all with my bags, which impressed me — I certainly couldn't manage them all at once. We passed a window and the afternoon sunlight glittered oddly on his skin.

"I hope you don't find this blunt, Edward, but what manner of character are you?" I'd not met anyone who had skin that glittered before and it was more than a little odd.

He flashed a grin over his shoulder and I caught a glimpse of elongated canines. "Vampire, new breed. My author decided to upset the whole mythology."

I was more than a little concerned, as most of the characters written as bloodthirsty creatures weren't allowed to mingle so freely. Even though they technically didn't rely on blood to survive here and sunlight wouldn't *actually* make them go poof, instinct often kicked in and they'd end up attacking the nearest virgin. "I see. Did she go so far as to make you not want blood?"

"I'm sort of a vegetarian, like, I only go for animals even though the craving for human blood remains. That's why it took me four times as long to get through the stinking assimilation program, because it took me that long to convince them that I wasn't going to go hunting after the nearest beautiful woman. They had to take my Bella back in though, when our author turned her into a vampire in the fourth book. I'm still waiting for them to let her come out so we can be together." He sighed, and turned forlorn puppy eyes on me. "We're soul mates."

I was struggling not to laugh at how seriously this youngling took himself. "And how old are you?"

"Physically? 17, forever a teenager, unfortunately. But I was turned back during the influenza outbreak, so I'm quite old. I've seen things." We finished climbing the stairs and arrived at my door.

I gave him a smile and a curtsy, tipping him a couple coins. As soon as the door was closed, I couldn't stop myself from saying, "Not near as much as I have, boyo." Christ, where were authors getting their material these days? That sap was oozing so much puppy love all over the place, Gustav would have to have the carpets cleaned when the vampire left his work-study.

I unpacked and then called up to the Hearth's offices to double-check that my appointment was still set for tomorrow with the First Mother. The sun was low in the sky as I finished getting settled, and I decided to head out to the market for dinner before the light was gone altogether.

Not two streets over from the inn, I was drawn into the chaotic swirl and dance that was the Central Market. Every genre, every type of character you could imagine was there. Humans from Dickens rubbed shoulders with ghoulish fiends from King and elves from

Tolkien, and even a few of the alien races whose biology could function, like Vulcan and some of the giant insectoids. However, if a character's race wasn't too well thought through, the character could end up leading an unfortunately painful—and sometimes very brief—life on this side of reality. They usually ended up in the Moreau Foundation until the scientists there figured out a way to blend their biologics with human or other animal organs to help them live, instead of constantly being reborn into agony.

There's been a recent trend in publishing called steam-punk. Frankly, I think some human got a glimpse at our central market and that's how the steam-punk trend got started. Before characters started stumbling into our world brandishing steam-powered computers, we were already well on our way to blending technologies. The streets are lined with neon signs advertising book binderies and hand-carved wooden shingles for computer stores. Enterprising inventors and salesmen were not about to lose a sale to someone who was uncomfortable using a modern interface. You wouldn't find a shoemaker who didn't make ample use of rubber and synthetic materials even though he made his shoes in the style of the French Renaissance, just as people who made phones not only made cell phones, but rotary phones as well—though they were filled with modern electronics. You could even occasionally find someone to make the old school ones that required an operator...though I don't think anyone wanted one of those anymore—some things all the characters could agree were a waste of time.

I found a food vendor (thankfully not from Terry Pratchett's works) serving obscure meat pies and gyros and bought myself a flatbread full of ground, seasoned meat and Mediterranean veggies. I continued to wander, letting my eyes do a little window shopping while I started planning out the interview I had tomorrow. There was no worry about running out of time for shopping, since the market never closed. Sure, some of the street vendors and smaller shops would lock up a little after dinner time, but the big stores always stayed open and some more interesting vendors might come out even later, if one was so inclined.

Unfortunately, I was so preoccupied by my thoughts and the wrap in my hand, that I entirely failed to notice a tall man in leather pants and jerkin blocking my path before I tripped over the handle of his axe.

"Cross and damn!" I yelped as I stumbled. I managed to save my wrap, but only by falling entirely on my ass. I thanked my stars that I was still wearing my leathers instead of any of my court dresses. The tumble would have ruined them in an instant.

"Careful, Soph, you'll give someone the wrong impression about what class of princess you are." I froze. I refused to look up and acknowledge whose axe I had just tripped over. A hand appeared in my line of vision and I took a moment to screw up my courage before accepting it. My older sister always told me thinking too hard would end up making me look the fool, and sometimes, damn her, she was right. "You alright?"

I couldn't avoid acknowledging him anymore and lifted my gaze up to his face. Framed by luscious dark hair and square chin. His eyes (oh his eyes) crinkled at the corners as he openly grinned at my discomfort.

"Hi, Jack." I managed. "No, I'm fine. I'm sorry about that." I waved at his axe with the hand not currently holding food.

"No, no, it's my fault for bringing it into the market, I wasn't think-ing. I should have left it behind. It's not as though there are any bean stalks needing chopping in the middle of Central City, are there?" Jack pulled his axe from his belt and cradled it to protect it from the crowd. He looked exactly as he had 200 years ago, a rugged youth with a sparkle in his eyes and a quirk to his mouth that made you question whether he could ever be serious.

"I wasn't watching where I was going, it's entirely my fault." I con-templated my sandwich for a moment before deciding that I wasn't going to be able to eat any more of it now and wrapped it up before dropping it in my handbag for later. "What are you up to in the city, Jack. Trading?"

"Always, love. I've got a caravan full of elf-woven silk destined for the bodies of ladies such as yourself weighing me down. How about you? Back for some more carousing to tweak daddy's beard? Because I'm available for an encore." He let the axe slip to the ground and leaned in, becoming more serious than I was comfortable seeing, the laugh lines fading from around his eyes. "I've missed tearing up this town with you."

For a moment I couldn't breathe. Yes, during my bout of debauchery when I was trying to differentiate myself from my 11 nearly identical siblings, I had found myself in a hot and steamy affair with Jack the Giantkiller. I had still been fairly innocent, and hadn't taken notice of the murmured gossip about Jack the Ladykiller being a more apt handle for the man.

Okay, maybe I had taken *some* notice. But after a decade or so, I had come to realize that I wanted more out of my life here than constant partying. I'd had that with my sisters, and then I'd had it with Jack—I wanted to put this brain I'd been written with to some kind of use, and had headed home to start life with *The Daily Scribe*. I may or may not have left in the middle of the night because I knew I couldn't say no if Jack had pouted. He was really good at pouting.

He was pouting now.

"Jack, I'm sorry, but I...I don't know, grew up. Maybe it was a versioning thing. You know how that goes." I groaned inwardly at myself for using the cheapest card in the deck. Only young characters used a new version being told of themselves to justify their behavior. It was so childish.

"Now that you're back, what say we at least have dinner? You going to be in town long?" He was back to his usual devil-may-care self and busily tucked his axe into his belt, adjusting it to a jaunty angle.

"A week. I'm writing an article about the anniversary, lots of interviews to do, I'm not sure I'll have the time." I really, really wanted to have the time.

"You still need to eat." He bopped me on the nose with his finger. "You're at the Boar and Unicorn, I assume. I'll stop by tomorrow night and we'll head over to Neelix's for a late drink. Be ready at 8?"

"Fine! Fine, you win." I couldn't help but grin as he bowed, kicked his heels up, and started away down the street whistling.

THE HEARTH HUSTLE

The next morning, I indulged in a leisurely tea with Gustav, chit-chatting about the characters we knew in common, then dolled myself up in the finest of business royal dress to head into the Hearth proper. I'd only met the First Mother once, during my welcoming ceremony, but I remembered her as an imposing figure and wanted to make sure I'd girded myself for a two hour interview with one of the most important characters in our world.

Which is why it was quite a surprise when I was ushered into her offices at the top of the main building, 20 stories above the First Fire itself, to find it festooned in doilies with a cozy-looking armchair occupied by a buxom yet willowy middle-aged woman.

"Sophia! Child, how are you?" She stood from her desk and immediately enveloped me in a hug. It was one of the best hugs I've ever had in my life. Warm and full and loving. I was sorry when she let go, but I had a job to do and an interview to get through.

She returned to her armchair and gestured to one of the overstuffed seats in front of her desk. I took the proffered chair, pausing to remove a crochet hook I found the hard way. "Hello, Mother, I...it's good to see you again, it's been a very long time."

Mother laughed as I handed her the hook. "I know, funny how time goes, right? I look different, don't I? I know. All those unnamed mothers, most of whom die long before the story starts, are getting softer and more loving. Once upon a time, we were a terrifying force, but I'm glad. I enjoy the softer sides of me that I've been written with in the last few years." She fussed with the needlework basket beside her for a moment before settling down. "But tell me, how are you, child? I'm so happy to see you've found a decent job to occupy your time. So many of my children are at loose ends after their transitions. Are there any special men in your life? I was glad you'd come to your senses about Jack. I do love him, but he's such a hellion."

I grinned—I was written without a mother myself, and it was rare for me to have this kind of attention. I imagine most of Mother's conversations with characters followed similar lines, but that didn't make these moments any less...motherly. "Not at the moment. I actually just ran into Jack."

She made a silent *whoops* face. "Oh my. How was it?"

"Awkward." The less-than-comfortable conversation topic provided the impetus I needed to change the subject. "About this anniversary we're celebrating."

"Ah, yes, sorry, I tend to get carried away. We're in the midst of planning a citywide celebration, a whole week of events and parties. We have our largest group of characters ever matriculating from our program this month, and their transition ceremony is going to be the kickoff event for the week. Over 2,000 characters! I'm so proud of them; they are adjusting so well."

We talked about the plans for the next hour, and I only had to redirect the First Mother's attention twice more back to the anniversary and away from my love life. After three cups of tea though, I was ready to move on to walking the facilities, which Mother put in the hands of one of her assistants so she could get back to her responsibilities.

Gretchen, the embodiment of every nameless yet effective office manager, met me at the door. She carried a clipboard with a map carefully marked with our route and little notations next to circles along said route. I sighed a little as I realized I would be here for a lot longer than the two hours I had scheduled. But isn't that always the way it goes when you visit your mother?

"Princess, if you'd please come with me, I have all the details you'll need about the historical markers and specific anniversary plans."

I gave her my biggest smile and laid a hand on her arm, to try and short-circuit the curtsey- and title-ing. It only served to make people hard to talk to if they were constantly dropping the princess thing on me. "Thanks, that would be wonderful. And, please, it's just Sophia. You are the woman I wanted to see. Have you been noticing anything overly exorbitant in the spending for this year's celebrations?" I tried to keep the smile on my face journalist-neutral.

Gretchen made a face. "You mean besides ordering solid gold napkin rings for the banquet, or renting enough snow machines and air conditioning units to turn one whole banquet room into an ice skating rink? No, none that I can think of. Wasteful, it is. All of it. Thank goodness the Charmings are footing the bill, or we'd go bankrupt."

I felt a little of my journalistic excitement fade. "They're really paying for all of it?"

"Oh yes." The assistant nodded her head forcefully. "Every last penny of it."

"Well then." If the Charmings were actually paying for it, that meant there couldn't be any embezzlement from the city, which was slightly disappointing. Maybe I could spin the story into the wasteful habits of the rich instead. I'd have to see if Gretchen would give me the budget numbers later. For now, I was determined to enjoy my tour of the building. "Tell me, are we going to get a chance to go to the Hearth? I would so love to look on the Fire again."

She consulted her map and then the timetable on the sheet below it. "I guess if you could do lunch while we walk it could be arranged." I hid my amusement as best I could. "I think that can be managed." We started at the corporate level and worked our way down through the building. We walked past more doors than I could possibly count, more intake and processing waiting areas than I thought could fit in the buildings, and all of them somehow managed to be inviting as well as professional. I think it was the presence of shelves upon shelves of books everywhere we turned. Characters were always more comfortable surrounded by story.

It had been ages since I was last at the center and I had no concept of the sheer number of characters coming through each year. I mean, I was concsiously aware of the numbers, since we published them each month for the curious readers, separated by genre with details about how many had to go into holding centers due to criminal or insanity issues in their make-up. It was quite a different feeling to see the sheer mass of offices and facilities necessary to support that influx of characters laid out in front of me. It was thousands, tens of thousands of characters now, that came through the center in a year, and each and every one of those characters had to be incubated as a spark until their authors finished conceptualizing them and told their stories, by pen or by mouth.

Then they had to be debriefed as to what was going on in our world, and that took longer with some than others. They would be working one-on-one with a licensed narrative therapist. It was fortunate, then, that so many people nowadays were writing stories with a psychologist in them—we needed them. Can you imagine having your life story in your head, knowing exactly who you are and what you've done your whole life. Then you are told that none of that actually happened?

That you have to start over from scratch? More often than not, they had to go through a full psychological break before they could accept it. Everyone heard stories about characters like Anansi, who, in his story, could change himself from man to spider and back again. He came through the Fire as a man...and a spider. Two separate entities with the same mind; talk about a split personality. He spends most days playing chess against himself now.

It was only once characters had accepted their new world that they were then shuffled into group homes and started on their transition into society. Since we were unable to have children of our own, child characters were adopted into families who wanted to raise a kid. We didn't even age unless it was written, so there was no shortage of willing families to take in the little tykes.

Any character over the age of 16 was given a work-study position in the city to earn some money and find a neighborhood they were comfortable in. Once they had passed all their proficiencies and a final stability screening, they were given bus fare to get to their chosen province and a send-off ceremony to make them feel successful.

The main Hearth skyscraper rivaled the tallest building in Newer York, and the entire tax-funded adjustment process was run from the top 30 floors. The middle of the building was entirely taken up by classrooms and therapy offices, with the bottom 20 floors full of incubators. There were additional incubator buildings branching out from the main building, and then there was the complex of dormitories. Halfway houses, with in-house therapists and industrial-neutral architecture, were scattered throughout the city so the characters wouldn't have too far to travel for their work-study jobs.

Gretchen happily zipped between departments, rehashing their history and all the plans that they had for moving forward and continuing to modernize the processes. For example, the incubators that had once been lined wooden bowls of increasing size were now medical units large enough to fit your stereotypical 7-foot barbarian hero, wherein the spark stayed until fully grown. If it appeared the character was going to outgrow the unit, there was a whole specialty wing for odd-sized creatures like anthropomorphized animals and the giant races.

We stopped in some of the training classes and saw flightless fairies hopping on keyboards, trying to use a computer, and aliens of various tentacled and furry sorts learning English, as that was currently the most common language to come through the Fire, accounting for about a quarter of new stories. I even got a few minutes to speak with the head therapist at the center, who, unsurprisingly, was Dr. Sigmund Freud.

My feet were screaming by the time Gretchen stopped us outside the Hearth Room. I don't know how she still looked like she'd stepped straight out of some hiring brochure, but she did. Her clipboard list was now full of little checkmarks, made as we had marched past each designated spot in the Center for Character Transition. It was well past dinnertime, and my stomach was crying for something to eat. I couldn't help it, I had to have protein—and right now I'd settle for a Slim Jim—regularly or I started to get cranky. Unlike some robo-admins I could name.

But we were almost done and I was too excited for our last stop to care. We were at the very heart of the city, the exact center of our world, where the flickering and pulsing First Fire burned. The Fire connected us to the human world, and each and every one of us was born from it. Gretchen opened the doors and waved me in.

"Ten minutes, Miss Sophia. I'm afraid that's all we can allow the general public at this time."

As the only light in this room came from the central Fire, I was careful to watch my step. The room was a full two stories high, with balconies circling the domed ceiling at five separate levels. The walls were a stark white and there was no chimney hole. This Fire produced no smoke. Handfuls of sparks flew up towards the ceiling, and those that didn't immediately wink out were caught gently in the long-handled gourds swung by the tellers stationed along the balconies.

There were a few benches scattered along the walls, but I chose instead to sit on the banks of the rivers where they joined together, not far from the edge of the enormous Fire. You could easily have roasted an entire cow over it, that was certain.

Gretchen stood at the door, glancing occasionally at her watch, determined to pull me out exactly at the ten-minute mark, and I was just as determined to ignore her for those ten minutes, as best I could.

The room was almost silent. I say almost, because beyond the slight rustle of cloth as the tellers worked wordlessly above me, there was a gentle whisper, at the edge of my hearing. If I concentrated, I could almost make out the words, cadences of stories told on the other side of the Fire. I hadn't realized I was leaning into the Fire to try and hear them better until a log popped and a cascade of sparks flew up towards the waiting men and women. They swung frantically for a while, trying to catch everyone, but a single spark drifted back down and I held out my cupped hands so it wouldn't fall to the dirt.

It was already cold when it landed, a hard and pulsing speck of light. A gourd descended into my field of vision and I glanced up, startled, into the eyes of Kith.

"You, I—" I hastily lowered my voice at the growled warnings from above me. "Storyteller Kith, how good to see you again." I let the spark in my hand roll gently into the gourd she proffered.

"National Novel Writing Month kicked off on the other side. They're going to have a hell of a time keeping up with the influx of characters for the next few days. But I'll take this one to the Incubator for you. Not everyone would reach out for a spark you know."

I shrugged. "I knew they were cold from the moment they started falling back to the floor. It wasn't a big deal, I just thought they should get a better start than covered in dust."

Kith smiled and peered closely at the little fella. "Good thing you did, too, this poor sap is going to have a hell of a time. His author is a bit of a sadist." An acolyte appeared at Kith's elbow and she handed the gourd off to him. "How have you been finding the city?"

"With a map. Seriously though, I haven't seen much of it this time around. I wandered around the market for a little bit last night, but ran into an old acquaintance I'd prefer to have avoided and decided to go back to my inn early. I was planning on a little more shopping tomorrow."

"Jack, yes. You know, he's a much better man than you give him credit for, especially these last couple hundred years. I would advise giving him a second chance. I believe you'll enjoy the character he's become. And not all of it comes from them." She waved at the Fire, alluding to the humans on the other side.

I was irked that Kith was poking her nose into what she shouldn't know in the first place and I decided this time I didn't particularly care how rude I sounded. "The story of our failed romance isn't recorded anywhere, so how in hell could you know about it?"

Kith's laugh was soft enough not to draw the wrath of the tellers above us and she leaned into my ear to whisper. "Oh darling child of mine, have a little imagination, will you?"

It was a line from one of our pageants where a character is asked to identify someone who turns out to be the Storyteller in the flesh. But that couldn't be right. Everyone was in agreement that He was, in fact, a He. I backed away from what I now assumed was a slightly off balance teller and found myself pressed up against someone else's chest. I immediately stepped to the side, disliking the prospect of putting myself in whispering range of Kith again and turned to face both Kith and whoever had snuck up behind me.

It was at that point that everything in the room paused. Cliché, right? The sparks flying from the Fire, the gourds sweeping through the air, everything came to a stop and the whispering from byond the

Fire finally became audible.

"Our Father left us and so I have become God."

"He was asked three times, and three times he denied Him."

"God does not play dice with the universe; He plays an ineffable game of His own devising..."

The figure to my left, standing between me and the Fire, was almost entirely obscured by the backlighting. He wore the robes of a traditional teller but they moved constantly, stirred by a breath I did not feel. And it was downright creepy. "You're right, Sophia, she is not Me. But that is because I am Me. Anything else would get terribly confusing."

"Much unhappiness has come into the world because of bewilderment and things left unsaid."

"Storyteller, forgive me, I was not presuming to label her as you. But if you're here, that makes her..."

"That makes me one connected teller." Kith interrupted, smiling. She placed a conspiratorial finger to her lips and winked. I don't know why, considering it didn't seem as if anyone in the room could hear me name her as First Character anyway.

"12th princess, youngest princess," The sound of my first names drew my attention back to Him and I shivered at the power in them. I felt more awake, more alive than I had in months. "I have a task for you, clever one. A character is...cheating and I don't like it. He is influencing his own stories, and I have not been able to correct them. I'm not sure how he has managed it. I need you to go forth, determine how he has done this, and edit things back into their proper place."

My mouth was hanging open, I know it was. It had been centuries since the Storyteller last appeared to anyone and now He wanted me to take down a renegade character? One who was beyond even His knowledge? I wondered if His centuries in hiding had made Him slightly mad. "Me, Teller? I'm just a clever princess playing at reporting. I'm sure there are plenty of heroes you could go to for this. I mean, if you need a wicked article exposing someone's mischief, I'm your girl, but I don't do the whole confrontation thing."

The whispers surrounding us grew louder for a moment before settling back to play at the hems of His robes.

"The forest they came to was dark and foreboding, but the road was the only path that led to his goal."

"You are a ring-bearer, Frodo. To bear a ring of power is to be alone. This task was appointed to you. And if you do not find a way, no one will."

I threw my hands in the air. "Okay, I get it, you want me, for some reason. I don't suppose you'll tell me why?"

Kith laid her arm around my shoulders and leaned in conspiratorially, her eyes on the Storyteller. "You have a unique blend of talents, beyond being a remarkably stable character. Your retellings have all reinforced your cleverness and your ability to see through invisible cloaks and sneaking tactics; you've been around enough to know most of what's going on; and you have a desire to be...more."

She had hit the nail on the head. (If they were allowed to use so many clichés, so was I.) So many characters were content to live their lives exactly as they were written, to stay married to their written spouses regardless of how happy they may or may not be. And Kith was right in that I was uniquely suited to see through things, considering that I had caught my brother-in-law red-handed, despite the discouragement of my sisters, in several million tellings and counting. That sort of thing adds up.

I crossed my arms and gave the two of them the stink-eye. "Okay, fine, I'll admit I may be able to unearth his editing, and if you have set the narrative in the direction of his reprisal, let it be so told, or at least attempted. But it's a bit hard to tackle if you don't give me his name."

The whispers shrieked around Him for a moment, too confused

and angry for me to make out, before subsiding. "Prince Charming."

I felt a thrill run up my spine. "I knew it! I *knew* there was something rotten going on around this whole celebration. No one spends this kind of money on a party. The whole thing is a distraction, right?" The Charming family commands a controlling interest in every province. They had adapted to every change in genre and time period. For telling's sake, they ran half the character support agencies for transitioning characters. Everyone knew them, and everyone owed something to the Charmings. And no one that well connected and that controlling could be 100% squeaky clean.

"Not the whole family, though several of their stories have gone astray, as well. Prince Charming himself is your target. Correct him and everyone else's stories should fall into line. Find out how he's changing his story and why. Here, to make things easier on you," He reached out and grabbed my left hand, reached into the Fire, and picked up a coal, pressing it hard to my wrist.

I yelped at the searing pain it caused and yanked away, cradling the injured arm in my good hand, trying to see the damage in the dim light cast by the Fire. "The hell'd you do that for?! Oh that hurts like a mmm." I bit my lip to keep more profanity from pouring out. My father was constantly reminding me that cussing wasn't exactly best behavior for a princess.

The Storyteller simply tossed the ember back into the Fire. "I need your help, Sophia. Something is rotten right here in Central City."

Even through the pain in my wrist I managed to roll my eyes at the blended quote and glared at Kith and the Storyteller. "I'll think about it, but if you don't mind a word of advice, burning your chosen ones right off the bat doesn't inspire much confidence."

Kith chortled, though I couldn't see what she found so funny. "You'll find that mark useful on your journey, love. If you show it at any hearth in the world, they're obliged to help you in any way they can. It's worth it, I promise."

"Fine, if you say so. But where am I supposed to start? It's not like anyone has anything even remotely bad to say about that family, let alone the prince."

"Silly me, almost forgot." Kith stepped forward one more time and handed me a folded sheet of paper that had not been there a moment ago. There was no magic here, I firmly reminded myself. The First Character was excellent at sleight-of-hand, though. "These three characters have been sending out prayers for years to the Storyteller here, asking that their stories be told accurately. They all have to do with Charming, so I'd start with them." I glanced over the short list, noting Rumpelstiltskin, deWolfe, and Regina White, with a notation at the bottom that they were currently being held at the Stroke of Midnight Prison.

When I looked back up to ask another question, the Storyteller was gone. The gentle swish and sway of the tellers above me indicated that everything had started moving again. Gretchen started out of her stupor and glanced at her watch, making a hurried little noise when she noticed she had lost nearly twelve minutes. I hastily tucked the paper away as she came near and hid my injured arm behind me. I certainly wasn't going to try to answer her questions about it. In fact, if I didn't have the *incredibly* painful mark as well as a scrap of paper to prove it, I wouldn't believe it had happened myself.

♛

I somehow made my way back to the Boar and Unicorn and all the way up to my room. Gustav tried to hail me, but I couldn't understand anything he was saying and I waved him off.

Sitting on my bed, I unwrapped the handkerchief I'd secured with one of my hair ribbons. A simple quill was burned, almost branded, on my wrist. The nib of the quill was angled towards my thumb and the whole thing wasn't longer than an inch, but it smarted something fierce. I went to the tap and ran cold water over it until it started to feel numb.

What did the Storyteller think I was going to be able to accomplish that he couldn't do Himself? For 'Teller's sake, He was basically a god, as he'd just demonstrated. There was no such thing as magic, and yet he'd seared my flesh into a quill-shaped burn with nothing more than a touch. And then disappeared. How was it that he couldn't reach out and...and flick the Charming family on the ear and make them behave?

But if we were taught one thing during transition, it was that He always had His plot and it would be revealed in due course. Reading a story out of order ruined the ending. That was fine and all, but it kinda sucked when you were a part of said narrative.

A knock at the door startled me out of my mental whining and I turned off the tap, gingerly wrapping a towel around my wrist before opening the door. Jack was standing there, a bouquet of my favorite flowers, wild roses, held out extravagantly in front of him. I must have been wearing more of my distress on my face then I thought because he immediately dropped the playful attitude.

"Hey, Soph, you okay?" He stepped into the room and gently pulled the door out of my now shaking hands to close it. He did a quick scan of the room before setting down the flowers and pulling me over to an armchair. I let him. "You look like you've seen a ghost. Talk to me, Sophie."

He only used to call me that when he was getting all sappy and it broke the last of the restraint I was holding onto. I couldn't stop myself and let the whole story come pouring out, annotated by my confusion and distress. Shaking harder at this point, I started to slip into full-on shock with the pain and what I had just witnessed, so he pulled a blanket off the bed and wrapped it around my shoulders, propped my feet up on another chair and pulled over a footstool. When I got to the point where the Storyteller had marked me, he carefully took my hand and unwrapped the towel. He hissed in sympathy at the welt there and retrieved a washcloth that he liberally soaked in cold water before wrapping it loosely back around my wrist.

Once I had finished the tale, we were silent for a moment until Jack stood, dusted off the seat of his pants and then propped his hands on his hips. "First off, I need to go down to the pharmacy on the corner to get something to wrap that properly. I'll be right back. Don't you go anywhere."

I nodded, already stuck back in a mental feedback loop trying to decide what I was going to do. Where I could even begin. As he opened the door, I called out. "Jack, I...thank you. I don't—"

He cut me off with a motion. "I don't want to hear any whining about how you don't deserve it 'cause you ditched me, yadda yadda. I'll be right back." He smiled and there was a twinkle in his eye. "Promise."

In ten minutes he was back, with a plastic bag full of modern medical miracles. He ripped them open and pulled the footstool closer to me. "What are you thinking?" He twisted opened the burn ointment and gently started to spread it across my wrist. It hurt briefly, then the whole area started to go numb.

I'd been thinking a lot of different things in the ten minutes he had been out. About how crazy it all was, how long it had been since the Storyteller had asked anyone to do anything. If I remembered the stories right, it would have been before I had come into the world; he had sent out emissaries tasked with prepping characters for the transition from spoken to written stories. It had, by all accounts, been rough. But each and every one of them had been branded, just like this. What the stories didn't say was how much it hurt.

I sighed and pulled my marked wrist from his hands before he had a chance to start wrapping it up. I examined the mark, wiggling my fingers and watching my tendons flex under it. "Something the

Charmings have done has upset the balance of things. I always said I wanted my own adventure, something daring and exciting. To stop playacting at the investigative reporter shtick and do something real. I'd be a fool to turn down exactly what I'd been asking for, so, I guess...I guess I'm in. I'll do it. I'll go up against the Charmings and the 'Teller only knows who's going to come out on top, but I don't think he would have asked it of me if he didn't think I could handle it."

There was an audible noise, along the lines of a soft clap, and my wrist stopped hurting entirely. The burn had been healed to a raised scar, as if it had been placed on my skin years ago. Jack hesitated a moment before running his fingers over it. "Does it hurt?"

I shook my head. "Not anymore."

Jack picked up the gauze he had been about to pad it with and carefully wiped off the excess burn ointment. "I guess that means that if you're playing by His rules, this gig won't be so bad—now that you've accepted it, that is."

The laugh that made it out of me sounded sarcastic, even to my ears. "It certainly won't be easy, that's for sure."

"Speaking of which," He stood and started clearing away the first-aid supplies. "I made a decision myself while I was picking all this up. I decided that if you were going to take him up on his adventure, I was going to go with you. I'm bored with the city and could use the excitement."

I was taken aback, but he'd always been impulsive. "Jack, you don't have to do that, I mean, what with how I treated you before, and your trading business."

"I'm not going to argue with you, Soph. If you ditch me in the middle of the night, I'll follow you this time. Regardless of how pretty a note you leave me. You're going up against one of the oldest and strongest families in our whole world. There's no way in hell I'm letting you go on that adventure alone." He grinned. "Besides, think of how much good this will do my reputation."

Really, I was relieved. I'd been worried what I'd do if things got physical because I'm fairly useless on that side of things. No one tells a story about an ass-kicking dancing princess, though I'm not sure why. I think it would be one rockin' story. I stood and put one hand tentatively on his arm until he stopped fussing with the bandages and looked at me. "Thank you. That makes this a whole lot easier to bear."

His shoulders relaxed from a tension I hadn't even been conscious of until it was gone. "It's decided then. We'll storm the castle together. What's our first step?"

I sat back and rubbed hard at the newly branded mark, to see if it would hurt. It didn't. "He said to start with the three characters who have been making a ruckus down at Stroke of Midnight, so I figure that's where we should start." I stared a moment more at the brand and then held my wrist out to him. "Do you think you could wrap this, for now? I'm not sure I want people seeing it yet."

♛

THE JAILBIRD QUADRILLE

I spent most of the night writing up the article on the anniversary celebrations so Geppetto couldn't grouse that I had bailed on my assignment to chase after yet another folly, as he would call it. I had just finished repacking when Jack knocked and handed me a Dunkin' Donuts bag and an enormous tea. Dunkin' was one of the few chain stores to come through the Fire that I enjoyed; when that first Dunkin' employee was written into our existence with the recipes in his memory, I could have kissed the author.

Jack warily eyed my stack of luggage as he drank his coffee. "How many clothes do you need to travel? I mean, I'm not judging. I like to look as good as the next person, but this seems excessive."

I shrugged into my travel vest and buttoned it closed over my muslin blouse. I made sure the shirt was tucked firmly in the band of my pants before throwing my rucksack over my shoulder. "Don't worry, we're going to swing by my place and ditch most of the frilly stuff before we do any serious traveling. I never know when I'm going to have to look like a princess on trips such as these and those dresses take up a lot of room. If you grab the large trunk, I'll get the smaller."

He made complaining noises, but hoisted it up, balancing his coffee on top of it. We made our way down to the front desk and we piled everything by the front door before I went to the desk to check-out. Gustav was already up, checking through the roster for who was supposed to be checking in and out that day. "Are you leaving us so soon, Sophia? I thought you were to stay the week."

"I'm afraid so, and it has nothing to do with your hospitality, don't you worry. I've been given an urgent assignment and have to get cracking on it, so I'm off for home." I signed the printout that Gustav handed over to approve the charges for the two nights I'd been there and Jack came up to the counter to retrieve his axe and pack that he'd stashed before coming up to my room.

I gave the axe a dirty look, remembering its role in our interlude in the market, and Jack gave me a wide-eyed look of innocence. "What? I told you this was going to get sticky. I'm not going to leave my baby behind."

Gustav beamed at us. "You two are teaming up again? I pity the provinces if you're headed out there. You two are a force of nature when you get your dander up."

I rolled my eyes at Gustav's obvious glee. "I didn't exactly invite him, but you know better than anyone that he's tough to shake if he doesn't want to be shook." I was not going to admit to Gustav that I was glad for Jack's presence. If Gustav knew I was headed into serious business, the entire town would know by lunch. I trust the old dear, but he loves to gossip. I hopped up on the counter to plant a kiss on his cheek, then turned to signal to the doorman. "I'll be back soon enough. Gustav, take it easy, okay?" He leaned forward onto the counter and gave us a lazy wave as we caught our cab.

The cab brought us around to the livery stable and I shelled out for a private coach for the two of us. I had hardly made a dent in my budget for this trip since I was leaving the city early, so I figured it was worth it. Plus it would get us on the road faster since the first scheduled coach didn't leave for another two hours. We were loaded up and on the road in no time, with instructions for our driver to stop at the first post office he passed that was open for business.

That left me and Jack facing each other, alone, in the coach's in tight quarters. He graciously let me finish the donut he had purchased for me before propping his feet up on the bench beside me and stretching out. "Wake me when we stop at the post office, I need to catch some sleep before we start getting into any action."

I grumbled at his boots beside me and tried to squeeze more tightly into my corner. His eyes were closed for a grand total of maybe five minutes before I couldn't hold back anymore and poked his leg until he opened one eye to glare at me. "Can it wait?"

"No, it can't. I left you in the middle of the night with a harsh note about having to grow up after running the night scene in Central for a decade and you never once tried to find me. Now, here you are, diving into a very sticky situation, insisting on guarding my back. I don't understand. Why?"

He sighed and sat back upright. "Why didn't I come after you? Your note made it very clear that you needed time away from me. I could respect that. I figured once you were done with space, you'd let me know."

I shifted uncomfortably. He was right that I had needed space to finish growing up, but I had hated him for not making any attempts to woo me back. I would have turned him down, but I desperately wanted him to try. It's a girl thing. "Two centuries is a lot of space, Jack."

"I know." He leaned forward, his arms propped on his knees with that dratted half smile pulling at his lips. "After a while, I figured you probably weren't going to come back and by then, it was kind of okay. But you had done the leaving, it was up to you whether you wanted to come back or not. If it helps, I was hoping that you tripping over my axe was an indication you were falling for me again, but it turns out it was just you being clumsy."

Damn him, he was right. I hated that. I was a complete child for leaving in the middle of the night, and the truth was, I had missed him every day since then. Enough that it had made dating anyone else intolerably boring. But those thoughts weren't for now. We had much more pressing matters at hand. "I can deal with that, but what about the second half of my question? Why are you coming with me now? Don't get me wrong, I'll be very grateful to have someone to watch my back, but it would help to settle my mind if I knew, for sure, why you're here."

"It can't be because I want another shot at your ass myself?" He laughed and threw up his hands to ward off the crumpled Dunkin' Donuts bag that I pitched at him. "Several reasons. One, I've missed you. The trouble you get up to in one night is way more fun than anyone else I've ever met. Secondly, the whole trading thing was boring me. I needed to mix it up, get out of the city. It doesn't have the same spice to it when you know that every magical artifact is a fake. So this adventure was perfectly timed."

I suspected that boredom with trade wasn't the only reason he wanted to get out of the city. Some of his trades ran a little hot and close to the legal line. But if he didn't want to share what trouble he had managed to get himself into this time, I wasn't going to push. "Fair enough. Thank you."

"Can I go to sleep now?" It wasn't really a question as he was already putting his feet back up on the bench.

"Fine, yes. And for the record?" I stared out the window at the passing houses so I wouldn't have to look at his face. "I missed you, too."

"That's my Sophie," he murmured and curled up in his corner to sleep.

I was woken by the coach coming to a stop at a post office, and I kicked Jack, gently, to wake him up as well. He startled awake, more on edge than he'd ever woken when we'd slept together before. But he sheathed the half-drawn dagger when he made sense of his surroundings and gave an exaggerated stretch and yawn instead.

I hopped out of the coach and entered the little post office. At the counter, I sealed the article about the anniversary into an envelope and paid for next-day delivery to the Scribe offices, and then sent a telegram to let Geppetto know that I'd bailed on the city, but his story was on the way.

As I came back out of the building, I found Jack and our driver genially debating the merits of various forms of weaponry against mythical animals. "All right, we're all set. Jack, I was thinking of stopping at that place that the guy recommended on the way back to my castle to begin our research. Any argument?"

It took him a moment to parse my obtuse sentence, but he nodded. "No time like the present. I'll get our driver updated." He turned to the driver, but put his hand behind his back and rubbed his fingers together. I rolled my eyes and dropped a handful of coins into his hand to compensate the driver for "getting lost," then started rifling through my trunks.

Jack came to the back of the coach to see what I was up to. "The driver is all set when we are, it's only an hour's detour out of the way. Can I ask...?"

"I'm not headed to the prison that holds the oldest and most prestigious villains in our world looking like an adventuring ragamuffin." I pulled out a gown and held it up, debating whether there were few enough wrinkles. I decided it looked acceptable and grabbed the accessories I would need as well. "You can ride up front with the coachman. I need to get dressed."

♛

When I stepped out of the carriage at the prison, I was struck by the sheer...sheerness of the walls. It was a giant stone block, fifteen stories high and about as long, with nothing to break the façade except for the occasional recessed window. The characters that had designed and built the super-max prison had wanted to make doubly sure it was hard for anyone to escape, which apparently included scaling down the walls from the roof.

It took almost a half hour to get inside, through multiple checkpoints guarded by the biggest humans I'd ever seen, including those that passed for giants. By the time we finally reached the warden's office, I was regretting the decision to wear the full-royal, as I called it.

"Do you understand the ground rules?" The warden was standing with his back to me, looking out the arrow slits in his office.

I was perched at the edge of the hard wooden chair by his desk. "Yes, sir. No riling up the interviewees..."

"Prisoners."

I sighed. "Right, no riling up the...prisoners, no giving them information about their victims, the interview is over when you say it is, or the...subject..."

He didn't even turn around to correct me a second time. "Prisoner."

"...prisoner gets violent." His attitude was starting to get to me, so I decided to dig at him a little. "By the way, what kind of restraints do you use here? Are they approved by the egalitarian guild or are you still using the old human-standard manacles from the last administration? I'm sure our readers would love to know..."

He turned, stepped down from the stool that allowed him enough height to peer out the holes, climbed into his desk chair, and placed his hands on his desk. I could smell the toadstool soup on his breath. "Princess Sophia. You are only here because I had a foot shoved so far up my backside that I got Ogre's Foot in my nose precisely one hour ago by my supervisor. You are here to interview the three specified prisoners. You will only speak to them. Not to the guards who will escort you. Not to any other prisoners you may encounter. Three interviews. That is all. Don't know why *The Daily Scribe* is interested in these bumwarts anyway."

I slipped into full princess mode, since reporter-me was getting nowhere. "Is that kind of language supposed to shock me, Wsrden? Trust me, I have heard much worse. I am interviewing them because they have sworn, under oath to the Storyteller, that they are innocent of the crimes ascribed to them by their tales on record. I simply want their side of the story."

The warden threw his hands into the air, snarling. "Fine. Remember, keep valuables away from the goblin, don't bring any food into smelling distance of that deWolfe character, and, for wizard's sake, throw on some rouge before seeing the queen." He sat down roughly in his chair, feet dangling high above the hewn stone, and motioned for the guards at the doorway to escort me out.

I stood and waited for them to flank me before leaning in towards the more intelligent-looking troll on my right and stage whispering, "How did a gremlin get wardenship, anyway? Aren't they on the watch list?"

"No questions!" the warden hollered from his desk as the iron-bound door slammed shut behind us.

I glanced around the cell that had been provided for the interviews with growing distaste. It was small, dank, and smelled an awful lot like my cat's litterbox. By the fur on the floor, the last occupant had been at least part beast and had spent a distressing amount of time scratching at the wall beneath the single, barred window. This was my first time visiting one of the institutions for the Criminally Written, and I hoped they weren't all as oppressive as this. I know the common theory was that these characters were written beyond hope of redemption, but that was all the more reason to ensure their lives were as pleasant as we could manage. It wasn't their fault they had been written this way.

As time passed, I started to get antsy. It was taking them an awfully long time to bring up the first name on the list the Storyteller had given me. I turned to my current cellmate. "Who had this cell last?" The guard at the door could well have been made from the same stone as the walls behind him. I sighed and tried a different gambit to get through to him. "How much longer till Kriemhild gets here?" Nothing. I double-checked the location of my satchel and straightened the parchment, quill, and inkwell I had laid out on the table. "I hope they hurry up. I'm supposed to do three of these today, you know."

His mouth cracked open. "I know." It snapped shut.

I was about to ask the golem what word was inscribed inside his head that made him so uptight, but the door swung open with the obligatory squeal and scurrying rat soundtrack. Two troll guards shoved a small goblin into the room. Well, small for a human, large for a goblin — he was about the size of a human 12-year-old and had taken pains to comb the greasy remnants of his hair and individualize his prison rags with bits of glass, tin, and other detritus. He pulled himself haughtily erect, brushing down the front of his regalia, causing it to jingle together like a kitchen junk drawer.

"Thanks ever so," he said to his guards. He turned to the table and yanked on the chair opposite me, which almost fell over before righting itself and scooting an inch or two back. He leapt into the chair and curled up in the lotus position, his twiggy fingers knitting themselves together three or four times before settling on the tabletop.

"So. Are you actually going to listen to me? Or are you gonna be like all those other prats, assuming the 'official' story is true?" His gaze slid over me, dollar signs racking up in his eyes as he took in the gold embroidery in the hem of my dress and the necklace at my throat. I had dressed to impress for these interviews. One learns when one's nobility is most useful. "Most royals wouldn't bother to come. In fact, nobody ever visits, not even a teller. Why you, my precious, why you?" His sudden suspicion hardened his face. "You don't believe any of that crap about me turning straw into gold, do you? 'Cause I can't on this side of the Fire, as you should well know!" Kriemhild Rumpelstiltskin finally paused to take a breath and I leaned across the table.

"Yes, Mr. Rumpelstiltskin, I am going to listen to you. As for why," I leaned back, gave my most nonchalant shrug, "You swore to the Storyteller you were, what was the word you used?"

"Framed, I was."

"Yes, framed. And anybody trying to get the Storyteller's attention sure has mine." Especially now, I couldn't help but think. I straightened my cuff, making sure my new scar was as covered as I could make it. "Besides, *The Daily Scribe* is always interested in a good story, so I've come to talk to the three inmates here who claim innocence." I picked up my quill, dipped it into the inkwell and flourished it over my parchment. "Shall we begin?"

Kriemhild blinked once, twice. "Teller be damned, you really are going to listen, aren't you?"

"Yes, I am. In your letter you said you never turned straw into gold in your story, is this correct?"

"Nah. I mean, yeah, I couldn't turn straw into gold. Not literally. That's what people used to say about me, what my first teller told about me anyway. Mind you, this is my story as I remember it, before things got all wonky, 'bout 100 years back." The goblin leaned back in his chair, hands running repeatedly through his hair. "I can turn a profit on anything, even straw. Even items that were, shall we say, of a questionable provenance. If you brought it to me, I'd buy it, and I'd find someone to sell it to for double, sometimes triple the cost. Then along comes this miller's daughter, right?"

"Grania Miller, correct?" I played with my quill, waiting for the little man to get to something worth writing down.

"Who cares about names? I sure don't, not anymore. Anyways, so here comes this Grania character and she's pinched some stuff from the castle where she's working as a chambermaid to his royal ass-ness King Charming. And I tell her, sure I can move it." Kriemhild snorts and leans the chair back on two legs and one of the troll guards smacks him in the back of the head, knocking the chair forward onto all four legs. The goblin glared balefully at him while rubbing his head. "But I told her, jokingly, you see, that to move it, she'd owe me her firstborn 'cause moving royal goblets and such ain't easy."

"So you were joking." I paused and looked up for confirmation. He nodded, once more knitting his fingers together.

"Yeah, I was joking. Apparently, the wench thought this was a great idea. Apparently the king's silver wasn't the only thing she was lifting, if you catch my meaning," The goblin chortled and winked broadly at me, and I couldn't help but blush at the obvious innuendo. "Seven more months go by and boom, there she is, baby in hand, informing me she had kept our deal and here was her firstborn. Strapping young boy, with a grip you couldn't pry off a piece of gold if you tried. But I didn't want him. I tried to tell her this, she wouldn't listen."

"She just *gave* you her child and walked away? Didn't you try to return him or anything?"

"I tried, but that idiot wench disappeared, poof!" He threw his hands in the air and looked beseechingly up at the ceiling. "I figured, if there was a god, this was his almighty joke on me. A baby, seriously? I had absolutely no friggin' clue what to do with a baby.

But I tried. Lasted about a year, too, before the chick comes back, begging for her boy. And I'd grown kinda attached, you know? I'd named him after my father and all, too. Wieland. But she didn't care. Said everybody expected her to come back with her baby boy, now that she'd married this Charming king and they wanted an heir. Now she needed a boy." The goblin crossed his arms to hug his chest, roughly shaking his head back and forth. "I told her no. I'd bonded with the kid, named him, and here she was taking him away again. We all know how she handled that!"

Sophia looked up once she realized her subject had paused, expecting a response. "I only know what the stories say. Something about a naming competition? And a bonfire?"

"Ha. Only the stories you hear now. Not the first story, the original story. Naming competition, right. She never could pronounce my name, so she makes a little game out of it, trying to get me killed by the soldiers, and finally rounded me up with a bunch of iron-heads, grabbed the kid and bolted. And fat lot of good it did trying to protest. Me, a lowly fence, against the royal Charming family. Right." He snorted and ran his hands over his face, wiping away the bit of moisture clinging to the tip of his quivering nose then rubbing his fingers vigorously over his eyes.

"And you know what? Strange as it sounds, I miss that little tyke. He wasn't so bad, considering the idiots who created him. He'd have turned a good profit when he was older. At least they let him keep his name. He wouldn't answer to anything else." He shook his head. "Prince Wieland Charming. That's the story they used to tell, anyway. A stupid git of a peasant trying to figure out a way around an unwanted pregnancy." A gong sounded deep within the castle, marking the quarter day and the guard change. The two trolls strode forward and pulled Kriemhild up by his armpits and started frog-marching him out of the door.

"Wait, we aren't quite finished," I protested and the trolls paused, confused. Kriemhild wrenched himself once more out of their grip and turned back to me.

"You know, there is one thing I'm quite proud of, though, I've followed that tyke's life from inside, and he's quite the character. Do you know, he's had two wives written? And a daughter? But he keeps on. Excellent man, excellent man. He'll make a helluva king if his father ever Fades. Anything else you wanted to know, missy?"

"I guess not, thank you. You may take him out now." The trolls once more grabbed hold of their prisoner and nearly lifted him off the ground. I fell back into my chair, shuffled my parchments, and set the filled ones aside after numbering them.

"Could I have a little warning when the next interview is coming to an end, please?" I didn't even look up at my attendant, wondering as I reorganized my parchments whether I would even get an answer.

"Dunno. Can't tell time." Figures.

Two golems came through the door, each holding a length of chain that trailed back into the hall. As they moved farther into the room, they backed up against opposite walls, to keep the chains taut between them. A shackled man was dragged into the center of the room by this action. He stood tall, regardless of the collar, chains, manacles, and wooden hobble that caused him to take mincing steps across the uneven flagstones. He slid carefully into the wooden chair opposite Sophia and scratched futilely at the iron collar with both hands.

"I hate this thing, you know? They put it on me every time I get a little walky...which isn't often. They don't seem to trust me." Eduard deWolfe smiled broadly and started to lean across the table, but the chains attached to the collar pulled him up short. Instead he closed his eyes and inhaled deeply through his nose, the tip twitching ever so slightly. He opened his eyes again, and leaned all of his weight against the collar and slowly licked his lips, the stiffened red tip of his tongue looking just like a strawberry. "Mmm...cinnamon, cloves, hot tea with your donut this morning. Sugar *and* cream in your tea. That's not all that good for you darling, but I adore them chubby anyway. Softer." DeWolfe's grin widened as I tried to discreetly slide my chair back an inch and picked up my quill. The room seemed hotter with deWolfe in it.

"Mister deWolfe. Please contain yourself. I'm simply here to hear your side of the story. Not discuss my diet or my weight, which, as you can tell, is fine." I cringed a little as the older man's sharp gray eyes slid over my trim frame. I subconsciously checked my stays and he licked his lips again, more slowly this time, and started panting, his tongue lolling over his lips, dangling slack, nearly to his chin. The golem at the door stepped forward, and landed a hard slap on the back of deWolfe's head, knocking it almost to the table before the man could catch himself. He slowly pushed himself back upright, tossed his shaggy, unkempt hair back from his angular features and sent a shake down his spine before settling back into the chair. I fiddled with my quill, wishing they'd let me bring my little trimming knife in so I could do something with my hands while I waited for him to start talking.

"All right." His bound hands made a vain attempt to brush his hair into some semblance of the stylish cut it had once had. "My side. I like my side. The version they're telling here now, the one that didn't come over through the Fire, it's lacking something. You see, I have a condition. A disease of the mind. I'm simply unwell and they decide that it's grounds to throw me in here." He shook his head woefully, but instead of rotating on his neck as a normal human's would, his chin waggled like a dog's. "Some people are so close-minded nowadays. They claim to be open-minded and liberal, and yet they cling to the stodgy old concept of things."

"Such as?" I leaned into the table to take notes now that it appeared my interviewee was going to behave himself.

"Well, like sex." I started blushing and was furious with myself. I was not the virginal fairy book princess anymore, but the way he said it was so...juicy. "You see! There...that's what I'm talking about. We can't even have an open discussion about a basic human function without people getting all embarrassed and uptight. Is it any wonder that I am locked up in here for my...well...let's call it a fetish, shall we?"

I paused and stared curiously at deWolfe. "A fetish has you in here?"

"You want to know what turns me on, besides blushing young princesses?" I blushed even harder and focused determinedly on my note taking. DeWolfe chuckled deep in his throat. "Food."

This was not what I was expecting to hear. I've heard of ropes and things being used in sex, and there were a surprising number of princes out there with foot fixations, but food was a new one. "But we all need food, how is that a fetish?"

"There are times when I smell food, certain food, that I can't help myself...and if it's carried by a maiden through the woods, even better." He leaned back and closed his eyes. "Bread, that's what she was carrying, you know. Fresh-baked whole wheat, still hot enough to leave trails of delicious, ambrosial perfume in the air. And when she told me...she told me she was off to visit Granny Grania in the back of the woods, I figured nothing could be more convenient. Granny was deaf, confined to her bed upstairs, I'd go wait for her to make her way to me, and then I would have all that wonderful, sweet..." His eyes snapped open and he trained them on me, and, curse him, I was hanging on his every word. "sweet, luscious, young bread."

"But, you ate her grandmother, didn't you? And you tried to eat her?" I had dropped my quill on the table at some point and hadn't noticed that I was leaning into the table, hands around my inkwell.

"You would like that, wouldn't you? The big bad deWolfe ate the little girl all...up." DeWolfe lunged forward and dragged his tongue up the side of my face before he was dragged back by the golems on the wall. I am ashamed to admit I shrieked and leapt up from the table, lunging to the back wall where I rubbed my face vigorously with the handkerchief I always kept in my sleeve. Meanwhile, deWolfe sat calmly in his chair, chuckling quietly to himself, hands placed carefully on the table. I almost stuffed the handkerchief back into my sleeve before dropping it to the floor of the cell instead and stomped to my chair, righting it roughly before sitting down, once more out of reach. He had caught me unawares once: it wouldn't happen again.

"That, deWolfe, was completely uncalled for." I tidied my papers that had scattered across the tabletop, trying to keep the anger out of my voice. "Now. Behave or you go straight back to your cell. Last warning."

"Smack the poor puppy across the nose with a paper, why don't you? I was just having some fun. And you do taste good, if that helps..." he broke into gales of laughter as I leapt up from the table and gestured furiously at the golems to drag him out of the cell. "Calm down, calm down. Hey!" The troll had forcibly picked the man up from his chair and was preparing to toss him bodily out the door. "I thought you wanted to know the truth!"

"You have apparently lied, even under oath to the Storyteller. You tried to devour that young maid and it's a damn good thing the huntsman was there to stop you."

"I never said I didn't...I didn't!" he protested as the golems started marching out the door.

"Hold." I commanded, staining my voice with every ounce of disdain I could muster.

"Look. I only said the story they tell now was incomplete. It never said I knew she was coming, did it? Who told me she would be comign into my forest. It never said she was sent into those woods, on that path, with fresh-baked goods knowing that I was nearby, that I was waiting for her, waiting for little Ellen Charming and her little red riding hood, now did it?"

"No. It didn't. Take him out." I sank back into my chair, wiping at my face again, but utterly unable to get rid of the feeling of his tongue sliding over my skin.

♛

I had finished reorganizing the papers that deWolfe scattered when there was a timid knock at the cell door. "Uh, come in?" I looked up to see a middle-aged woman drift into the room. She would have been strikingly beautiful in her prime, and still managed to retain a regal cast to her features, but the intervening years between her mirror days and now had been unkind. Her hair, while swept into a graceful twist, was secured with a young girl's ribbons and barrettes. Wisps of the graying black strands straggled into her eyes. She blinked owlishly as they tickled her long lashes, but did nothing to brush them away. It looked as though she had tried to apply cosmetics to her face, but had done so with an unsteady hand, and had completely ignored the right half of her face.

I stood as Snow White's stepmother trailed around the room, standing for a moment in front of the guard and toying with his breastplate while he steadfastly ignored her. She flicked it with a fingernail, causing it to ring loudly in the quiet room. Giggling, she danced backward.

She was certainly not what I had been expecting. "Your majesty?"

"Where?" The older woman spun in a circle, half crouched into a curtsey. "Is momma here?"

"No, your majesty, I was referring to you." I slowly started to walk around the table to stand in front of the older woman. "You are Queen Regina Charming White, correct?"

The woman straightened up, giggling once more. "No, silly, I'm just princess Regina Charming. If you're looking for the queen, you want my momma." Regina's smile disappeared and her eyes shuttered. "She doesn't come out very often."

This woman was broken, no two ways about it. Most of the stories say that when her mirrors broke, it broke something inside her, but that was commonly understood to mean her magic, her youth. This complete mental dissociation was another matter entirely. I wasn't sure how the Storyteller thought I was going to get anything from her. "Regina, would you like to sit down?" I took the woman gently by the arm and led her to a chair.

"Are we going to play tea party now?" The bright smile was back on the woman's face and she bounced delightedly.

"No, sweetheart, it's story time." I walked around the table and sat opposite the deposed queen, who was now clapping her hands together.

"Story time, story time! Storyteller be praised by the stories in our hearts. Are you telling me a story? What's the story about?" Regina leaned forward excitedly, hands wedged between her legs. "Is it a scary story? I don't like scary stories! I like romantic stories with weddings and pretty girls!"

"Actually Regina, I was hoping you could tell me a story. A story about Snow White?" I picked up my quill, prepared to write if anything cogent came out of the woman's mouth.

"I don't know anybody by that name. Gee, funny isn't it, her named after snow like that? Who'd name a girl after snow?" She giggled again. "No, you tell me a story!"

I sighed, toying with my quill. "How about we trade stories? If I tell you my story, will you tell me yours? All about your family and such?"

"I guess that sounds fair...But you better have a good story!" Regina crossed her arms belligerently across her chest.

"Of course it's a good story." I gently placed my quill on the table, and hesitated briefly. "Every story is a good story, so long as you give it honor and respect."

"Storyteller be praised!"

"Exactly, Regina, exactly. Storyteller be praised. I told you I'd tell you my story, right? I'm the youngest of 12 sisters, all daughters to a good king, but we weren't very good girls."

"Ooh, ooh, what did you do? Did you steal desserts from the kitchen? I did that a lot..."

"Who's telling the story now, Regina?" I waited while the queen deflated into her chair.

"Sorry, it's your turn. Please keep telling."

"Right, we were bad little princesses and we snuck off every night to a great big party where we would dance all night and wear out our dancing shoes, wear them right to pieces! We had to go through these three big rooms full of trees made of silver and gold and emeralds. And then we crossed this enormous lake, rowed by our sweethearts. And, oh, that party was lovely. Endless wine and cakes, the newest music...we could have spent our entire lives there. Well, our daddy didn't like the fact that he couldn't figure out where we were going at night, and he was tired of spending money on new shoes for us, so he put a reward out on us. Anyone who could figure out where we went could marry one of us and inherit the kingdom. If they failed, they died."

"That's not very nice!" Regina protested.

"Daddy was very strict. Nobody wanted to try because they didn't want to die, even for the chance to run a kingdom. So we kept dancing. But then this old soldier decided to have a go. He had been hurt very badly in a faraway war and decided that he didn't have much to live for anyway, so he might as well try his luck at winning a fair bride. He even met an old lady who decided to help him. She told him about the drugged wine we gave the men and gave him an invisible cloak so he could follow us."

"Was he terribly old? And gray?"

I couldn't help but smile at her eagerness. It wasn't often that a character was asked about their story, especially older characters such as myself whose stories were fairly well-known. "No, Regina, he was old for a soldier. Most soldiers die young or retire long before this old general had. He was quite handsome, for a common man. Very distinguished bearing, and his eyes..."

Regina waited impatiently for a moment. "Yes, his eyes? Were they pretty?"

"No, not pretty, per se. They were more...haunted. Chiseled from the most beautiful blue crystal and full of death. You could see the war in his eyes." I shook my head, trying to dislodge his gaze from my mind and continue the tale. "Anyway, he only pretended to drink the drugged wine and donned the invisibility cloak so that we never noticed him following us. He stole goblets from the party and bits of the shiny trees our dancing partners had set up for us. I was the only one who thought something was wrong, I could tell we were being followed. But no, my sisters wouldn't listen and we got caught."

"What did your daddy do? Did he take away your dollies? Did he... did he hit you?" Regina's lip quivered slightly and then firmed up, tears locked into her eyes.

"No Regina, my father never hit us. My oldest sister married the soldier because they were nearly the same age. But that's the end of my story, Regina, are you ready to tell me yours?"

"I'm not supposed to tell." Regina shifted in her chair, lodging her hands under her thighs on the chair, and looking away from me. "Daddy said, never tell anyone about our family. It's our secret."

I picked up my quill, idly examining it. "Are you allowed to talk to family about your family?"

"I guess so. Daddy said don't tell others about our family. They wouldn't understand." The queen started chewing on her bottom lip, drawing it in between her teeth.

"But don't you know, I am family!" I smiled widely, trying to look as open and honest as I could, even though I was cringing at the manipulation I was about to try.

"You are? But...I don't know you...I don't think." Regina looked hopefully up at Sophia through her straggling hair.

"I'm your cousin, silly. Didn't you know that all royalty are cousins? I'm a princess and you're a princess, so you can tell me anything!" I smiled reassuringly, fingers crossed under the table.

"I didn't know that! That's so neat! So...I can tell you anything and daddy won't get mad?"

I relaxed into my chair. "Anything, Regina, and everything is safe. Tell me about our family, cousin."

"Okay, so long as we're family, I guess it's all right. Do you know my daddy and mommy?"

"Prince Wieland Charming, right? And Ella?"

Regina nodded. "I never get to see mommy that much. Daddy said it was because she was sick a lot and needed to stay in her room to get better and not get excited by little girls. But I would sneak in sometimes, just to lay in bed with her. She would be covered in bruises and smell funny, like Daddy did after a banquet, only stronger. And she'd talk funny, too. I didn't like her like that, but when she was out of bed, sometimes she'd be better. She'd play games with us. But then Daddy would come and yell at her, call her little cinder, and she'd go away again."

"That's too bad. The bruises, did she get them falling down?"

"No, Daddy said it was part of her illness, that she was suffering for being a bad wife."

I paused, not sure I wanted to know the answer. "Did Daddy give her the bruises?"

"I don't know." Regina's voice got very quiet and she hunched into her chair. "Sometimes at night I could hear them yelling at each other, Daddy telling her he never should have picked her up out of the cinders, that she was nothing but a...a chambermaid who would... would...I can't say that word. It's bad."

"That's okay, Regina, don't worry about the bad words, we can move on." I consulted my notes from earlier in the day. "Tell me about your sister. Ellen, right? Was she named after your mother?"

"Yes!" Regina sat up straight again, smiling. "I loved my sister Ellen. She was the perfect princess and she was teaching me to be one too. Curtseying and dancing and languages too! And she was so pretty. Even Daddy said so. He said Ellen was the fairest girl in all the land."

"You say 'was', Regina, what happened to her?"

Regina ignored me, and kept chattering on. "Ellen was the *best-est* at everything. Daddy said he bought her all the pretty dresses 'cause she was a good little princess, and she got to take naps in Daddy's room and everything. She even got to sit on Daddy's lap in the throne room and he gave her kisses."

I was starting to get a very bad feeling about the direction this story was going, but the Storyteller had told me not to be surprised by what I found out. "Did your mommy know about this?"

"I don't think so, Daddy only did it when Mommy was sick. And sometimes Ellen would cry at night and I'd ask her what was wrong and she would say she was sad 'cause Mommy was sick again. But Daddy didn't like it when we cried. If he caught us crying, he'd hit us. 'Cause good little princesses don't cry." A single tear trailed down the queen's cheek, carving a path through the caked-on makeup.

"Regina, what happened to Ellen?"

Regina closed her eyes and started rocking back and forth, singing, "Mirror, mirror, on the wall, who's the fairest of them all? Tell me quick and tell me true, before I turn all black and blue."

"Regina? Regina, sweetheart, stop singing." I got up and came around the table, and laid a hand on the woman's shoulder. The haunting little melody was worse than hearing that girlish little voice coming from the middle-aged woman.

"Take your hands off me, girl-child." The queen sat up straight in the chair, brushing away my hand. "What are we doing here?" She swept the hair out of her face with one swift motion, unveiling eyes hardened to silver gray.

I was startled by her instantaneous transformation, but I tried to roll with it. "You were telling me about your life, your majesty." I quickly bobbed a curtsy to the queen, and retreated to my seat. "We had come to the point when your sister left the family."

"Yes, that little tart had it coming. We sent her off to live with our grandmother in the woods. Imagine, sleeping with the huntsman. She was a princess for goodness sakes. We were well rid of her." She sniffed and twitched her shoulders. "I was father's favorite then, his 'fairest in the land' and he made sure I was, shall we say, well taken care of? He found me a wonderfully lucrative marriage with a sweet man when I was sixteen. Poor man had already lost one wife, but at least he already had a child to dote on. I wasn't all that...welcoming of his advances. Poor man tried, telling me I was the prettiest girl he'd ever seen but I wasn't interested. I'd spend hours in front of the mirror with tailors and hairdressers. I loved fancy dress and asked him to host balls as often as possible."

At least this version of the queen was giving straight answers, even if she was frigid. "Did you have a good relationship with King White and his daughter?"

"As good as could be expected for an arranged marriage. Snow and I got along alright, but she was a strange girl who didn't particularly care for things a princess should, such as sewing and dancing. Instead she preferred fraternizing with the maids and hostlers, begging rides on the horses, or helping tend the castle's animals. She was an odd child, but compassionate." The queen trailed off, tapping her finger to her lips. "It's too bad what happened to her."

"You mean, the part where you ordered her execution?" I froze as Regina's hand slammed down on the table.

"I did no such thing. I was...I was only trying to protect her. She..." The queen broke off and looked away, eyes closed, whispering under her breath.

I waited a moment, then whispered, "What happened, Regina? What happened to Snow White? Why did you send her away?"

"I thought I was protecting her."

"From who? Regina, who did Snow White need to be protected from?"

"Did you know my Father visited the castle regularly after Mother died? We would get together for a family dinner. Sometimes...he'd visit me later in my private chambers. One summer, that summer he had Snow White sit on his lap, hugging her. He turned to me, he said, 'Regina, darling, I think you're in danger of losing the title of 'fairest in the land.' Little Snow White here is growing up to be quite the young beauty." Regina was shaking, quivering from head to toe. "The next morning, I had the huntsman try to take Snow White to my grandmother's, with a note for Ellen and her to take care of Snow White for a little while, that I'd explain later. They never made it. And Father..." Regina stopped talking, muttering to herself and staring at the wall behind me.

I stared at the queen, and quoted "'...and that summer Prince Charming rescued Snow White.' They married."

Regina stopped moving entirely, the hard mirror of her eyes shattered, and tears poured down her face. Her sob-choked voice set the entire prison cell echoing: "mirror, mirror, before I turn all black and blue, who's the fairest of them all, tell me quick and true, who's the fairest of them all, mirror, mirror black and blue, who's the fairest on the wall?"

♜

THE DEFLECTION TANGO

I stood outside the gates to the Stroke of Midnight prison, clutching a writing kit filled with secrets that the Charming family had paid, with power or money, to bury. It was amazing to me that they could manage such a sweeping cover-up, particularly when their stories were told so often. These must have been the first iterations of their stories, a violent and predatory young prince, but the stories had mutated so far from the original that I was amazed. Yes, stories change, especially now with the human movement to justify and explain evil. Not excuse it, but at least give it a sympathetic background. But this was a bit much.

I watched as the gates slowly swung closed on the retreating figure of the spindly warden and his lumbering trolls. I waited until the prison door had closed behind them before crossing the street to the waiting coach. The coachman and Jack were standing near the horses, sharing a bottle between them. I threw them my hardest look and Jack raised his hands in defense, a huge grin on his face. "Coffee, I swear it. I wouldn't jeopardize my neck with a drunk coachman."

"Unfortunately," the man muttered before returning the bottle to Jack and climbing back up to his post. "Where to now, your highness? An inn for the night?"

"Yes, I think that's best." I briefly debated changing out of my dress but decided to wait. "I'll even let you pick the inn for the night, since we dragged you out of your way."

"Thank you, miss. Would you mind if we pushed on a little further, then? I've got a cousin runs a way house about five miles up the road."

I smiled at the blatant kickback ploy. "That sounds perfect. First round's on me if we get there before dark." I hauled my skirts into the coach and tried to arrange them as best as possible to keep them out of Jack's way. I was snapping open my satchel as Jack climbed in. He had barely closed the door before the coachman had us off and rolling.

"How'd it go? Find out anything interesting?" Jack nudged the edges of my skirts farther over to me so he could settle his feet on the floor.

"Quite. It seems the stories we know are abbreviated and leave out important details such as Charming setting up his daughter to get eaten by the big bad wolf, and Queen White being his other daughter. Did you know she was only trying to protect Snow?" I pulled out my sheaf of notes. "I have some very interesting tidbits that seem to have evaporated from our group perception of the Charming family. I was going to go over them, add some things while they're fresh in my head."

Jack held out his hand. "Can I take a look?"

"Only if you can remember my shorthand." I handed over a few sheets and rifled through the rest to get to the Queen's story.

"But this isn't in your shorthand, it's long hand."

I frowned, which my third-eldest sister was always fond of telling me would give me wrinkles—as if it could. "It can't be, I took all my notes in shorthand."

"It is, here, look." He handed the sheets back to me. The top page was definitely long hand, and even worse, it wasn't my handwriting at all. It was an elegant script designed for carefully copying over verse. And then I registered what it said:

"I spun straw into gold for her. So she wouldn't die. Of course, I don't do this kind of work for free. And the price was her little golden boy."

"No. No, no no no, no. This is impossible." I started flipping through the pages and finally caught one changing mid-sentence. My ink was actually dissolving on the page and rearranging itself:

"Ran across a little girl, with a basket of goodies. Didn't know where she was headed, so I decided to find out. She gave up the answer easily enough and I decided to beat her to it."

"This is all wrong!" I was trying not to freak out, I really was. This was impossible. There was no magic on our side of the Fire. Or any side of the Fire. This was quite literally the definition of impossible. Yes, the power of a human's imagination created us, and sustained our world, but unless a human mind worked out actual, workable physics for magic, it would never exist over here. So how was this happening?

The change had reached the notes on my last interview: *"That child was always a nuisance. I just wanted to be rid of the dratted girl who had the gall to be prettier than me. I was the fairest in the land, not that little chit."*

Jack was studying the pages intently, brow furrowed, holding them up to the light. He'd gotten to see a few of the pages change in his hands, and I could tell he was as unsettled as I was.

"Jack, say something please. What could have done this?" The final page of the notes had turned into a giant scrawled *"Happily Ever After"* and I was feeling sick to my stomach. The only person who might have anywhere near the kinds of...influence to do this would be the Storyteller and I highly doubted it was Him, considering he had set me on this path.

"Nothing." Jack tasted the paper briefly, rubbed the damp spot carefully between his fingers, and watched the ink smear. He frowned harder when the smudge didn't reassert itself as a word, for which I was grateful. I was unnerved enough. "I wonder, can I borrow a pen?" I pulled one of my disposable quills out of the side of the satchel and gave it to him. He damped the end of it and wrote in large letters across the page, *Prince Charming is a Prat.'* Within moments, the last word had rearranged itself to form the single word *'Hero'.* He tried again, this time with the phrase, *'Princess Sophia is one Foxy Princess.'*

"Cute." I smirked, and we both waited and watched, waiting to see if it would change. Nothing.

"Let's try a lie about me then, shall we?" Jack thought a moment and then scrawled *"Jack couldn't make a trade even if he was offering golden straw."* "We know that's not true." We waited again, but nothing changed.

"Damn, how come the Charming family gets this spiffy autocorrect juju and we don't?" Jack complained.

I snatched all the pages back from him and glared at them. "Obviously, they shouldn't. It's almost as if the sheer weight of the tellings on the other side of the Fire are influencing our written word here, but that can't be right, can it? And why would the inmates tell such different stories, why aren't they affected by this...this...whatever it is?"

"Since I can't read about it, care to fill me in on exactly what it was that they told you?" Jack propped his hands behind his head and relaxed. "I could use a decent story."

So I filled him in, from the entrance of Rumpelstiltskin to the full break of the queen. I stared out the window through most of it, trying to commit all of the details to memory since I apparently couldn't keep notes through this adventure of ours. They'd just change.

Jack let out a long low whistle when I got to the end. "The Storyteller doesn't give out half-assed assignments, does he? How in hell don't we all know about this? Why isn't this jerk already locked up someplace where he can't hurt women anymore?"

I watched a stone wall weave past the carriage window for a while. I wasn't ignoring the question, I was unable to answer. Jack didn't seem to notice I wasn't responding and instead was flicking blindly through the altered notes.

We didn't have access to magic, so that was out. Nor did we have any advanced tech that could be doing this. Humans were even worse at figuring out how the fancy science stuff worked than they were at the physics of magic. So if what appeared to be magic could not be explained by magic or science, what was left?

I didn't look away from my window before broaching what was starting to look more and more like the most likely explanation. "Could it...Have you ever heard of a character gaining the ability to affect things here?"

"The First Character and the Storyteller can. He helps keep us from fading, so his recitations certainly have a power of some sort. But anyone else? No." Jack dropped the pages onto the seat next to him and briskly rubbed his face. "It'll be an odd new day if Charming has figured it out. I can't even begin to imagine..." He stopped and laughed ruefully. "Imagine. Damn. Whole new ballgame, isn't it?"

"If that's what this truly is, then yes. And I'm not looking forward to trying to defeat one of our own who has the power to harness imagination behind him, that's for sure."

We were silent the rest of the way to the inn, lost in our own speculations about the possibilities and dangers that had reared their ugly head. It was a testament to how distracted we were that Jack didn't make any crude suggestions when the innkeep informed us that they only had one room left for the evening, though thankfully it had double beds.

I went up to the room fairly early, leaving Jack gambling in the bar, and lay in bed tracing over the new scar on my wrist. I'd been careful to keep it covered so far, because I still wasn't sure what would happen if anyone saw it or whether anyone would believe where I'd gotten it. I started worrying about why it had been given to me. Charming was obviously powerful and in a way we couldn't even imagine. I laughed at myself because that was exactly what the crux of the problem was. It appeared he was tapped into the fabric of our reality somehow, so how did we cut that off?

The goal was to get Charming to stop messing with the stories, as it appeared to be wreaking havoc on the characters around him. He always seemed to do so much good for our world, though. I wondered if the Storyteller was right in believing that he had to be taken down. I mean, the stories I had heard that day were painful and cruel, to be sure, but so many characters benefited from his donations and charity organizations. And if I couldn't write any of this stuff down, there was no way for me to disseminate the real story of his character to the world at large. So the option of a public defacement was out.

That meant I had to figure out how to cut him off from his power source. However Charming was doing it, he was tapped into pure imagination. Nothing else could have such an effect on our world. Therefore, the first step was figuring out how he was doing it. Did he find a text, stumble on to the talent, or was it taught to him? And then we had to stop him from using it, which could prove a mite trickier.

As long as he was living, he would use the ability to shape this world, I was sure of it. That meant he would have to die.

It's difficult to kill a character, but not impossible. Of course, the moment someone tells their story again, they're reborn into our world, sans any memory of having been there before. There have been accidents and suicides, cases where a character has faded into obscurity, only to be reborn decades later when their book becomes a cult classic. Death isn't entirely permanent, which made me feel a great deal less uncomfortable with the notion. And, when he was reborn, he'd be born out of the stories as they were told now, all sweetness and light. I was getting ahead of myself, though. I needed to figure out my first step first, then worry about the end game when it came down to it.

I must have fallen asleep scheming because I woke with the first light of dawn creeping in through the open window and Jack snoring fitfully on the bed across the room. I threw a pillow at him to wake him before dressing in my leathers and heading down to talk the innkeep into packing a basket of food for the rest of our trip.

The ride to my father's castle was fairly uneventful. Jack was not a morning person and I was brainstorming a list of characters that I wanted to start talking to as soon as I was packed up and ready for the next leg of our trip. The footmen at the castle started unloading the coach as soon as it pulled up, and I left Jack arguing with the doorman about the etiquette of bringing his axe indoors.

Whenever one of us sisters got back from a trip, it was customary to go straight to Father, give him a kiss on his cheek, and lie outrageously about where we'd been. "Hello, da, how are things? I spent a few days at the spa with my sisters and we discovered a cure for not aging! Can you imagine? All those little orphans will finally get to grow up."

The king smiled at me. "You did nothing of the sort, young lady. Don't lie to an old man now."

"You're right, how horrid of me, I've been found out. Finished up an assignment for Geppetto in the city, about to head out for another." I winced at the sound of Jack shouting out instructions from the courtyard. "And I have a, well, guest is definitely not the right word for it."

At that point, Jack swept into the hall, and I have to admit, he did cut a handsome figure. No matter how hard I tried to forget how gorgeous he was, no woman could ignore his presence for long. A fraction of an inch shy of six feet, he was a very well-cut young character. His clothes, while designed for hard work, were tailored to his slim waist and broad shoulders. And the axe swinging from his belt made him seem at once honest and dangerous.

"Daddy, I don't believe you've ever had a chance to meet Jack the Giantkiller."

"Your Majesty, it is quite the honor." He swept a courtly bow, then came forward to shake the hand my father offered him.

"Good to meet you, my boy. I've got nearly all the rest of them paired off and out of my hair but her."

"Daddy," I groaned. It was an old argument.

"In that case, Your Majesty, I'll have to reconsider my designs on her honor." Jack stepped back and rested his hands on the head of his axe.

"Enough, you two. Da, we won't be here long, I just need to trade out my frillies for a more sensible pack and I figured we'd grab some horses instead of relying on coaches. Do you mind if Jack borrows the fiend?"

The king grinned. "If you think he can handle him, that's fine."

"He's a better horseman than he cares to let on. He'll do great with that beast, they're two of a kind." I winked at my father and turned on my heel. "I'll stop to say bye before we head out! Time to go repack."

"I wish Geppetto would give you more of a break!" he hollered after me and I rolled my eyes. It had taken him a century to accept that his daughter wanted to have a job, and he still wasn't 100% behind me at this point. He'd prefer I did something more lady-like such as clothing design, or flower arranging. "Jack, why are you tagging along on this journalism adventure of hers? Don't tell me you've given up trade for it..."

I hoped Jack would be sensible enough to lie and continued up the stairs to my suite of rooms. It was probably time that I moved out of the castle and found a place of my own, considering I was in the ballpark of six centuries, but my father would be lonely if I left. There were only two daughters of his still living in the castle and I was the only one left with a brain in her head.

Speaking of which, my next eldest sister was waiting for me in my room when I got there. Like me, she was a moderately tall, leggy blonde with crystalline green eyes. But at that point the similarities ended. I was hardened by my days on horseback and helping out at harvest time whereas Beth was leaning towards pudgy from her days pining at the window and eating too many chocolates while reading the trashiest romance novels to hit our world.

"Sophia! You're back. Did you bring me some new stories, did you?" She bounced off my bed and danced around me. You'd think she was the younger sister, but no.

"Yes, Beth, give me a moment. I only had an hour or so in the bazaar, but I managed to snag some of the new ones for you. The characters are less than a month old." I dug through my trunk until I found the novels I had acquired for her. I sighed as I handed them over and she let out a gleeful squeal, running off to her favorite window seat to embark on a long week of reading and sighing longingly.

I had finished unpacking all my trunks, since I wouldn't let the maids do it—they always messed up my organization—when my sister came tiptoeing back in. "Soph, you've got a visitor."

"Why are you whispering?" I whispered back to her.

"Because its Prince Charming! Here, can you imagine?" You know, when a character says they've a chill that runs up their spine, it's mostly for dramatic purpose, but this time it felt like my body literally cooled ten degrees.

"Thanks, Beth." I almost decided to change into something more formal, then decided that I would prefer to get this out of the way, so I settled for tidying my hair and brushing the road dust off my leathers.

The prince was chatting with my father in the main hall and Jack was nowhere to be seen. I'll give the prince his due; he certainly didn't look evil. Bright blonde hair that naturally drifted into a sculpted wave accented his strong nose, and his rugged chin was emphasized by an easy smile. He was tall, with a tunic and hose to outline the muscular strength of his thighs. There wasn't a girl alive (not to mention a large number of boys), who didn't dream at some point of having Prince Charming swoop in and save them from their doldrums. And the power of their imagination showed in the confidence and sexuality that oozed from his every pore.

I was standing in the doorway, trying to decide how to interrupt politely, when he looked up from the conversation and saw me dithering there. "Princess! It's been a century or two since I last saw you. How are you?" He met me halfway down the great hall and took my hands in his and laid a gentle kiss on my knuckles.

This was definitely not the time to let him know that I was on to him, so I opted for an empty-headed approach. "Fine, my Prince. I've been filling my days helping out that dear old Geppetto at the paper. I do get so dreadfully bored staying around here all day. Plus he sends me to all the good parties. What more can a girl want? Except, of course, a beau to go with it all..." I let myself trail off hopefully as I made cow eyes at him, trying my best to emulate Beth. I was sick to my stomach from tension and I wished he'd let go of my hands before they started to shake.

The prince held onto my hands a bit tighter. "What, so the rumors I'd heard about you back together with Jack are unfounded? I thought he'd followed you home from the city!"

I smiled, but it felt halfhearted. "No, your highness, we just happened to be headed in the same general direction. We chose to ride together to reminisce about my scandalous days in the city, but that time of thoughtless adventure is behind me." I contemplated yanking my hands out of his, but it would seem rude to pull them away myself and my father would ask questions. I wasn't entirely surprised that the prince had heard that Jack and I had left the city together—as I said, Gustav was a terrible gossip—but I was wondering how much more the prince had heard about my recent activities.

"I was actually hoping we could take a brief walk in your marvelous gardens. I need to pick your brain about that last article of yours, the one about the pumpkin-growing competition. I had heard rumors that the winners were using imported chemical fertilizers..." He deftly transitioned from holding my hands to securing my arm in his. He made a brief bow to my father. "That is, if you don't object, my lord."

The monarchy out here had an odd hierarchy. Technically, my father outranked Charming since he was a king, but Charming had been around long before our story was told and thus was considered higher on the totem pole. It sometimes made it hard to tell to whom you owed what observances, but Charming played this one exactly to the line. My father bowed his head in response and gestured to the side door. "So long as you return her in the condition you found her, I certainly cannot object."

Now I really wanted to know where Jack was. I sincerely hoped he had heard Charming was in the castle and was somewhere close. He was the only other one who knew, at this point, how dangerous the man pinning my arm to his side actually was. I found myself being deftly maneuvered out the door and into the manicured flower beds that bordered the castle.

"You've started to make quite the name for yourself as a reporter, Sophia. I'm glad. It always makes me happy to see one of the royalty do something worthwhile with their time. Too many of us are content to rest on our written laurels. I'm looking forward to your piece on the anniversary of the Central Hearth buildings." He was guiding us farther from the castle with each step and I caught myself looking for gardeners nearby. Hoping to have, if not defenders, at least witnesses, if things got ugly. I couldn't stop hearing the Queen's little broken song in my head.

I forced myself to relax onto his arm and smiled pleasantly. "It's almost done, your highness. I sent a draft to Geppetto yesterday morning in fact."

"It certainly didn't take you long in the city to do your interviews." I rolled my eyes and sighed with as much disdain as I could muster. "You wouldn't imagine the tour I was subjected to. All this minutiae, and I could have told the woman a thing or two she never would have imagined about the early days. It was so boring, except for the fact that I got to spend a lovely few minutes with the Fire. That's always so calming and peaceful. But now I get to go back to covering the society rounds, and that should prove to be much more fun."

"I would have thought they'd let you stay in the city for the parties we'll be hosting in a week. They will be a spectacle you don't want to miss."

"I'm hoping I'll be done with whatever Geppetto thinks up in the meantime to keep me busy, but I had to come back at least for a little while to pick out my outfit for the fancy dress ball. I don't want to go with a standard swan or something passé; I want to stand out since I'm still looking for *my* prince charming." I forced a giggle and dragged the prince to a bench near two gardeners working on one of the topiaries. "Let's do sit, I'm tired from all my travel."

"Of course." He finally let me retrieve my arm and sat on the bench next to me. "Speaking of your interim projects, I heard you had a stop at Stroke of Midnight yesterday. I'd be very interested in learning what article that was for." The man was a master actor; there wasn't a flicker of anything but polite interest in his features, whereas I had to keep myself from hesitating while I scrambled for a lie. If he knew I'd been there, he probably knew who I'd been speaking to as well.

"You know that new show that's been going on, what are they calling it...'Once Upon a Time,' that's it. I was curious how the story they were telling was affecting some of the characters so I decided to drop by and talk to a few that are featured in it. I must say, that deWolfe character is downright disturbed. I could hardly get anything out of him except for some weird sexual twinges, though that might be echoes from the liberties they've taken with the Red Riding Hood reinterpretations lately.

Really though, it doesn't seem to have impacted Rumple or the Queen much at all. I guess they have too many tellings on them to be able to change all that much." I shrugged and fiddled with the hem of my vest. "I don't even think I'll get a decent story out of it. But enough about failed projects, what are you going to the fancy dress ball in? I'm sure all my readers will want to know."

A vague line of tension I hadn't noticed in Charming's shoulders relaxed and he smiled, playfully cupping my chin. "You'll have to come to find out, then write about it in your next article, won't you?"

"Oh, you." I playfully batted at his hand and he stood, offering me a hand up. I took it, dusting myself off as I stood. "I must say, your interest in my work is quite flattering, your highness. I hope my articles continue to entertain you."

"I'm sure they will. But now I must take my leave of you. My work calls me back to the city. Good day, Sophia." He clicked his heels together and offered me a brief bow, then turned and strode out of the gardens to the front of the castle where a carriage waited. I watched until he was in the carriage and out of the gates before I collapsed back onto the bench and threw my head back, strangling the urge to go into hysterics. At least he had appeared to buy everything I had laid out for him. I was going to kill the Storyteller the next time I saw him. While I'd wanted a bit of adventure, I had wanted to start out with something easier than this.

"Didn't that look cozy."

I yelped and scrambled to get upright but only ended up landing in the dust of the path. Jack hauled me upright, once again, and I glared at him. I needed to stop letting him pick me up, he might get the wrong impression. Or the right one. I didn't know which was which any more, but that was something to figure out at a less stressful time. "Where were you?"

"I was getting to know that demon horse you so kindly offered to let me ride when I saw Charming's coach pull up. I decided to play least seen unless you needed me, but it looks like you handled yourself well enough. I couldn't quite get close enough to hear you guys, so fill me in." He sprawled on my bench and I opted to let him fill it rather than complain. Instead, I paced in front of him rubbing my temples as I filled him in on the lie I'd concocted for our visit to the prison.

"Nice one, Soph, that was pretty smooth."

"Lucky, you mean. It's not like I could come out with, 'The Storyteller thinks you're shady and we're supposed to pull the rug out from under you.'" I flopped onto what little of the bench Jack had left me.

"Nope, you had the right idea. Where do we go from here?"

I made a face and ran my fingers through my hair. "Why do I have to decide? Can't you come up with something smart?"

He flexed his bicep and mugged for me. "I'm the muscle on this trip, remember? I'm not the one chosen by Him for being oh-so-clever."

I shoved him, hard enough to rock him back a couple inches. "You're apparently the comedic relief as well as the muscle. Fine then, come up to my room with me while I figure out what I need to pack. I don't quite know where to head yet myself." He laughed and righted himself.

We made our way back up through the castle and by the time I had arrived at my room, the maids had managed to finish my unpacking and carted away all of my laundry. Thankfully, they had left all my writing gear and personal supplies on the table, rather than hiding them away from me. I threw my large panniers on the bed and started rummaging through my bureaus for adequate travel clothing.

As I threw things on the bed, Jack started deftly rolling them up and packing them into the bags. "We know a few things at this point. One, Charming is definitely crooked. The stories those inmates told painted a less than charming picture of our dear prince."

I went to the bathroom and retrieved my toiletry kit from the shelf where the maids had stashed it. "Two, he has a source that told him I had been interviewing people at the prison. You, me, the warden, the guards, and the driver were the only people who knew we'd been there, and for him to be here right after meant he had to get going in a hurry when he heard about it."

Jack wedged my writing kit into the other pannier along with my tools. In this case, multiple ballpoint pens and a Moleskine notebook. Much more practical than parchment and quills, but not nearly as satisfying to work with. He added, "Three, he thinks you're not a threat considering he issued no warnings during your talk. He seemed to be gauging your level of knowledge."

"Which is something at least." I stopped buzzing around the room and leaned against my desk with my arms crossed. "We need to stay under the radar as long as possible, don't you think? What do you say to a vacation?"

He buttoned the covers closed on the panniers before standing and swinging them over his shoulder. "It seems a bit abrupt, but I'm game. Where to, my fair lady? A small seaside village on the coast? A spa resort in the mountains? Someplace romantic, I do so hope." He leaned forward to pin me to the desk, but I danced out from under his arms.

"Not a real vacation, jackass. A cover. Charming already thinks we've rekindled our torrid love affair, why not perpetuate that? And I was thinking more along the lines of a visit to Libro Vocali. It's large, a tourist destination, and it's home to Storyteller U where Charming happened to spend about a century in the stacks, if I'm remembering his bio properly. Part of his whole spiritual phase before he started up all of his charity work. I think it's worth a visit, at least as a starting point. What do you say?"

Jack snapped to attention and offered his arm in a mockery of the prince. "Libro Vocali it is."

I laughed, grabbed my bags, and left Jack standing alone at the desk.

THE  HIJINKS JIVE

It should have only taken us half a day to make it to Libro Vocali, but Devil was living up to his name by nipping at Jack, shying at shadows, and generally raising hell. Jack and I spent those brief portions of the ride where his horse was behaving to create a plan of action for our time in the city. We were agreed that we should probably spend the first day shopping and poking around the city together, to set up the cover of being a newly reunited couple.

"But you know, that means we should probably be getting comfortable with a little public display of affection." He leaned over in his saddle, trying to lay his head on my shoulder and Devil took offense to the redistribution of weight and decided to try and unseat him. Again. I had given up restraining my laughter miles ago, and enjoyed the spectacle of Jack clinging grimly to Devil until he decided to calm down again. "This damn horse! Soph, why on earth did you pick this one for me to ride instead of a gentle gelding like your beast?"

"Toefer isn't a beast, he's family. And would you believe I wanted Devil for the entertainment value?" I tried to choke down a laugh as Devil floundered off the road trying to get to some clover.

"Yes, yes actually I would, if we hadn't suspected our lives to be in danger. In this case, I'd hoped you'd take the safety of my neck more seriously. *No, Devil! Damn you to hell, you mangy cow!*" I finally took pity on Jack and decided to show him the trick to getting along with our Daredevil. "Here, here stop, get off him a moment." I dismounted and led Toefer to the side of the road and let his reins trail on the ground; he wouldn't go anywhere without me.

Jack dismounted with some difficulty and tried to hand the reins over to me, but I held up my hands and stepped back. "No, you've got to do this on your own. Alright, stand in front of him, make him look you in the eye." I waited until he was in position. "Alright, now sing to him."

"What? You've got to be kidding me." Jack had tried to back away from Devil, but the horse stepped on his foot, pinning him in place, and slowly started shifting more weight onto the leg until Jack yelped and pushed him off. "Fine, if it's the only way to get me to Vocali in one piece. What in god's green earth should I sing to this monster?"

I sat on a fallen tree and played with Toefer's reins as he grazed behind me. "Dealer's choice. But don't half-ass it, he can tell."

After a few moments of grumbling, Jack straightened up and struck a player's pose, arm out for dramatic delivery. After a moment's hesitation, he broke into song.

Frere Jacques, Frere Jacques,
Dormez-vous? Dormez-vous?
Sonnez les matines, sonnez les matines
Ding dang dong, ding dang dong.

Devil's head swayed down and his eyes closed, and when Jack stopped, he perked back up, prancing. "There, you brute, are you happy now?"

"Excellent selection, sir. I think you'll be fine now. Go ahead, mount up." I turned my back on him while I remounted Toefer and was glad I heard no more cursing. When I had made it back onto the road, I turned to see how Jack was faring. Devil was behaving admirably, with his head up high and prancing as he worked his way back to the road. "You'll have no more trouble out of him now. He's a sweetheart." I reached over and gave the horse in question a brief pat on the neck. "What on earth is the singing about?" Jack wiped the sweat off his face with a handkerchief and then stuffed it in one of his packs.

"He was a runt when he came out of the Fire and his author hadn't decided what to do with him over the series yet. I sang to him a lot during those days, since we weren't sure whether he was going to make it or not, but he was told into a fine strapping stallion. Father decided he wanted to train him up as a warhorse, even though we have exactly zero need for that. I think it was a way to pass the time for him. That's when we learned he would play merry hob with anyone who hasn't serenaded him. Must be fond memories from when he was a little tyke." I nudged Toefer into motion as Jack shifted uneasily in his seat.

"Warhorse, really? Why don't we trade places and you can ride the bomb, since you're so fond of him."

"Because Toefer won't put up with anything male, period. You're stuck with him!" Jack swore and urged Devil into motion, trotting to catch up with me.

With all of the antics between Devil and Jack, it took us until after dinner to get within sight of the second-oldest city in our world. In the early days, characters had lived close to the Fire, creating a small village and helping each other adjust to their new lives. But after several thousand of us had been told into existence, a small subsection of the population decided they wanted to dedicate their lives to the Storyteller and followed him into the wilds to start another city, this one dedicated solely to the study of our stories.

Like the rest of our world, Libro Vocali has grown and changed over the years. It was still home to the Storyteller's School, and any character wishing to dedicate their lives to perpetuating our existence went there for training before choosing a hearth or the mendicant lifestyle. A thriving metropolis had sprung up around the school, big enough to rival the old human college towns. It was a tourist destination, for the first telling of every character's story was kept in the grand Stacks and the finest binderies set up shop in the winding causeways.

We made it through the city gates as the sun was setting, and we were still debating about the best way to approach the university. I was determined to get a look at the original copies of Charming's stories, to see how far back the contamination went, but getting permission to handle the oldest volumes could be tricky, particularly if they weren't your stories. Jack was all in favor of lying through our teeth and poking around the archives once we were in. I wanted to play the journalist card and see if I couldn't get a look at them honestly.

We decided to change the subject as we rode through the gates, to a commentary on Quidditch as a non-magical sport, which both of us could agree was silly-looking. We were laughing as we entered the city of Libro Vocali, which I chose to take as a good sign. I was feeling fairly confident, slipping easily back into the habits and customs of our old relationship.

We were about to pass a 1950s Las Vegas styled hotel when Jack pulled up short. "Did you call ahead for a reservation anywhere?"

"No, I figured we could find something when we got here." I looked from him to the gaudy facade with a billboard proclaiming that they had the original Elvis impersonator on the stage. "No, oh no, please Jack? Can we find someplace a little more...well...tame?"

"And why, lover, would we want tame on this wild adventure on which we are embarking?" Jack grinned and dismounted, grabbing my reins. "Why don't you go see if you can snag us a room for a few days, and I'll take these guys back to those stables we passed."

I groaned, but dismounted, taking a moment to remove my packs before walking into the hotel. Jack was right. This was high-profile, loud, and touristy: perfect for a couple pretending to have fallen madly in love again. Even the staff were wearing uniforms ripped straight from some 1950s Vegas noir; the polyester looked itchy. I walked up to the counter and was greeted by a chirpy redhead. "Hello, and welcome to the Palm. Do you have a reservation?"

"Hello yourself. My boyfriend and I would like a room for a few days. Do you have something available? And I'd love one of the suites, if it's available." I slid my First Edition credit card onto the counter and suppressed a smile at the clerk's awed expression. It was quite hard to get a First Edition card and it could unlock almost any door in this country. It helped that my 'Member Since' date read 'Day One,' which if I remembered correctly was about 200 years ago now.

"Of course, ma'am. I believe our royal suite is available, if that would suit your needs."

"That sounds perfect." The clerk swiped my card into the system and handed me the room key. "My boyfriend should be along any moment, he went to stable our horses. Could you send him along up?"

"Of course, ma'am, who should I be expecting?"

"Jack, he carries an axe."

"Oh, my. Him, absolutely, I'll send him right up."

I was puzzled by her strong reaction, but I brushed it off. Jack was a well-known character and had been around for a very long time, so it would make sense for characters everywhere to know him. The room was gaudy, but spacious, and it was at the top of the building with a wonderful view of the university. I was unpacking my limited wardrobe when Jack knocked on the door.

I let him in and he let out a long whistle. "Nice pad you got us here, Soph."

"Yeah, I figured why not go the extra mile, right? I've got plenty of cash for it, that's for sure. Investing in computers at the very beginning paid off." I closed the wardrobe and flopped on the enormous round bed. "You could get lost on this thing."

"I think that's the point." He let out a Tarzan yell and pounced on top of me on the bed.

"Jack!" I shrieked, laughing and tried to wrestle him off of me, but he had me good and pinned. I tried to blow the hair that had escaped from my braid out of my eyes. "Could you please get off of me?"

"Awww, but I like the view, reminds me of that time we were in the Boar and Unicorn on my telling day and you—oof." This last was the air rushing out of his lungs as I executed a neat twist and jab with my leg that levered him off of me and flung him to the side. I did not need him reminding me of the sorts of things I had done for him on his telling days. I remembered them quite well enough on my own and they were more than a little distracting from the task at hand.

He rolled over on his back, grinning, and laced his hands behind his head. "Should we draw straws for who gets the bed, or should I assume I'm sleeping on the couch?"

I stuck my tongue out at him, but didn't answer his question. "I was thinking of hitting up the District tonight, do some shopping, get a nice dinner out, maybe hit up a pub or two, make sure the right people see us around town tonight. What do you think?"

"Sounds perfect, as long as we avoid Manny's."

And here it was. I knew there had been something off in the clerk's reaction. "Great, why can't we go to Manny's?"

"I may or may not have traded him some moonshine-filled bottles of vodka the last time I was here."

I rubbed my eyes. "And he thought it was high-end quality stuff. What did you get out of the deal?"

"It wasn't so much what I got as what his daughter was giving..."

I threw my hands in the air and turned my back on him. "Enough! I don't want to hear any more. Change into something appropriate and we'll head out." I opened the wardrobe back up and pulled out the soft gray slacks and embroidered blouse I had brought along for just this reason. I headed into the bathroom to change and firmly shut and locked the door behind me.

When I had primped myself well enough, I came back out to find Jack in khakis and a button-down shirt. How he had produced a perfectly dry-cleaned shirt from his saddlebags, I have no idea, but he looked good in it. He was trying to decide if he had somewhere to hang his axe when he looked up. "Oh, Sophie, aren't you a vision."

I tossed my carefully tousled hair and purred at him, "Not so bad yourself, stud. Come on, let's get going. I want to get to the District before the binderies close."

The District was one part boutique shopping heaven, one part Bourbon Street, and one part craftsmen shops. It was eight square city blocks full of bookbinders, apparel stores from Saks 5th to local designers that blended traditional with modern, enough bars for the entire university to drink itself into a coma on a nightly basis, and some of the best restaurants in the province.

We entertained ourselves by watching the binders at work and Jack made a show of buying me a journal that we watched an older man sew together. It was quite pretty, with a cover made of rich red leather covered in embossed roses. The thick creamy paper that filled it begged to be written on and I looked forward to filling its pages. With what, I had no idea, but maybe I would join the fad of characters recording the stories of characters they met on the road.

We stopped for dinner at a place called Amelia's, which boasted a menu of fusion cuisine from all sorts of cultures. We were contemplating dessert when a female voice cut through the happy buzz of the restaurant. "I thought that was you, Jack."

Jack cursed under his breath, wincing. "I forgot the daughter's name was Amelia..."

I tried to hide my smile with my hand, but it wasn't working.

The woman approaching our table was diminutive. She couldn't have been more than five foot, if that, and it looked like she was from one of the elvish-inspired races, or maybe pixie. Pretty though, I'll give her that. "Jack the Giantkiller. I didn't think I'd ever see your mug again."

Jack stood and faced her, looking more sheepish than I think I'll ever see him again. He towered over her, shifting awkwardly, and I hope I was the only one who noticed him checking for an absent axe on his belt. "Hi Amelia, I didn't realize this was your joint. We were just about done. If you'll excuse us, we'll get out of your hair."

I cleared my throat and declared, "Actually, I was hoping to try one of your lava cakes. I hear they're sublime." This show was too good to give up on.

Amelia raised her eyebrow at me and her mouth twitched. I could tell she was having as much fun winding Jack up as I was watching it. "Oh, sit down, you big scoundrel." She broke into a huge grin, and slapped him on the back. I watched him sway from the blow and wondered how strong this woman was. She pulled an extra chair out from the next table over and signaled to our waiter. "Three lava cakes, Joe, thanks."

It took a moment for Jack to regain his composure and reclaim his seat. While he was carefully folding his napkin back into his lap, I turned to Amelia. "You have got to teach me that trick. How did you get him to jump like that?"

Amelia grinned and leaned over to me and said in a stage whisper, "Pure fear. It's the only way to get them to sit up and pay attention to something other than these." She did a brief shimmy, which, combined with the sequins on her dress, was blinding.

"To clarify, am I in trouble or not?" Jack politely interrupted.

"Hell no, boy, loosen up. I'm glad to see you, believe it or not. We're about to run out of that rotgut you left us with and we need more. Who'd you get it from?" Joe returned with our lava cakes and she dug in with gusto, carefully mopping up each drip of the chocolate fudge.

"You want more of it? I could get you legit stuff, you know." Jack poked at the steaming mound of chocolate cake and waited until I had taken a bite before trying one of his own. Chicken.

"Naw, that stuff is easy to come by, but whatever the hell is in those bottles you sold to Daddy, that stuff the yabbos are drinking up like nobody's business. We made this cocktail, call it the Giantkiller, in your honor of course. It can floor a troll, and we have to get the customers to sign a waiver to try it. If you can drink two in one night, your tab is on the house. It's become somewhat of a competition over at Dad's place."

"I guess I'm honored? I got that wagonload from some dwarf miners up Mountain Way. I'll have to send you their address when I'm back in Central City, though. I don't remember it off the top of my head. I think they use it to help clean ore." Jack dug into his cake with gusto, now that he had decided he was well and truly out of trouble.

"We should go try one." I declared, scraping the last bit of chocolate from my plate.

Amelia laughed, and waved at Joe for our check. "It's your funeral."

Ten minutes later, the three of us were seated at the bar in Manny's, and Jack was happily trading greetings with Manny himself, who insisted on making the drink for us. I looked at the tumbler warily and wasn't sure I liked the rainbow sheen on the surface of the multicolored concoction, but shrugged and took a sip. The flavor was somewhere between an underripe starfruit and an overripe dragon fruit, sweet and tart and, yup, there was the punch. Boy, did it pack a wallop. I can see why they decided to call it the Giantkiller. I was tipsy a moment later, and drunk not long after that. I don't remember much more of that evening, but there may have been another Giantkiller or two before Jack and I managed to drag ourselves back to the hotel.

☙

The next morning was too bright, and I burrowed back under the pillows, trying to ignore the pounding in my head. After deciding I probably wasn't going to throw up, I rolled onto my back and into Jack. I froze, not remembering how he had gotten there and quickly checked myself for clothes. Thankfully, I was still in my outfit from last night and I sighed. If I were going to break down and sleep with Jack again, I would rather remember it.

Jack groaned as I got out of bed and headed towards the bathroom. "Lord, what was in that shit?"

"You sold it to him, why are you asking me?"

All I got in reply was a moan and I shut myself into the bathroom and started the shower. Several painkillers, glasses of water, and twenty minutes later I was feeling almost human again. I ordered us breakfast from room service while Jack tried to make himself somewhat presentable. He was shaved and dressed by the time the food arrived and we sat down to a full Irish breakfast. I knew I'd feel better faster if I managed to eat a decent meal, so I set to with minimal resistance. Jack looked a bit green, but he managed to put a decent amount away before pushing back from the table.

"Today we're going to go hit the Stacks, yes?"

"I thought that was the plan. I think I'll tell them I'm working on some profiles of founding characters to go along with the anniversary piece, ask to see a bunch of character's folios, not just Charming's. That way we can avert some suspicion. What do you think?"

"That might work." He drained the last of his cup of coffee. "My hangover is not going to get much better today than it already is; you ready to get to it?"

I wrinkled my nose and drained my own mug of tea. "As I'll ever be."

After gathering my new notebook and pens, packing a shoulder bag with everything I'd need for a day in the university Stacks, we headed out. I gave Jack a skeptical expression when he slipped his axe into his belt, but he shrugged. "I feel naked without it."

I rolled my eyes, but didn't say much. It was comforting to know that he had it.

For all that we had partied hearty the night before, we were still at the Stacks before they opened to the general public for the morning. University students could access the treasure trove of books at any time, but us lay-characters were only allowed in during restricted times, and were permitted very limited access.

The acolyte at the front desk asked for our IDs and when we handed them over, he recorded our names into his daily log before handing them back.

"I was hoping I might speak with the Head Librarian, is he about?"

"The Librarian is probably busy, but I'll ring up. Give me a moment." His murmured conversation through the intercom lasted a bit longer than strictly necessary, but when he hung up, he gave us directions to the office and bid us a good read.

"So far, so good," Jack murmured and I shushed him.

The Head Librarian was one of the highest positions at the university, second only to the Head Storyteller himself. They were in charge of watching over the first copies of all of our stories and ensuring that any subsequent variations were recorded and attached to our folios. Some of the compendiums were quite large and, with the advent of fanfiction, some characters took up entire rooms all on their own. The Stacks itself was 30 stories tall and there were rumors that it went 100 stories down into the ground as well.

So I was somewhat bemused when a young woman who looked to be in her late 20s greeted us. The last time I was here, the Librarian had been the Pagemaster, a character uniquely suited to the task. "Good reading to you, Librarian. How is Mr. Dewey? Happily retired, I hope."

"Fine, Sophia, he decided to take a sabbatical for a decade or so and travel some of the other provinces. I think he needed to spend some time away from these hooligans here."

I smiled, put well at ease by the young woman's quick smile and no-nonsense nature. "Yes, I could see that. It's a pleasure to meet you, miss..." I held out my hand and she gripped it firmly.

"Marian. And the pleasure is all mine. It's not often we're visited by such well-established characters. You and Jack have quite the set downstairs, up to several shelves apiece I believe." She gestured at the chairs in front of her desk and we sat.

"We're here today because I was hoping to get access to the deeper Stacks. I'm working on a piece for the upcoming anniversary celebrations, and I thought it might make for a fun insert to include the absolutely original stories for a few of our world's foremost characters. A who's who collection."

Marian adjusted her reading glasses and pulled out a card index drawer and started flipping through it. "That sounds like fun. And I think we can certainly trust you down there. Who did you have in mind?"

"Prince Charming, certainly, since he's planning the shindig, but I was also hoping to be able to access a few of the other royals as well as some of our more common heroes, like my Jack here." Jack smiled and winked at me and I blew a silent raspberry at him while the Librarian was absorbed in her index cards.

Marian pulled a couple cards and slipped the drawer back into its spot. "I think we can manage that. I'll get one of the acolytes to show you down to the rooms you'll need. I'm afraid it's a bit cool down in the basement levels."

"I remembered, I brought a shawl with me."

Marian pressed a button on her desk and another acolyte instantly opened the door. "Yes, Librarian?"

Marian handed her the cards she had pulled. "Could you please see these two characters down to sublevel 2? They're to be given free access to the original fairy tale folios."

The acolyte bobbed a quick bow and gestured for us to follow her. With a quick thanks to the Librarian, we followed the acolyte through the vestibule and down a tight stairwell. The acolyte whispered over her shoulder, "Any character you wish to start with?"

"Prince Charming would be good, thanks." I whispered back, and the acolyte nodded, and ducked out of the stairwell into a hallway. She finally stopped in front of a door marked with the Charming crest and opened it, leading us into a cozy room.

The walls were lined with folios and there was a reading table with chairs, as well as a few armchairs scattered around the room and ornate rugs on the floor. The acolyte saw my raised eyebrow at the decorations and smiled. "The Charmings like to come here on a regular basis, so they donated all the seating and even the paintings." She gestured to several portraits hung around the room.

"I guess they wanted anyone who was doing them the favor of reading their stories to be comfortable." She gave a small laugh and excused herself, noting that there was a call button on the wall should we need her, but most of the other characters we would probably want to look at were all within a few doors of the Charmings.

After she left, Jack went over to the bookcase to the right of the door and pulled out the first folio. "If we want to see how the story goes, we might as well start at the beginning, right?" He flipped it open to the front of the book and frowned.

"Seriously? We have a problem right off the bat? What is it?" He handed it to me without saying a word and I ran my finger down what was left of the torn-out pages. From the looks of it, at least twenty pages had been haphazardly removed from the folio where the first Charming story should be.

"You've got to be kidding me!" I slammed the book shut and dropped it on the table, sinking into one of the chairs. Jack pulled out the next folio and started going through it. He stopped about a third of the way through and laid it on the table next to me. It, too, had a story not-so-neatly removed from it. He pulled out a third book and I got up to take it from his hands and put it back on the shelf. "It's not going to help us to know that there are missing stories. What we need to do is look at what is here and see if it can be of any use to us."

Jack was scowling, but he nodded. "Agreed. We can probably leave out the daydream folios and the bedtime retellings, am I right? Focus on the older, more original pieces? Man, is the Librarian going to be pissed."

I went back to the table and reopened the first folio. "Mmm, yeah, I'm not looking forward to being the one to report this vandalization." I started reading at the beginning, a story about Prince Charming ravishing a princess of some sort or other.

Jack brought another three folios to the table and sat down next to me. "Well, at least we know one thing."

"Agreed. If he could have changed these words like he did the others, then they wouldn't have been pulled out. And it looks like they were ripped out recently. Look, the parchment isn't discolored on the edge."

Jack took a closer look at the ripped edges in the book he was holding and grunted his agreement. We were both quiet for a few moments while we drifted through story after story of Prince Charming rescuing princesses and living happily ever after.

I sighed and leaned back from the table. "These are so drab, and you know, he wouldn't have left anything in if he thought it could damage him. This feels like a waste of time."

"Well then, oh marked one, what do you suggest? I'm glad you think reading this dreck is useless. The sap running off these pages makes me feel dirty." He made a show of wiping off his hands on his pants.

"I don't know." I flipped my book closed out of frustration and propped my head in my hands, staring at the cover. I hardly noticed that my movements had dislodged a paper until Jack reached over and pulled it the rest of the way out of the book. On it, in Prince Charming's gracefully looping script was an odd series of marks that looked to be some sort of runic language, but not one I was at all familiar with. "Jack, do you have any idea what this says?"

"No, but I know what language it's in at least. That's ancient Sumerian. I did some trade in Sumerian manuscripts a while back." Jack turned the paper this way and that, but remained equally as puzzled as I was. "Maybe the Librarian can read it."

"Worth a try." I pressed the call button in the room and the acolyte returned with hardly a delay. "We found a notation in ancient Sumerian and we were wondering if the Librarian might be able to help us with a translation?"

She smiled and held her hand out for the paper. "No need, I just finished a semester studying Sumerian under Anu Himself. Let's see." Her brow furrowed and she mouthed a few words under her breath before she looked back up. "It's a title, one of our oldest texts in fact. *Word and Power* is a direct translation, though the connotation is more along the lines of power in words. It's a little-known treatise on the Storyteller's early days."

Jack caught my eye and I nodded slightly. "Would we perhaps be able to look at a copy of the text?" he asked, all smiles and wide eyes.

"Absolutely. I think we even have a translation in English if you'll give me a moment. I'll go find it for you." She was gone before I had a chance to give the affirmative and Jack gave a little hoot.

"Not so useless of a trip after all. Charming interested in a book called *Power in Words*? Sounds like what we're looking for. What are the odds of it falling out of a book like that?"

"Probably about the same as being chosen by a god to do their dirty work, I'd imagine." I laid my head on the table to wait, since the hangover wasn't quite gone yet, and was startled by the acolyte coming back into the room.

"I'm sorry, access to that particular text has been restricted. You'd have to ask the Librarian specifically for permission to see it."

"Well then, back to the Librarian it is! Lead the way." Jack bowed her out of the door with an extra flourish and she giggled, and pranced up the stairs in front of us. I swatted at Jack and got a stuck-out tongue in return.

Marian ushered us back into her office looking thoroughly apologetic. "I'm sorry about this, but it's a delicate situation. There are all sorts of questions about the authenticity of the manuscript in question and so we've restricted access to it to the higher-ranking Storytellers, to ensure that our newer characters don't get the wrong ideas about life here."

I quirked an eyebrow at her, my curiosity piqued. There was no censorship in our world—there couldn't be, considering that was a commentary on the very sanctity of the life born out of the narrative. "That's a curious way to put it. Seeing as we're hardly new characters, do you think we might be able to give it a go?"

"I'm sorry, it's not just me, or I would. The whole board of tellers has to approve access, and I'm afraid they're not in session right now. You'd have to wait until next month." To her credit, Marian did look truly sorry about the situation.

I bit my lip to keep from snapping at the woman and glanced over at Jack. He gave a discreet glance at my wrist, then flicked his eyes at Marian, and did it again when I feigned ignorance the first time. I sighed and started rolling up my left sleeve and laid my wrist on the desk. "I'm sure the board will understand."

The woman looked confused at first, then angry. "It is a sacrilege to carve the mark of the Storyteller on yourself, and you should know that. What are you trying to pull?"

"Pull? I'm not trying to pull anything. Trust me, the Fire that caused that was anything but self-inflicted. Isn't there some way to verify this thing is real?" I prodded at the scar on my wrist that I had been hiding for this very reason. The faint sibilant strains of a song filtered through the room. *Maaarian, madame libraaaarian.* A masterfully rendered version of her song, I thought.

The Librarian went deathly pale as the chords faded from the air. "But, he hasn't...not in over one thousand years..."

I briskly rolled my sleeve back down over the scar. "I wish he hadn't started now. Marian, I'm sorry, but I have to see that manuscript."

"Yes, yes of course. I have a copy up here." She got up and went to her personal bookshelves and hunted around for a moment before handing us a small chapbook. "I'm...don't take this the wrong way, but please, take that and read it someplace else? I don't know how I could explain to the board that I gave it to you; they'll never believe me. If anyone asks, say you stole it?"

I laughed, albeit dryly. "Sure thing. We'll leave right now." I tucked the chapbook into the back of my new journal where it fit discreetly. "Jack, let's get going."

"So much for the promised assistance." He muttered, levering himself out of his chair.

"Stop it, Jack. Marian, thank you. You've been most kind, and we don't want to get you in trouble." I grabbed Jack's arm and towed him out the door. As we were heading to the front door, the acolyte intercepted us. "Did you get access to it?"

I interrupted Jack as he started to open his mouth. "No, no we have to wait for some damn-blasted council meeting. For a *month*. No thanks, we don't need to see it that badly."

"I'm sorry to hear that. Do you need to go back down to the Stacks?"

"Not today, but I may come back tomorrow to finish my research. Thanks for your help." I towed Jack the rest of the way to the front door and we made it out into the sunshine.

"You know, you should trust me more. I'm not an idiot." Jack sounded vaguely put off, but I couldn't tell if that was irritation at Marian or me.

I sighed and made my way to a bench in a small park in front of the Stacks. "I'm sorry. It's not that I don't trust you, I never know what story is going to come out of your mouth and I'd rather not be blindsided by something I have to back up later."

"I'll take that as a compliment." He sat down beside me on the bench. "Care to read?"

"Not here, let's wait till we get back to our room. I have a feeling we shouldn't let anyone see us with this little book in public." I stretched, then stood, offering my hand to Jack. "Shall we pick up some food on the way?"

He grasped it, and nearly hauled me back down as he stood. "Sounds perfect."

I laughed as I caught my balance and we headed off to the District, picking up some delectable-looking sandwiches from Amelia's before returning to the Palm. I was holding the bags with lunch, so Jack opened the door and stepped through first, arguing over his shoulder about the merits of anchovies, which meant he didn't see the thugs in the room until one had already clobbered him over the head.

I should have turned and tried to run, which would have been sensible for a princess, but I instead found myself throwing the sandwiches at one troll then launching myself at the one standing over Jack. I never made it, and yelped as the first one caught me by my hair and hauled me back against himself, slapping a cloth across my face that smelled sweetly of chloroform. I tried to struggle, but trolls are deadly strong. Within seconds I was out.

♛

As I came around, everything seemed to be shifting around me, and then I realized that it wasn't me, the room was *actually* moving. My wrists were handcuffed in front of me and I was in a hammock in a cabin on a ship. In the hammock next to me was Jack, trussed up more securely than I was. He was still out and had a nasty-looking bruise on the side of his face. I sat up, trying to figure out exactly what sort of ship we were on, but I couldn't tell much more than that we were in either an officer's or guest quarters; it was much too roomy to be crew quarters. The portholes were covered with curtains, so I struggled out of the hammock, hampered by the handcuffs, and made my way over to one of the windows to look out.

I couldn't see land. Anywhere. I couldn't believe I had been out long enough that the scoundrels made it to the coast and then got far enough from land that it could no longer be seen.

I dropped the curtain before I started to hyperventilate from fear and made my way, staggering a little, back to Jack. I carefully made an examination of his head by touch, and while I found a small bump, his skull at least seemed to be in one piece. He groaned when I touched the bruise that spread from his temple to his jaw on the right side, but didn't quite come around.

"Jack," I hissed, trying not to alert anyone to the fact that I was awake. "Jack, come on, you stubborn ass, wake up."

He groaned, louder, and his brow furrowed before he cautiously opened one eye. "Oww."

"Yeah, I bet that hurts, but we've got bigger problems. We're at sea." Now that I knew he could wake up, my heartbeat slowed a little and I could focus more on the room. I went over and tried the door, but it was locked, so I made my way to a water jug instead. I wet a handkerchief I had stashed in the pocket of my leathers and came back to Jack and laid it on the enormous bruise.

"At sea? How the hell'd we end up at sea?" He pressed gingerly on the handkerchief, winced, and put his hand down.

"Best guess? We kicked a field goal with that beehive we've been trying to avoid." I checked his pupils with a lantern that was hanging by the hammock, happy to hear he wasn't slurring his words.

Jack waved the light out of his eye. "I'm fine, promise. I've taken harder whacks then this." He ran a hand through his hair and winced when it glanced off the bump on the side of his skull. "Though I can't precisely remember when at the moment. Think that's a problem?" He grinned at me when I huffed at him, and grabbed my hand when I made to leave the side of the hammock. "Teasing, Soph. I'm fine."

He slowly eased himself upright and stretched out his neck and back. "Door's locked?"

"Tight. I guess we're supposed to sit here and wait." I paced around the small room. The the cabinets were empty but for extra bedding, though I did find a small travel loaf and round of cheese, which I brought back over to our hammocks. I sat on mine like a swing and broke apart the bread and cheese, handing Jack half. "Not as good as the sandwiches we'd picked up, I wager, but I'm too hungry to care." We sat quietly for a bit, picking at the food, until we heard a key in the lock. We both got to our feet, slightly apart to give us room to maneuver, and waited to see who would come through the door.

I was disappointed that it wasn't Prince Charming who came in. Instead it was a white-bearded older fellow, with a wooden leg and a pipe firmly clenched between his teeth. He cast an eye over us, grunted, and then beckoned us onto the deck. I looked at Jack, wondering what was going to happen if we followed, all sorts of nightmare scenarios running through my head, but Jack shrugged. I took his arm, and we exited our prison for the salt air outside.

Most of the crew was busy with the rigging, bringing the ship to a halt, and I could see why. A dense ring of fog surrounded our small continent, about fifty miles out from the coastline; directly in front of us hung those mists. No one knew what was beyond them, because no one had ever came back. It was rumored that you weren't even reborn when your story was told the next time; you were just gone, for good.

A small contingent of sailors were loading up a lifeboat with crates and barrels while others rigged a shade of sorts over it. The old sailor stopped beside it and gave its hull a solid slap. "This should do you well, I think. The goal is not to have you dying on us. You'd be reborn next time someone needed a bedtime story and we can't have people wondering what offed you. We're loading you up with food and water, enough to last you a week, so hop in and we'll send you on your way."

"I'm sorry, but you plan to put us down this close to the fog? That's as good as killing us!" Jack's voice cracked on the last of his sentence. Whether that was from the last of his hangover, the residual effects of the chloroform, or his fear at being this close to the mist, I wasn't able to tell.

I put a hand on his arm to remind him to control himself, and stepped up to the captain. "Sir, do you mean to give us no way to maneuver away from the fog? There are no oars on that boat."

"The way I figure it, you can doggy paddle away from it, if you're that all fired to stay back. Hell, maybe you'll get lucky and find your way to Perdida." He turned away from us and I felt a chill down my spine. Isla de la Perdida Historia was our ghost story, an island that some claimed to have seen from the bows of their ships, disappearing into the edge of the mists. The Island of the Story-Lost was the place where fading characters went to die. No one ever left once they set foot on the shores of Perdida.

However, this was probably the last time I was going to be able to get any information about what was going on, and I doubted that the

Storyteller, next time I saw him, would take fear of death as an excuse for not doing my job. "What could Charming be promising you, to get you to consign us to a slow death?"

"Charming knows how to beat a certain white whale." The man grinned, the smile more of a grimace than an expression of pleasure. I wondered how a character this unhinged had managed to avoid being committed when he came through the Fire.

"Tell us this, at least, why are you only giving us food for a week? We'll reemerge from the Fire when we starve."

"He didn't say why, just that it wouldn't matter then. Now that's enough questions, missy, into the boat with you." His men had come up behind us and lifted us bodily, tossing us into the boat, regardless of our struggles.

I rolled to my knees and leaned over the side "Wait! Please, wait, I have one last request."

He paused, stroking his beard, then nodded his head. "As the condemned, you have the right, though I may refuse it."

"Could we please have our effects, my bags, Jack's axe, if you have them?"

Ahab laughed and gestured to one of his men. "By all means, though what use you'd have for them at sea is a mystery to me." He took my satchel when it was handed to him and pulled out my credit cards before handing it over. "I think, though, for the sake of thoroughness, I'll hire a trollop to use these a few places, send your trail to the other provinces, in case anyone starts getting suspicious."

His men tossed the rest of our effects into the boat; it appeared that they had ransacked our room of everything before capturing us. That was nice, as at least we'd have a few changes of clean underwear as we faced our death. It's the little things that can brighten your day.

"Alright, send 'em over!" the captain roared, and his men hauled on the winches, setting us down roughly on the water. "And to make things easier on you and lover boy there, have a key to those irons." He dropped it over the rail and it landed with a dull clink on the bench beside me. "Happy sailing! May your story end well, but not too soon!" The vessel wasted no time in hoisting its sails and turning back to the mainland, leaving us bobbing on the waves with nothing else in sight except an endless expanse of fog.

♛

THE CASTAWAY CONGA

The key sat there, glinting in the late morning light, while I stared at it. It's hard to think about doing anything when your prospects look as dim as ours. We had food and water for a time, apparently, but what would happen when it ran out? We'd eventually die, of course, and back at the Hearth, a new 12th princess, unnamed but clever, and a new Jack would be floating out of the Fire, brand-new and clean of any memories but those they were written with. Or we'd simply float into the fog and vanish, lost to everyone. Or maybe we'd get lucky and float back in to shore, though that would likely be long after we could be of any use to the Storyteller in stopping whatever it was that Charming had planned for the anniversary celebrations.

Jack finally tired of watching me stare at the key and leaned over and picked it up. He lost no time in unshackling himself and tossing his irons into the ocean. He then tried to hand the key to me, but I was still too lost in ruminating on all the awful possibilities and ignored him until he pulled my hands out and unlocked my handcuffs for me. Those, too, he tossed into the drink and was about to follow it with the key when he changed his mind.

Instead, he slipped it into his pocket. "You never know when a handcuff key will come in handy. Fancy a bit of a swim?"

"With the white whale, Jaws, and the Kraken somewhere out here? Thanks, I'll pass." I had no idea what we could do now to get back to the mainland. Confession time; I'm not so much clever as I am a paranoid worrywart. I think everything could mean two or three things, and I assume the worst. It helps that I've been right about a few things in the past, but it meant I wasn't so great at figuring out the positives of a situation and capitalizing on those. So, I did what I always do when I felt lost. I pulled out paper and pen.

"Oh goody, we can play hangman or something!" Jack made to grab the notebook he'd purchased for me and I pulled it out of his reach.

"What, are you bored already? We haven't been sitting in this boat for ten minutes yet! Why don't you bend that mind of yours to our predicament and figure out some way to get us out of this mess. I'd say you've failed spectacularly as a bodyguard." It was cruel, I knew it as it left my mouth, but I was scared and he could be so irritatingly immature.

He *finally* got mad. "I've already thought it through, your highness, and nothing is immediately forthcoming. We are well and truly stuck and I was hoping to distract myself from the fact that we are most likely going to die. If you want, I could make things clean and give you a too-short haircut with my axe here, let a new Sophia pop out of the Fire lickety split and send someone asking questions, and I'd be tempted to follow you shortly after. But I feel too self-preservational for that at the moment. I was considering rigging us a sail out of the sunshade, but they left us no rope; it's nailed directly to the boat. We have plenty of food and water for some time, longer if we ration, and perhaps someone will come along. That's about the best we can hope for. No, strike that, if we could add some *pleasant* company to that, that'd be great, or even if we do survive for a week, it'll seem like hell. But no, that's right, you refuse to think anyone else can have ideas that are original and interesting. I forgot that if it's not your plan, it's no good. Given all that, your highness, feel free to doodle away, if you think that's going to help."

He started to shift himself under the sunshade and curl up in the bow, but I wasn't going to let him run away from this argument—well, run away as far as he could. I moved forward along the boat myself, sticking my head under the shade. "For your information, I am quite capable of listening to other's ideas and suggestions and even finding the merit in them, when there is merit. I am afraid that the majority of *your* suggestions are so juvenile as to be worthless! You decided that since we couldn't immediately figure a way out, we should play a *game* where someone *dies*. You don't think, ever, you just act!"

"That's better than only thinking and never acting!" He shoved his way out of the canvas and stood in the boat, starting it swaying. "You have to plan *everything*! We couldn't even get a group of friends together without you insisting on planning this grand gala! It would take days!"

"They loved my parties!"

"They hated your parties! They were long, overwrought, and... and over the top! You tried too hard to make things just right and were never comfortable letting things be!"

I was crying at this point, though if anyone had asked, I would have blamed the tears on the horror of being left adrift on the ocean, and not on what Jack was saying. "I'm sorry if I like to improve myself and present a *proper* image to the public at large."

"That's just it, Soph, we loved *you*, not the damn 12th princess. We could have done well away with the drama and pomp. I never understood why you couldn't be the same way in public that you were with me, when we were alone. You were so happy and fun. Warm and sexy and loving. It hurt, so bad, when you left, Sophie." He reached out to wipe away my tears and I couldn't stop myself from softening to his hand.

"I had to, Jack, I was wasting my life. I had to find a purpose." I laughed, sharp and hard. "I guess I should have waited until I had one handed to me."

"It's not in your nature." Jack finally sat next to me on the bench seat and I curled up under his arm.

"I'm so sorry, Jack, for everything. For leaving all those years ago, for never coming back, for this mess, and we're probably going to die out here, and—"

"Hush." He brushed a light kiss on my lips and I froze instinctively. I'd spent so long trying to convince myself that he wasn't good for me, he was too much of a playboy, that I didn't know how I wanted to respond anymore. And then, it hit me that we were probably going to die shortly anyway, so who cared?

I threw my arms around his neck, dropping the journal to the deck of the boat, and kissed him with all the pent-up passion of 200 wasted years. And every ounce of it was returned to me tenfold. After a moment, I pulled back, needing the answer to one question before I could go any farther. "Jack, this isn't some conquest to you, proving that you can get me back, is it?"

"You were never some belt notch to me. You were so much more." He started in for another kiss, but I was distracted by what I had seen on the floor of the boat.

"Jack, look! They missed our copy of *Power in Words!*" I pulled it the rest of the way out from the back of the journal. "They must have believed us when I said we were denied access."

Jack blew out a lungful of air, letting it raspberry through his lips before sucking down another deep breath and consciously turning off the lustful side of his brain. "Out of curiosity, did you hear anything I just said? I thought it fairly eloquent, myself."

"What? Oh, yes, Jack, it was very sweet." I planted a lingering kiss on the corner of his mouth before pulling back again and starting to flip through the small booklet. "I'll bet you anything it was asking about this that got us stranded out here. We weren't a problem to him when we were looking at his stories because he'd excised all the contradictory ones, but this...this must be dangerous to him somehow."

"Well then, let's take a look, shall we?" Jack adjusted his belt, then flipped us back to the first page, but didn't try to grab for it from my hand this time.

I scanned the first few lines, and shook my head. "This seems like a pretty standard First Character story to me, about her creation of the Storyteller. I mean the language is stilted and all but..." I flipped to the next page to continue reading.

A moment later, Jack let out a long slow whistle. "Oh baby, I think we finally figured out how he's doing it."

The story was more than the history of our beginning. It was an instruction manual on how the First Character had managed to harness the power of humanity's imagination to make life on this side of the Fire bearable, and how the Storyteller could wield his power to keep characters alive long after they had been forgotten, if that was the character's wish.

"Alright, so it is possible to control the power of imagination here, somehow. I can see how the tellers wouldn't want just anyone to get their hands on these, but the instructions are vague, referring to focal points and capacitors." I flipped through several more pages of cryptic diagrams and equations, before handing the whole thing over to Jack to let him puzzle over it. "I really don't understand it right now. And it would require an incredible amount of power before you can do anything. Charming would have had plenty of time to amass it, that's for sure, but what does he think he's going to do with it? This isn't helpful in that regard."

"What would be helpful right now is a tip on how to get our imagination to bring us to land. First things first!" He screwed his eyes shut and scowled fiercely. "I am imagining a spit of land, extending out from the mainland and right to our boat, saving us from the mists and from starvation, and leaving us with enough time to figure out what Charming is up to and how to stop him." He sat there for another moment, cycling through various grimacing faces before he let his breath out in a great big gust and opened his eyes. "Anything?"

I made a show of looking around us, already forming a negative answer on my lips, when I saw it. "Holy shit."

Jack looked to where I was pointing, saw the beach ahead of us, firmly anchored in the mists, looked down at the book, back to the land and then looked up at the sky. "I'll have one roast turkey, please, with stuffing and gravy." He waited patiently for a moment, but when nothing happened, he sighed. "I guess we should try and make for that land then."

We detached the lids from the water barrels and tried to use them as paddles to speed our journey to shore, but it didn't seem to make a whole lot of difference. At least we felt we were actually doing something. We watched the shore drift closer with each bob of a wave until we finally felt our keel scrape the bottom. Jack leapt out and hauled us closer in to shore and then helped me out. Together, we hauled the dinghy up above the high water mark and, for good measure, dropped the anchor into the sand.

"This can't be the mainland...can it?" Jack asked, even though we were both sure it wasn't.

I shivered a little as I noticed the wisps of fog curling along the tideline. "It's got to be Perdida, you know that as well as I do. It's the only land that anyone has spotted out here, ever." I walked the rest of the way up the beach until I was standing at the edge of a dense rainforest where a path cut its way in, a sign inviting newcomers to head into the heart of the gloom. The darkness was made worse by the fog condensing on every available surface and dripping steadily into the undergrowth. I went a few steps down the path, and then turned back to Jack. "You were saying how I overthink things... How 'bout it, cowboy, you ready for some adventuring?"

Jack hesitated a moment, then went back to the boat, retrieved his axe, then passed by me to take lead on the path. "In case there's anyone out here that would like to jump us," he commented over his shoulder. We walked in silence for the most part, listening to the incessant drip of the forest. It was almost a mile before we realized we hadn't heard any animal sounds. When we finally heard something go rustling through the brush to our right, we about jumped out of our skins. But nothing came at us, and when our heart rates returned to normal, we continued forward. More rustling started up, some on either side of us, and soon there was a constant shushing sound of things moving through the ferns and bushes.

The path finally disgorged us into a clearing that had a small settlement at its heart, about thirty huts and cottages and some barns on the far side. At first we didn't see any movement in the village, and the rustlers stayed behind in the trees. With nothing to prevent us, and a burning sense of curiosity to motivate us, Jack and I cautiously approached the buildings. They were all oriented toward a round grass circle with a well at its center. There were no windows on the backs of the buildings, so we couldn't be sure if the village was even occupied, but I was starting to get thirsty and directed my steps to the well.

It wasn't until I was clearing the last of the houses that I noticed there was someone seated on the low wall of the well. I couldn't be sure, but I don't think she had been there when we first came into the clearing. She hadn't walked up and taken a seat, either. She was just— *poof*—there. Her back was to us, with tightly braided white hair that reached her waist and mingled with the green flowing fabric she wore. It wasn't a dress, or a robe, but this fluttering drapery of fabric that seemed to be caught in a breeze that I didn't feel.

I screwed up my courage, and decided the direct approach was best. "Excuse me, can you tell us where we are? I believe we're on La Isla de la Perdida Historia, but I'm hoping I'm wrong."

The woman turned to the well and hauled a bucket up from its depths. Her hands were dark-skinned and calloused, her movements sure and strong. Once she had pulled it over to the wall of the well, she turned to us with a sigh.

"Hello, Sophia. I had wagered on you making it nearly the full week before being caught." Kith smiled at me and offered me a ladle full of water. "I was wrong, sadly. Thirsty?"

I was caught flat-footed at seeing the First Character here, but at least that meant we had help on this island. And then I realized what she said and I started to get mad, again. "You wagered on me?"

"Things can get boring when you've been kicking around for a few thousand years. You take your entertainment where you can find it. Aren't you going to introduce me to your handsome companion?" She smiled at Jack and held out her hand.

"I'm Jack, and let me tell you, it is delightful to find conversant companionship on this island. I'm afraid we might be stranded." He brushed his lips lightly over her fingers.

"For goodness sake, she knows who you are, Jack. This is the First Character, otherwise known as storyteller Kith. If she's about, I highly doubt we'll be stuck here long, wherever here is." I raised an eyebrow at her. "At least I would assume that since the wager is now completed, your sense of fair play wouldn't be violated in helping us get back to the mainland?"

"Don't be cross." Kith responded, smiling at Jack as he backed up from her, looking somewhat more ill at ease. "And that all depends on you. Characters only find Perdida when they are in need of something."

"Yes, we're in need of a lift back to the mainland. We got ahold of a copy of *Power in Words*, which is, apparently, the guide Charming is using to manipulate things. Now we have to figure out what his plan is and stop it."

Kith tapped her chin thoughtfully. "If it was just a ride back to the mainland you needed, you wouldn't have stumbled across us here. All the prevailing currents head back into shore, and you would have found yourself back on the mainland soon enough. I think perhaps you need some help with something else."

Jack leaned into the conversation. "Perhaps we're here to make heads or tails out of that book. I certainly couldn't understand one whit of it. It was a translation, though, so it's possible that is part of the problem."

A sunny smile broke across Kith's face. "I should have put more money on you. But first, let me give the crew the all clear. They're leery of strangers; they rely on me to clear the new characters before they'll come out to say hi." She didn't raise her voice, but I could almost feel it whisper out past me to the forest beyond. "It's alright, come on home." Kith stood as a crowd worked their way out of the forest.

They were a mixed bag of folks, a few humanoid characters, but most we would classify as monstrous. Additional limbs, odd coloring, eyes in places where there shouldn't be eyes. These were sloppy creatures, appearing for all the world as if they would fall apart at the least touch. The humans among them didn't look much better; some were put together like a Dali portrait while others were almost transparent.

"Sophia, Jack, meet the Story-Lost. Characters, meet Sophia and Jack. They won't be staying long, as they're just visiting, but I'll make sure you have time to catch up on news from the mainland if you're interested." Most of the characters seemed to lose interest and drift away to their homes or tasks about the village. "Sorry, they're a shy bunch. I'm sure you can see why."

"Are those...are those imaginary friends? They have to be...they're so..." Jack's eyes darted back and forth between creatures and his grip on his axe had gone slack.

"Rough around the edges? Why yes, how astute of you. Most of the island's population is made up of imaginary friends. The rest are characters that have chosen to take their stories out of circulation with the Storyteller and are slowly fading out of human memory. This is one of several villages on this island." Kith bent to pet a dog-caterpillar crossbreed that sat at her feet, panting. "The imaginations of children are powerful things. A single child can dream one of these beautiful beings into life, sustain it for years, and then forget about it. One day, the child won't be able to remember the color of their friend's fur, or how many eyes it used to have. They have such a fleeting life, such a tenuous hold on our reality. That's why the Teller and I bring them here when they come out of the Fire. It's better for them."

"That's why we never see them. I mean, our philosophers have theorized, but to actually see one..." Jack squatted down and held out his hand to the pup. "Hey fella, want a scritch?"

The dog-caterpillar growled. "What do I look like to you, jackass, a cocker spaniel?" He sat down and started giving his privates a thorough wash. Considering he looked like a corgi with a caterpillar costume integrated into his coat, with antenna and all, it was an amusing sight.

"You'll have to excuse Fredderpillar. He's quite foul-mouthed even though I've asked him to find less crude ways to express himself." Kith frowned down at him.

The dog stopped washing himself long enough to roll his eyes. "Lady, for the millionth time, its just Fred. When you say my full name like that it makes me sound like a French whore."

Kith pursed her lips, but didn't respond. I squatted down and stuck my hand out. "Well, Fred, I for one am pleased to make your acquaintance."

Fred squinted at me, the perpetually cheerful corgi countenance taking on a frightening degree of shrewdness, which was somewhat moderated by his hind leg still sticking up in the air. Finally, he dropped his leg and stood, shaking out his fur and chitin coat. He trotted over to me, sat, and offered his paw.

"You seem like a smart broad. And hot. I like that." I gave his paw a brief shake and let go.

"Thanks, I think." I took the opportunity to examine him closer and reached out a hand before remembering. "May I?"

"Feel free to pet me wherever you like, dame. If you like what you see, we should ditch the charmer over there and go for walkies. What do you say?" He waggled his eyebrows at me, panting, and let his tongue roll out.

I laughed, more delighted than offended by his forward nature. "I'm afraid you're not my species, or I'd love to." There was chitinous plating fused into his back, in bright green and yellow, with plates that came up over his neck and finished with a small helmet where the antenna branched out, twitching. Bands of the plating encircled him at the ribcage, across his chest.

"That hasn't stopped anyone before, doll, trust me." Fred winked and leaned into my hand. "Can you scratch, right there? No, at the edge of the green stuff. Oh yeah, that hits the spot, perfect." He hummed in pleasure while Jack finally broke down into laughter.

I scratched him a bit longer, then patted him on the back and stood back up. "Out of curiosity, Fred, what function do your antenna serve?"

"Beyond making me look cute and innocent? Not a damn thing that I've been able to figure out. Let me tell you, my kid's imagination ain't so fantastic when it comes to some of the details of the thing, ya know what I mean?" He stood and turned to Kith. "Miss fancy pants, if you want my opinion, we should keep these two. Well, Sophia at least. The tall one over there should go to the kennel." He trotted off in the direction of the barns, pausing to bark briefly at a cat-like creature hanging linens out in her backyard. She ignored him.

Kith watched Fred go with a bemused expression. "He's strongly focused for an imaginary character. We think it has something to do with the fact that his creator is a young child with severe autism. Strong interior life, absolute need for a companion he can relate to. But I do wish he'd been created with at least a modicum of self-restraint." She smiled and hooked her arm into mine and Jack's. "But let's talk about you now. You said you have a copy of *Enum ina Awatum*? It's been ages since I read that. May I take a look?" She led us over to a porch on the largest house facing the well and offered us seats and then glasses of lemonade. We politely accepted, mostly because I wasn't entirely sure how one could politely refuse; though I would have preferred barley water.

I put the lemonade aside and pulled the booklet from my bag. There was a small water stain on the cover that must have come from the floor of the boat and I tried to rub it out before handing it over. Kith thumbed through the pages, alternately murmuring pleased sounds and shaking her head.

"They got most of it right. Whoever they have doing the Sumerian translation down at the Stacks has gotten much better over the years. The general outline and information is correct, but some of these specifics, such as here," she gestured to a diagram involving humans, the Fire, characters, and power flow, "and here," she gestured at a table two pages later, "are completely wrong."

Jack leaned forward, his lemonade forgotten at his elbow. "It is possible, then. For a character to gain some control over imagination."

"Certainly, look at the Storyteller and me. We wouldn't be here without it, and neither would most of you. At least, not as stably as you are. We help guide and channel the flow of imagination as it comes through from humanity. If Charming found a copy of this and managed to master the skill, that would certainly explain a lot. You see, I can't tell what the Storyteller does with the invisible force that is imagination, any more than he can tell when I've tapped into it. It blinds you to other wielders of it. We weren't sure if that was restricted to the two of us, since we were told at nearly exactly the same time, but it appears its true for anyone who's tapped in. I wonder..." she trailed off, nibbling on a nail.

"You wonder what?" I didn't want her to stop now, this was becoming too fascinating.

She waved a hand dismissively. "I was thinking that maybe that's because by taking control of imagination, it took you out of the general pool of things. You're no longer just a result of the inspiration, but also a creator or guide to it. But that philosophical mumbo-jumbo will get us nowhere. No, if we're going up against someone tapped in enough to completely flummox the Storyteller and me, you're going to need some heavy ammunition yourself; you're going to have to start learning how to channel it yourself."

I didn't particularly like the sound of that, considering the complexity of the diagrams in the book. How was I supposed to get a handle on that in less than a week? It seemed impossible. And then I had a thought. "Why do I have to learn this if you and the Storyteller already have the skills? It seems like something overly difficult to learn in the time we have."

Kith looked amused and leaned over to pat my hand. "That's sweet of you, dear, but we simply don't have the time. Unlike some human deity, we are not omniscient, omnipotent, and omnipresent. We are stuck in this timeline right alongside of you and both He and I are kept quite busy by the separate tasks we have undertaken. The Storyteller spends all day every day, and all night as well, cooped up in his caverns telling the stories of our people so that they can live richer and more full lives. The fact that he left there for even a few moments to speak with you is remarkable. And I have duties here. These characters rely on me to keep them safe and guide their passage into whatever lies beyond. We simply haven't the time to go mucking about in Charming's affairs, figure out exactly what he's up to, and then pit ourselves against him. And I have no doubt it's going to be a significant battle if he's already exerting the kind of influence you've found."

"So teaching Soph the skills is going to save you time?" Jack leaned forward and braced his elbows on his knees. "I'd think it would take more, if I catch the drift of some of those diagrams."

"We're thinking of it more as an investment." Kith stood and stretched, her gown once more flirting with a non-existent breeze. "We aren't going to start this today, however. You two are too tired to learn anything properly. Let me show you to your room and you should get some rest." She pushed aside the curtain covering the doorway and led us into a cozy seaside cottage. When I looked out the window, I could see cliffs with seagulls circling overhead.

I quickly stepped back outside and was once more in a steaming forest. Back in and I could hear the gulls crying out. "Kith? Um, that's disconcerting."

"Don't mind that. I change the scenery outside of the windows every few months when I get bored. That trick is an easy one, I'll show you sometime. Here is your room." She led us to the end of a hall and opened the door, revealing an enormous four-poster bed and dual wardrobe sets. "I hope this will be comfortable for you. My other rooms are all occupied at the moment and I don't have any room around the house for another addition, though I suppose I could always add another floor..." Kith drifted off and assumed a faraway expression, but we hurriedly assured her that one room would do fine. Personally, though I wasn't sure sharing a bed with Jack right at this moment was entirely the best idea, the concept of thinking a new addition onto a house was even more disconcerting.

Kith snapped to. "Very good, then. Can I get you anything else?"

"I don't suppose you'd mind if we went back down to the beach to grab our gear out of the boat, do you?" Jack asked, leaning against the doorframe.

"Not at all! You aren't prisoners here, only guests. Feel free to go anywhere you like, talk to anyone you like. I just ask that you respect that a large portion of the characters here are fading, or dealing with the fact that they will fade in a short time. They may not feel like talking with you, or interacting with you at all. It would probably be best if you let them approach you, instead." She patted Jack on the shoulder and started down the hallway. "Oh! And before I forget, dinner will be at 7 in the main dining hall. That's the big blue building at the edge of the village. See you then!" And she hurried out the front door and began talking animatedly with an enormous blue ape.

I sat on the bed, testing the mattress, and was pleased to find it was a memory foam; another of my favorite inventions to carry through the Fire. I lay back on it, happy to be out of a boat, happy to be someplace quiet and safe, and blissfully ignoring the fact that I was on an island for the lost and being strong-armed into learning what amounted to magic tomorrow.

Jack, for his part, paced around the room a couple times, then stopped at the window, this one featuring a landward view from the cliffs. It looked to be an old-world forest. "Can you believe it, Sophie? Perdida. It's real."

"So is magic, apparently. I wonder why all the magic users who come through the portal can't tap into it." I sat up on one elbow and turned to watch his silhouette at the window.

He turned, hopping up to sit in the open window frame. "It's not magic, not really. Do you suppose if I tumble out of this window I'll land in that meadow or back on Perdida?"

"Let's not find out." I got up and went over to him, pulling him out of the frame. "Are you up for going back to the beach to get our bags? I for one would like to get a change of clothing before dinner. These are all salty and smell of stress sweat."

Jack bowed and clasped my arm in his. "As my lady commands, so shall it be."

I laughed as we left the house and headed back to the trail that had led us to the village. We were not long on it before a young child came hollering out of the jungle on a vine and landed in front of us. He wore a loin-cloth that seemed reminiscent of animal print, but not one I could readily identify. "Halt!" he cried, throwing up his hand to make us stop.

Jack and I slowed to a standstill, looked at each other, and struggled not to laugh. The boy was small, but assumed the authority of a much larger, and much older, bully. Jack stooped to put himself at eye level with the child and put on a very serious face. "I'm sorry, sir, have we transgressed?"

The boy seemed momentarily confused, then smiled, bracing both hands on his hips. "Naw, you haven't transgrowed at all. I wanna come down to the beach with you 'cause I can't go unless I've got an adult with me."

"And why is that?" I asked, smiling.

"'Cause I can't swim for nothin'. Can I come? Please?" He was begging now, all imperiousness gone, the picture of abject child-hood misery.

I couldn't help it, he had the worst case of puppy dog eyes I had ever seen, so I gave in. "Yes, sure, why not, as long as you tell us your name."

He snapped to attention. "I am Zacinus the Absurdicus."

Jack stood back up and gestured grandly down the trail. "Well, Zacinus, care to lead the way?"

The boy whooped and started off down the path, running ahead and then skipping back, stopping occasionally to grab a branch and fence with the foliage. We continued after him at a less breakneck pace.

After a moment of watching Zacinus in silence, Jack murmured. "Did you ever think of raising one of the children? There are so many who come through the Fire on any given day."

I thought about it for a moment, absently tracking the boy's progress up and back, up and back. "I've definitely thought about it. Who doesn't after a couple hundred years? But, I don't know, I guess I was worried what kind of mother a partying princess would be."

"For what it's worth, I think you'd be outstanding." Jack didn't wait for a response, but swooped up behind Zacinus and caught him in a great big bear hug, swinging him around, to the child's glee. There was a rustle in the bushes next to me and Fred popped out.

He shook himself to rid his shell of leaves, then trotted to keep up with me. "Your Neanderthal is right, you know, with your experience you'd make anyone a good mother. Or a good lover." He waggled his eyebrows suggestively.

I pursed my lips in amusement. "Thank you, I think. Did you want something?"

"Naw, I was chasing after that ragamuffin up there, making sure he hadn't wandered off unattended. He tends to do that. He's a scoundrel." Fred's tone of voice was anything but reproving. In fact, he sounded proud of the boy's rule-bending personality.

"I see. If it makes you feel any better, we're watching out for him. We're heading down to the beach to get our belongings and bring them back up to the village."

"I'll tag along then. The salt water is good for my itching hide. You'd think if a child dreamed us up, our biology would work well, but no. This damn shell itches something awful." He stopped for a moment to scratch briskly and I waited politely until he had finished and was ready to continue down the path.

We chatted for the rest of the walk, mostly about politics as they stood on the mainland and about new stories that had made particularly large waves. When we made it to the beach, Zacinus and Jack were already romping in the surf. I smiled at their antics and went over to our boat, making sure all the bags were tied shut before pulling them out. I tucked all the food and water under the canvas so that it wouldn't be interfered with by weather or animals, since I wasn't sure if we would need it for our trip back to the mainland or not.

When I had finished, I looked up to see Jack sprawled panting in the sand and Zacinus busily burying him, starting at his feet. Fred had wandered a little ways down the beach and sat, staring out at the ocean. I walked over to him and knelt down, relishing the feeling of warm sand under me.

After a moment, Fred sighed and lay down. "What I wouldn't give to be able to get off this podunk island for a little bit and go for a few walkies on the mainland. It's just so damn depressing here, what with your neighbors popping off every few weeks."

I picked up a handful of the sand and let it drain through my fingers. "Is there no way for you guys to ever get over there for a visit?"

"Not that I can tell, but then again, most of the yahoos here are too feeble-minded to care that all we have to occupy us out here is subsistence living until the kids forget about us." He snorted and stood up, shaking himself. "At least I don't have that problem. My kid'll need all the companionship he can get in his head since he can't seem to manage it in real life. I'll be here for a good long while." Fred did not sound happy at the prospect. He got up without saying anything else, shook off the sand, and trotted off down the beach towards Jack and Zacinus, nipping at Zacinus's heels until the boy chased him into the ocean. Jack extracted himself from the sand that covered him up to the waist and made his way over to me.

"Is Fred as abrasive when he's not playing to an audience?" He held out his hand.

I let Jack pull me up from the sand. "I think he's bored, and a little depressed. I mean, what kind of life does a character get to lead here? It's like everyone is just waiting to die."

"That sucks, but I can identify with that; I personally can't wait until you learn whatever voodoo it is the First Character is planning on teaching you so we can get home."

I watched Zacinus and Fred and flinched when I watched a wave go through the young boy, rather than around him. "You and me both."

After we had returned to the village with our two waterlogged friends, Jack and I decided to wander over to the dining hall a bit early. It wasn't like there was much else we could do while we were waiting, as Kith had taken our copy of *Power in Words* with her. We sat on a bench outside and chatted with a few imaginaries that stopped by to ask questions about happenings on the mainland. Fred eventually trotted by our bench and stopped to take care of another itch.

"Her Stuffiness asked me to show you the ropes here tonight 'cause she got called away for some emergency or something. I heard a rumor it was an author that had gone berserk and was burning every copy of his own book. Needless to say, his characters are freaking out something fierce right now."

Jack stood and stretched. "That seems unfortunate. Dinner, then?"

I stood and smacked Jack's arm. "That's insensitive, don't you think?"

"What? It's not like we can do much for them from here, can we? And I'm hungry!" Fred yipped in agreement and led the way into the dining hall.

The room was enormous, and it needed to be, to accommodate some of the characters here. There were dinosaurs and giants, and some aquatic-based creatures in tanks connected by pipes reminiscent of a hamster's jungle gym leading out of the hall. There were also all sorts of humanoids, large and small, though it appeared that most of the fading characters were absent. I guess once your very existence started to dissipate, food wasn't very high on your list of things to care about.

We got in line at the buffet, Jack carrying a tray for Fred, who trotted along the elevated platform next to us, dictating what food Jack should dish out for him; it seemed to mainly consist of sweets, leafy greens, and fruit. Then we found seats at a long table wedged between a hulking man with diminutive fairy wings and a young girl who insisted on demonstrating her ability to belch the ABCs... every five minutes.

But the food was delicious and, besides the belching, the company was pleasant. As characters finished eating, one by one, they trickled out, disappearing into the twilit forest. I watched them go, and was wondering where they all stayed when my thoughts were interrupted by Fred. "Most of them don't have houses in the village. They go off and create their own nests or bowers, or what-have-you out in the woods. The better to sulk over their impending fading, I guess. But enough of the sappy bemoaning of fates. Come see what we get up to in the evenings." He leaped down from his bench and trotted out of the building, not waiting to see if we'd follow.

I looked at Jack, wondering if he was as tired as I was, but he shrugged and gestured for me to follow the...dog, so we followed Fred out of the building. There was an enormous bonfire set up in the center of the clearing and it was starting to really get going. About half of the imaginaries I had seen thus far on the island were clustered around it in small groups, chatting amiably, though they seemed to get quiet when we approached, until all the conversations had stopped.

The girl who had burped her ABCs finally came out of the crowd and stood defiantly between us and the fire. "What are you newbs doing here? You're *characters*, you don't belong."

Fred sat down in front of her, between the girl and us. "Now, Mindy, they're trapped on this island the same as we are. Why not show them a little kindness?"

I wasn't sure what was going on here, but it was clear we were not welcome. Any place on the mainland, I would have said we were in for an evening of storytelling, with characters sharing their history, story after story, but this fire had a different feel to it. The friends grouped around it seemed more tightly focused, more alert than any characters at a telling.

The little girl was still standing stubborn, nose as high in the air as she could get it without losing sight of us. "Because they'll get to leave. They won't fade in two year's time. That's why."

"All the more reason they should be here tonight. Wouldn't you like it if someone remembered your stories, even if it's a stuck-up character like them? Besides, you know Kith is training the pretty one to meddle in this stuff, so She would probably be grateful if we took a little responsibility for her edification. Get the princess started off on the right foot, so to speak."

Mindy gave us one more glare, then backed down. "Fine. If Kith thinks she can handle it, then she can stay. What about the other one?"

Fred gave us a look I had trouble deciphering. "I highly doubt you'll be able to get him to leave her side." Jack nodded, a little too emphatically, and I could tell he didn't want to miss whatever it was that was going down.

The imaginaries closed ranks around the fire, forming a tight circle around the flames, closer than I would want to get. A gust of wind wound through their ranks, fluttering their clothes, feathers, hair, and fur. But it didn't touch Jack, Fred, and I, standing outside of the close-knit group. They raised their hands together and a hum seemed to emanate from them, but I couldn't tell if they were making the noise or whether it came with the breeze.

The fire abruptly tripled in size, making me flinch, but none of the friends seemed to even notice. Instead, they linked hands, fins, tentacles, and started whispering and peering intently into the fire.

"What are they doing?" whispered Jack.

Fred smiled, tongue lolling out. "Planting stories."

It took me a moment to process what he had said. "You mean, they're reaching out to humans through the fire? They're *influencing* their imaginations?"

"Sort of. Imaginary friends have a more direct link with humanity, their own human in particular. Because we're the product of one imagination and we're so strongly linked with the psyche of that one human child, we can, given proper concentration and study, link in with that child's imagination and dream centers. Why do you think imaginary friends are such strong influences in a child's life? It's because after our child dreams us up, we feed their imaginations, their dreams. We *are* real."

We watched the whispering for a few more minutes, and then, one by one, the imaginaries lowered their hands and stepped out of the circle, retreating into the darkness. As they stepped away, the fire dropped lower and lower until it was almost extinguished, having consumed most of its fuel. Eventually, we were left alone with a few burning embers. Fred trotted up to the wood pile and picked up a log, dropping it into the embers, blowing on the fire until it flared up enough to catch the new wood.

He sat back on his haunches and looked back at us. "Wanna see how it's done?"

I was still trying to process the fact that there were characters in this world that were regularly reaching out to our creators and having a real influence. Jack, however, didn't seem to share my preoccupation. He immediately sat down on the ground next to Fred. "Absolutely."

I sat on Fred's other side and stared into the small fire in front of us. "Don't we need the other friends to help us?"

"Those wimps? Naw. That's for imaginary friends whose bond isn't as strong as mine. You'll notice a good portion of the friends weren't out here. Those guys are new enough or strong enough to do it all on their lonesome. Here, lay a hand on my shell and be quiet." He waited for us to follow his instructions, then he let out a small whiny howl and peered into the fire.

The flames in front of us shimmered, and then parted, showing a view of a darkened boys room, covered in posters of astronauts and glow in the dark stars artfully arranged in constellations. The view was rocking back and forth until Fred started whispering. The view stabilized on a stuffed animal, a corgi in a caterpillar costume, on the bed. Neither Jack nor I could understand what Fred was saying, but when he stopped, the child picked up the stuffed animal and gave it a fierce hug before lying down and leaving us with a view of the constellations on the ceiling. It slowly faded out and the flames shimmered closed on the room. Fred bowed his head and was quiet but for some heavy panting.

Jack and I sat silently, staring into the fire and lost in our own thoughts until the fire ate through the log and it fell apart. Fred shook himself, dislodging our hands from where they lay and getting up. "There you have it, folks, your first bit of practical magic. I highly doubt you'd ever be able to manage it, cause you two have so many tellers keeping you alive. It requires a one-on-one link to establish that sort of influence."

I hesitated before asking the question at the forefront of my mind, uncertain as to whether it would be considered rude. "What did you tell him?"

"That is a highly personal question, doll, and if you're *very* good to me, someday I'll tell you." Fred winked at me and sauntered away, without even a good night.

Jack and I sat by the embers a while longer and I scooted closer to him, to try and negate the chill that was creeping in as the fire died. He wrapped an arm around me and I lay my head on his shoulder.

"Jack, do you think I can do this?" I could feel tears building at the back of my eyes, born of exhaustion, fear, and an overwhelming sense that I was in so far over my head that I had no idea how to get out. "I mean, controlling imagination, as if it were some easily malleable force? I'm having trouble accepting it even after watching it happen right in front of me."

Jack gave me a light squeeze. "You're not alone, Sophie, trust me on that one. I am flat terrified of all of this, but remember, we're written with a healthy dose of courage, you and I. We'll find a way through all of this, and we don't have to do it alone. Tomorrow, Kith will help us tap into the magic stuff, and then we'll take out Charming, and then go back to our regular lives. Once we manage to do that, I say we get a little place in Central City for a year or two, you can report on everything happening in the city for Geppetto, or even find something else to hold your attention, if you're getting bored with that. I can think of *lots* of things to keep you busy, if you'd like." He grinned down at me and I elbowed him as best I could while wedged under his arm.

"Yes, I'm sure you could. You are such a cad sometimes, you know that?" I smiled in spite of myself and felt a bit less worried. That was one of the reasons I'd fallen for the boy in the first place. I could relax around him, stop watching my back for a few brief moments. "I think on that note, I'm going in to sleep. It's going to take all my concentration tomorrow to understand that book, I know it." I struggled out from under his arm and he sighed, getting up himself.

"You're probably right. Do I have to sleep on a couch tonight?" Zacinus must have taught Jack his puppy-eyes, and the man was exercising them now. I couldn't help but laugh as I dragged him back to the house.

THE DAY DREAM BOOGIE

The next morning dawned bright and clear through our bedroom window, but when we stumbled outside to find some breakfast, it was the same sodden, misty island that we'd landed on.

"That's damn unkind," Jack reflected. "Here I thought we were going to get some nice pretty rays and we're stuck in this nether mist." He swatted a hand through a tendril of fog that was wrapping its way around him.

I don't know how Jack was so perky in the mornings. It never made sense to me. Then again, he was a farm boy and I was written a night owl. "As long as they have coffee on this forgotten rock, I couldn't care less." The dining hall wasn't open yet, so I sat on the ground and started doing some of my favorite yoga stretches, trying to get the kinks worked out of my muscles from being slung around by brigands the day before.

Jack ran an appreciative eye over my legs. "And I thought the windows were unkind. Soph, dear, you'll give a man a heart attack."

I grinned up at him. "I don't think anything about a female could kill you, Jack, unless it was a dagger. I can totally see a pretty woman getting the drop on you. You'd be staring at her tits so hard you'd miss the pointy bit."

He grimaced. "You learn to spot pointy bits pretty quick after you've lived through the Renaissance era, what with the men playing at being women." He gave a brief shudder.

It was at this precise moment that Kith walked up and unbarred the dining hall's door. "Good morning, you two. I hope you found the demonstration last night interesting. I'm sorry I couldn't be here. Bit of an emergency."

I stood up and brushed myself off before following her in. "We heard. A rogue author burning his books?"

A few other friends and fading characters drifted in behind us. "Yes, but the characters are safe. The author forgot entirely that his agent had already sold foreign language rights to the United States, and it's well underway for publication in the spring there. We'll have to tide them over till then, and then they'll get a whole new language to play with. How fun is that?"

Jack and I followed Kith over to the self-service yogurt bar and chatted amiably about the pluses and minuses to having your story translated and what that meant for our own language abilities until we were all settled at a table with food and coffee.

I was loathe to break into the innocuous conversation to talk about training, but Jack was apparently anxious to get started. He had hardly waited for Kith to put a spoonful of granola in her mouth before bubbling over with questions. "Are we going to get started on this whole imaginary powers thing today? I mean, we have less than a week before Prince Charming decides to do whatever dirty deed it is he's planning. We should probably get this show on the road, dontcha think?"

I almost choked on my mouthful of fruit, but Kith calmly finished her bite before turning to him. "Someone's chomping at the bit this morning. I was going to hand you over to a certain swordsman friend of mine for a little imaginary battle training while I work with Sophia on a...more surgical technique." Jack frowned and Kith pursed her lips. "Do you have a problem with this plan?"

"It's just that I thought I'd be training beside Soph. It feels like you're fobbing me off." He leaned back in his chair, arms crossed. When Kith said she'd be splitting us up, I wasn't too comfortable with it either, but I had to trust her judgment on this.

"You can put your bruised manhood away, Giantkiller, you're not getting a lesser treatment. Far from it. You can practice with friend Amund in the field in front of my house while Sophia and I work on the porch, so you won't feel like you're too far away to protect her, and you'll be learning as much as her when it comes to manipulating the streams of imagination, just in a different manner. I don't have time to teach both of you everything you need to know in a week, so I'm breaking up the knowledge into two subsets, split between you. Sophia will be getting the knowledge needed to create things out of the fabric of our world, while you learn how to move along and through that fabric to defend her back while she's building things. Deal?"

Jack relaxed and leaned forward over his breakfast, looking at me first and then Kith. "Sticking close and learning magical karate? I'd say that's a good deal. Done." He started shoveling food into his mouth and ignored us for the more pressing concerns of fueling himself up for what sounded like a rigorous day.

A small fairy-like character danced over to us and whispered in Kith's ear. Kith nodded and stood, taking her coffee mug with her. "If you'll excuse me, I have something I need to take care of before we get down to business this morning. Shall we meet in one hour on the porch? It'd probably be best if both of you limber up well before beginning today's lessons."

"We'll be there." I promised and Kith drifted away. Here and there she laid a gentle hand on the shoulder (or nearest relevant body part) of an imaginary, trading good mornings as she went.

One hour later, Jack and I were doing some preliminary stretching in front of Kith's house when a sprightly old man, who closely resembled a walnut, wandered up, clutching a gnarly cane.

"Which one of you is Jake?" Jack and I glanced at each other and I shrugged, indicating he should handle this one, since I had a sneaking suspicion that this was Amund.

"Good morning, sir, I am Jack, not Jake." Jack executed a flawless bow but leapt straight up, letting out a startled yelp. Amund was now standing behind him leaning on his cane while Jack rubbed a rueful hand across his backside. I would swear up and down all that anyone found holy that the old man hadn't moved, but there he was, five feet from where he started.

I blinked and the old man was on the porch, settling into a chair and pouring himself a lemonade. "Don't correct your elders, boy, it's not polite."

Still rubbing his rump, Jack bowed, more stiffly, and managed a fairly polite, "My apologies. Do I have the pleasure of addressing Amund?"

"You do, you do. Come sit with me, you two, and we'll talk while we wait for the mistress." Cautious, we joined him, settling onto a bench seat across from him. He drained his glass, and then rattled off: "Yes, I'm an imaginary friend, yes, I've been around for a while. I'm the product of a set of octuplets, believe it or not. It's given me a little extra leeway with playing with this marvelous 'verse. Got some extra muscle to flex, as it were. And I'm going to try and hammer it into your head, dear boy, so get ready. Does that answer all of your questions?"

Jack was starting to look more interested in, rather than disgruntled by, the old man. "Enough, thank you."

Kith arrived at the appropriate moment, before the tension became uncomfortable. "Amund, are you terrorizing these kids?"

He grinned up at her. "I have to have something to entertain me in my old age."

"Yes, the grand old age of three. Now hush, I've got to start teaching these pups how to tap into that fountain you so gleefully splash about in." Amund grumbled as Kith settled herself cross-legged on the divan in front of us. "Alright you two, it's time to get down to serious business. And here's your first question. How do you go about tapping into the slipstream of imagination that supports our little world here?"

I frowned, thinking. I had expected Kith to pull out the chapbook she had confiscated yesterday and start outlining how the diagrams worked, but she obviously had a different tactic in mind. "Last night, the imaginaries all seemed to be using fire to tap into the imagination of their children. Is fire the link?"

"Fire is a link, but by no means the only one. Fire is useful when you're trying to tap directly into the consciousness of a human or humans. What we're going to be learning how to manipulate are the free-floating radicals of imagination that drift along here. All the untapped potential that comes through from the other side but isn't solid enough to become a character. That's what the sparks are that come out of the Fire. Pure potential imagination solidified and given form. But there are millions upon billions of humans on the other side of the Fire, most of whom are constantly dreaming and imagining, and most of those dreams and figments remain just that, figments. They never become solid enough to share. Part the second: how does one reach out and grab a figment?" She reached out her hand and cupped it in the air and a moment later it was filled with a glowing, pulsing light. "Here."

I held my hand out to hers and she carefully poured half the light into my hand, then giving the other half to Jack.

"It's...it feels fizzy." Jack murmured, trying to examine whatever it was that was producing the light. It seemed to trickle out of his fingers and was gone in moments; he let out a grunt of frustration.

I closed my eyes to try and feel whatever it was that Jack had felt, focusing all my thoughts on the handful of light. Jack was right in that it was fizzy. But that wasn't all that it was. It tingled and tickled and itched in my hand. The harder I fixed my mind on it, the more elusive the sensation became. I relaxed and let the sensations wash over me. A vague sensation of warmth spread up my arm and I opened my eyes. The light wasn't cupped in my hand anymore, it was *inside* my arm. The light slowly diffused into my body and faded from my sight, but I could still feel it there, somewhere in the back of my head, buzzing about. I shook my head, trying to dislodge the sensation, and it faded. I flexed my hand and examined it, looking for marks on it, but there weren't any.

"What did you just do?" Kith asked.

"I...um...I relaxed? When I tried too hard to focus on it, it started to slip away. But when I let it do as it wanted, relaxed into it, it was like...it found a home in my brain. I think it's still there somewhere, but I can't quite feel it now." I shook my head for good measure, but I felt like regular old me again.

Kith grinned and clapped her hands. "Exactly. Perfect. Imagination can't be forced, the harder you try and understand and mold it, the less you'll be able to tap into it. I imagine humans are the same way. All those poor people who would be incredible writers sitting there with blockage issues all because they're bearing down too hard with their worries and fretting about how they can't get something right. Want to try again?"

I nodded eagerly and Jack was already holding out his hands. Kith held a fist above each of our palms, closed her eyes briefly until her hands started to glow, and then opened them, releasing a rain of golden particles onto us. I immediately closed my eyes and set my mind adrift.

It was like immersing myself in a tub full of bubbles, and romping in a field full of dandelions gone to seed, their white wisps brushing against my skin, the soft fur of puppies, the fizz of carbonation, and the tingle of an electric shock. I was simultaneously comforted and aroused. I opened myself as far as I could, absorbing every last drop of the light that Kith poured on me, feeling it spiral down into my core and up through my spinal cord until it wound itself tightly at the base of my brain and settled down to a slow simmer there, sending out the occasional pulse of happy thoughts and kittens.

I opened my eyes to see Jack grinning at me, a soft light that wasn't entirely imagined shining out of his eyes. Or maybe it wasn't actually real light. I was starting to lose my ability to differentiate anymore. I returned his grin, then closed my eyes to savor the feeling of the fizzing. Kith's voice came in from what sounded much farther away than the next couch over. "If it feels like something, let it be that."

The light in my head swirled and settled into a vague form and I smiled. I held out my hand and felt the light drain down into my palm until I felt a solid stem in my hand and opened my eyes. I raised the seeded dandelion to my mouth and blew gently until the last of the perfectly formed seeds had drifted off into the breeze. I looked over at Jack and was just in time to watch him take a bite out of a barbecued turkey leg.

"Really?" I asked him.

His eyes were closed in blissful contentment. "Really," he said around his full mouth.

I laughed and turned back to Kith. "This isn't so hard, not like that book made it seem."

I'd forgotten about Amund in the other chair until he gave a hard bark of laughter. "What's hard about getting charged up like a battery and letting that go, girl? Now you have to learn to *catch* it. And make it *last*. That is a whole different bailiwick. The flower, that turkey leg, they're going to disappear in a few hours, and he'll be as hungry as when he started. But here is where our lessons diverge. Up, boy, onto the grass with you. Go. Git." He emphasized each verb with a sharp poke from his cane until Jack was hopping down the stairs trying to avoid him.

I watched them go until they settled by the well, out of comfortable hearing distance. "What's so different about what we're going to learn?"

"Amund is going to be teaching him how to grip the fabric of our reality and slip behind it. Jack has to learn how to hold all that imagination and channel it away from him, whereas you're going to be learning how to spindle it inside of you and make it work for you. But you and Jack were chosen for your strengths in these respects."

I was nodding along until what she said penetrated my overloaded brain. "But the storyteller only marked me."

Kith smiled. "The storyteller chose you not only for your innate talents, but also for the people who you surround yourself with—and your cleverness."

"Wait, does that mean the Storyteller knew Jack would help me? How?"

"He tells all our stories, all the time. Do you think he does not intimately know all of us? That's what makes the current situation so important and distressing. Now, we must begin."

I shut my mouth, bottling the last few questions I wanted to ask, and settled more firmly into my chair, more than ready to begin my lesson proper. The feeling of being able to create something from nothing was way too good to pass up on. "Fair enough. How do we go about collecting figments?"

"Close your eyes and let your mind drift, like you did when you let yourself absorb the figments, but this time let your consciousness expand out around you instead of staying focused on yourself. Try to focus on the sounds of the wind and the leaves and the sound of water."

I sat as still as I could manage for a few moments, trying to do as she asked, stretching my perceptions out and away from myself. I could hear the very distant sound of breakers on the beach, the creak of the water pail being drawn up from the well, the wind playing in the shrubs by the porch, but I didn't feel a single tingle like what Kith had poured into our hands.

The thwack of something hard on my knuckles echoed through the clearing and I startled upright with a yelp. "What was that for?" I demanded, rubbing my throbbing hand.

Kith shoved a fan back into her waistband and leaned forward. "You were doing the exact opposite as you did when you were trying to understand the figment I gave to you the first time. You were grasping onto the world around you *instead of being in it.* Don't re-create the whole scene in your head, detail doesn't matter. It's the *idea* that's important, letting your brain fill in the spaces as it wants. It wants a castle over there? Let there be a big damn castle. Try again."

I sighed and sat back in the chair again, eyes closed, letting myself drift. If she didn't want me paying attention, then fine, I wouldn't pay attention. I worked a small kernel of grain out of my teeth from breakfast and swallowed, contemplating the ingredient list for the granola I had eaten. I couldn't tell if they had used maple syrup or brown sugar for the sweetener, maybe a little bit of both. It had been delicious.

A gust of breeze blew across my face and it tickled. I giggled and without thinking reached up to pull the gossamer strings from my face. I opened my eyes and saw a slim glittering string of nothing twisting in the breeze. As I focused on it, it flickered and melted out of existence. But I had done it! I had caught a figment all on my own. By thinking of granola. This was counter to everything I had thought one needed for a serious mental discipline, but hey, I'll take anything that requires daydreaming.

I grinned at Kith and she smiled back. "Very good, one figment. Now you need to figure out how to find and draw the ones to you that don't run into *you*. One little figment won't do you much good, particularly if you can't hold onto it."

"Well, excuse me, I was excited." I rubbed my tingling fingers together. "If it was that easy for me to catch it, why haven't more people figured this out by now?"

Kith laughed. "Several reasons. Firstly, it takes a fairly old character to have a firm enough grasp on this world to even begin to feel the tides of imagination that fuel it. When characters are still young, the imagination within themselves is so volatile that if they tried to reach for the ambient imagination, they wouldn't even be able to feel it beyond their own bodies. All the compound readings and interpretations you've gone through have stabilized your characterization matrix enough that you can reach beyond yourself. Secondly, unless you have someone, like me, who gives you a taste of what it is you're looking for, it's nigh on impossible to figure it out yourself. I'd love to figure out how Charming managed it, that's for sure, because it wasn't the Storyteller or myself." She frowned briefly and shook her head. "Enough of that, try again."

I sighed and sat back once again, letting my brain drift. Over the next two hours, I managed to catch several more figments and even begin to spool them within me. After the second time I let one loose and received another sharp rap on the knuckles from the First Character's fan, I was careful to remain relaxed and drifting until the figments had worked their way under my skin. I don't know what wood it was made out of, but that fan hurt like the dickens.

After two hours of work, I still couldn't feel any figments beyond an arm's reach away from me, let alone start to call them in from anywhere else. I sat up, sore from staying in one place for so long, and was glad I had taken Kith's advice to stretch beforehand. I glanced over to the field to see how Jack was progressing and was startled to see Amund seemingly holding a golden curtain aside while Jack stuck an arm through that reappeared on the far side of the well. He waggled his fingers, drew it back out, then started to step through it. Jack's toes should have reached the other side of the well when the old coot let the curtain snap closed and Jack yelped, yanking himself back out of thin air. Amund was laughing fit to burst as Jack hopped around and hollered invectives that would have surely burnt the air if I could have understood any of them.

"I seem to be doing better than him at least," I murmured to myself. There was the sharp thwack of the fan against my knuckles, again, but by this time they felt numb.

"Don't measure yourself against other people's progress, measure against your own. You've got to learn how to spool a decent amount of energy today or you'll never be able to make a flower, let alone do anything remotely useful."

"I must have gathered enough to make another flower by this point," I objected. I'd been gathering figments for two whole hours whereas she had only gathered figments for a few moments before handing it over to us. I closed my eyes, gently fondled the pool of imagination in my head and teased a shape out of it. It was a pansy this time and I let it flow into my hand. When I opened my eyes, a puddle of purple dust filled in my palm then rapidly dissipated in the breeze.

"What? I don't understand." I was genuinely confused. It hadn't felt like I'd done anything different and it seemed to have worked the same as the first time, until I opened my eyes.

Kith took my hand in hers, gently. "It took over one hundred collected drifting figments to create that single dandelion of yours this morning. How many figments had you caught on your own?"

"Twelve." I was pissed. I was never going to be able to gather enough power to be able to do anything significant in the next week! Who was I kidding? "It would have been better if the Storyteller had picked someone else because apparently I don't have the talent for this. Ow!"

Kith had taken the opportunity to whack me on the nose. What was it with these people and physical reinforcements? It was cruel, and completely unhelpful. I was tired and cranky and I was done with being the tool of anyone, even if they were akin to gods. I stood up, shoving my wicker chair back. My anger was fizzy and I could almost taste it, like a good orange soda, bubbling up at the back of my throat.

"Stop it, just, stop it." I yanked the fan out of Kith's hand and swung it through the air at her for emphasis. It was an oddly fulfilling move and I did it again. "I'm trying my best to learn, but hitting me repeatedly does nothing to help me relax and channel brief bits of imagination! It makes me all tense and it hurts, damn it." I slammed the fan down on the table, only it wasn't a fan anymore. It was a length of crystal, carved to look exactly like the intricate fan that had been tormenting me all morning. It shattered when it hit the table, cutting my hand. I stared at the blood dripping onto the shards of fan, uncomprehending of what had happened.

"Did you..."

The smile Kith leveled at me was almost as gentle as her hands as they guided me to the chair beside her and took my injured hand in hers. She rubbed her fingers together and dribbled a stream of golden light across the cut, healing it instantly.

I was still in shock, but I was in charge of enough of my senses to murmur, "That would have been handy when you burnt me."

"The only magic you needed for that was to stop fighting your destiny."

I snorted. "None of us have destinies over here. We've lived past the scripted portion, remember?"

"Sometimes I wonder if that's true." Kith replied. She let go of my hand and gestured at the table. "That was all you, darling." The crystallized shards of fan gathered themselves together, became whole, and then changed themselves back to wood.

She handed the fan to me and I examined it closely, but I couldn't tell if it was marred at all by the experience. "But I don't understand. I used up all I had gathered and it looks like that took a heck of a lot more energy than creating a simple little flower."

"First, flowers are hardly simple. They're stunningly complex, but yes, transmuting a substance like that does take quite a substantial bit of power. It's easier to make things from scratch than change what's already here. Law of inertia or something like that. Once the figments have been given some form, they like to stay the way they are. But beyond that. How did being angry feel?"

I thought back to my minor break, for which I now felt slightly embarrassed. "Fizzy, bubbly almost." I frowned. "It's odd now that I think about it, I don't think I've ever felt anger quite that way before."

"That brings us to your second major lesson for the day. There are certain emotional states that can feed the imagination. Anger is one of them. Some of the others are lust and greed and all those nasty emotions you've always been taught to control. Think about it. Who is more imaginative than a spiteful child? A lover scorned? Or, failing that, a young man trying to get laid? They can be seriously ingenious when it comes to their schemes. States of being like this can draw oodles of figments to you. The downside is, it's virtually impossible to control them once you have them. They're completely feral and take whatever shape is fed by the emotion. Make sense?"

"I think so. But what about happy states?" I was uncomfortable with the notion that the next time I got all hot and bothered it could lead to trouble.

"Less of a problem for feral figments. If you're happy, you're not likely to want to change what's happening, and so your own imagination is somewhat dormant. Though it is easier to manage whatever figments you've managed to spool up if you're calm and happy. Quite a bit easier to shape them into your desired designs, in fact." Kith plucked her fan out of my hand and leaned back. "Before we retrieve your delectable friend there for lunch, what say you give this whole gathering thing another go round. Close your eyes..."

We sat there for the rest of the morning, took a short break for lunch, during which we got a lecture on the basics of shaping the figments to our will, then we went straight back out into the gloomy afternoon for more practicing. By that evening, both Jack and I were baby steps closer to our ultimate goal. I was up to gleaning figments from about five feet away, which still wasn't good for much, and Jack had managed to transport an orange a good five feet, but it had turned itself inside out in the process. And then exploded. Amund had rolled on the ground, bellowing with laughter.

When our instructors finally dismissed us for the evening, both of our heads were aching and we were stiff and sore from concentration. The last thing either of us felt like doing was being social, but we weren't sure where else we could get food, so we trooped over to the dining hall.

Sitting outside the hall, his tail sweeping an idle path in the dirt, Fred jumped up when he saw us. "Thought the harridan had worked you to death. Up for some food?"

Jack turned a little green and put a hand protectively over his stomach. "Some broth, and maybe some rice I think is all I'll be having. Amund shoved me through a couple of wormholes today and that is quite the trip, let me tell you."

I patted Jack consolingly on the back and winced when the movement jarred my own head. "Aspirin, aspirin and wine. It feels like I've been raking a hot poker through my brain all day."

Fred let out a bark of laughter and led the way into the dining hall, and we straggled in after him. We each filled our plates, Jack less than usual, and settled into a quiet corner. It seemed like most of the imaginaries and characters had already had their fill for the evening. A soft wash of conversation filled the room. Quiet enough to make it easy to converse, but not so soft that it made you uncomfortable.

We ate quietly, each of us lost to our own thoughts, and then Fred broke in. "When do you think you yaboos will have mastered all this and head back to the mainland?"

Jack sighed heavily and dropped his spoon into his bowl of soup. "Never. It's like trying to grab spiderwebs you can't see out of the air and when you try to bend them aside, it's like trying to bend steel rebar."

Fred turned to me and I shook my head. "I'm not doing much better, I'm afraid. I can gather a few figments but gathering enough to actually do anything..." I shrugged and left it at that. I have to admit I was disappointed in my first day as well.

"It's a shame Kith can't use a dose of imagination to *make* you guys good at manipulating imagination, ya know?" Fred wolfed down another section of cantaloupe, then sat back contemplatively. "Though I might be able to help you, sweet cheeks. What do you say to sitting in on my session with my human again tonight?"

"I'm game for anything you think might help at this point." I pushed my tray away. "There are only a few days left before the big anniversary celebration, so we have *got* to get a handle on this."

"If I do manage to get this right, we don't have to worry about travel time 'cause we can be there just *pft* instantaneously." Jack made a weighing motion in the air. "However, if I don't get this right, we'll need at least two days of travel to get to Central City and stop Charming before he does...whatever it is he's getting ready to do."

I frowned, rubbing at my temples. "It sure would be nice to know exactly what it is he's planning. All we know for sure is it's going to be big. And probably not very nice."

Fred cocked his head and frowned, as much as a dog can. "This is that same Charming person who everyone seems to think the world of? What's he done that's so bad?"

"For one thing, all the stories he was born out of? The originals? Not near so nice, but you literally can't write them down. He's somehow rigged it so that if you do, it morphs into the newer sweet tales. His family has framed people, and he's a pedophile and at the very least an attempted murderer, if not worse. And he's using imagination to cover it all up."

"Oh, well." Fred licked his nose and nodded. "Yes, I'd say that's worth looking into then. Even if he's all charity and light now."

"I wish we had more time. Yes, I know I sound like a broken record. Sue me." I stood abruptly and grabbed my dishes. "Speaking of, care to go show us this shortcut you think you might have?"

We binned the dishes before heading out into the night. Most of the other imaginaries were already finished at the large fire, so we stood back until the rest were done. As we had the previous night, we stoked up the embers and settled down in front of the tidy little fire.

Fred shifted spots for a few moments before deciding he was comfortable. "Alright, I've never tried this before, and I don't know if it'll work, but let's give it a go. Put your hands on my back like last night. Good, now, when I make the connection, see if you can tap into my kid's imagination. It's pretty damn strong so it shouldn't be hard to find, especially now that you know what you're looking for. Ready?"

Jack and I nodded, and I stared into the fire, hoping I didn't seem as nervous as I felt. Trying to tap directly into the imagination of a living human? It sounded intense and more than a bit dangerous, but then I would take whatever help I could get at this point in the game.

Fred went through his regular ritual and soon had a link into the kid's head established. He started his low-key murmuring and I reached out a hand towards the image, almost in sync with Jack. I could feel the warm pulsing glow of the child's imagination beyond my fingertips and I beckoned to it, eager to feel the direct influx of imagination, not just the random fragments that floated around in our air. I could feel it uncurling and responding to my call and I relaxed my mind, ready to receive it.

The first tendril that reached out of the fire and wrapped around my hand felt cool, like a wisp of cloud trailing along my skin. That lasted for a moment or two, until the tentacle of light anchored itself and started channeling a flood of imagination up my arm.

It was a hundred times more intense than anything else I'd felt and I struggled to keep my mind calm and spool it as fast as I could while it continued to rush, streaming up my arm. The tingling and tickling the figments created couldn't hold a candle to the pure bliss shooting through my nerves. It was better than the best sex I had ever had, no offense to Jack—rich and warm and filling every crevice of my being with the urge to create.

I didn't notice that Fred had stopped speaking. I wasn't aware of anything beyond my link to the human on the other side of the fire and the glory that was pure imagination until my hand was knocked away from the fire and a bucket of water was splashed onto the embers, dousing the flames and sending up a sheet of steam.

"What the *hell* were you thinking?" Kith threw her bucket aside and knelt down next to Fred.

I fell back, swirls of gold streaming across my vision and making it difficult to focus on the First Character. Picking myself up, I smiled, feeling like I was leaking light out of every pore. I was filled with an incredible lassitude that was at once the calmest I had ever felt and also the tightest I had ever been wound. The potential to create absolutely anything I wanted simmered under my skin and I couldn't help but feel joyful for it.

"We have to stop Charming and we weren't doing very well. We don't have much time and Fred here," I gestured grandly at the canine laying on the ground beside me, "offered a possible shortcut. We were only seeing if it would work." Jack giggled—he actually giggled—and nodded in agreement.

Kith was seething in rage, her folded cloth dress writhing in the wind swirling around her. "Look at him, damnit, *look*."

I looked back at Fred and noticed he was panting desperately and his eyes had a funny glazed look to them. After a moment, I realized that he must be ill, but it took another moment yet for my daydream-addled brain to connect the dots and realize that he must be ill because of what we had been doing.

"Oh." As I realized that I had hurt a friend and been completely unaware of it at the time, the golden happiness started to trickle and drain out of me. "Can't I just, like you did, use some of this stuff to make him better?"

Kith slapped my hand away as I held it over the dog-caterpillar. "You've done more than enough for the evening. You'd likely kill him with the ridiculous amount of power you've pulled in. You have no idea how to shape what you're holding." Ever so gently, Kith picked Fred up from the ground and cradled him like a small child. "You two, go to bed, sober up. I will deal with you in the morning."

Jack and I stood, incredibly lightheaded, on our feet and sniggered at each other, trying to maintain our balance. The ribbons of gold still danced across my vision and made me stumble several times before I made it back to the porch. At that point there were handrails and walls to assist in our struggle to reach our bedroom. We utilized them well. Jack may have knocked down a picture. I wasn't quite sure if the tinkling of breaking glass was real or an echo in my ears.

The next morning was worse than the morning after the Giantkillers, and worse than waking up after being chloroformed. I had a moment of rational thought in which I acknowledged I had not been kind to my body in the last week before the entirety of my stomach rebelled; I barely made it to the bathroom in time. The cold tiles of the bathroom floor felt amazing, so I sprawled on them for a while as my eyes throbbed so hard I thought I could see the distortion of it in my vision.

I stumbled back into our room and fell back on the bed, planting a pillow over my face and hoping halfheartedly that I would accidentally smother myself before having to face Kith. My jostling woke Jack and, with a strangled hiccup, he too went bolting for the bathroom. I groaned and rolled over onto my stomach, wondering if there were any painkillers that could take the edge off of what I was feeling and then wondering if it wouldn't be more economical to cut off my head.

Jack stumbled back into the room, half supported by Kith. In her other hand, she carried a pitcher with two glasses balanced over the mouth. She let Jack flop roughly to the bed and then took a seat in a chair by the window. She said nothing as she poured out two measures of a sticky-looking green substance, and was even more pointedly silent as she carried them over to us.

I stared at mine for a few moments, wondering if she had planned on poisoning us for our transgressions. If it meant I was free of this hangover, it was a blessing. It took several mouthfuls to choke down whatever it was, but I felt miles better by the time my glass was empty.

Kith waited for us both to finish, then took the cups back and refilled them, handing them back again. This time when she settled, she started to speak. "The most interesting things happened all night in the village. There were colorful lights in the sky and at one point there were unicorn grazing by the well and, I'm told, a plethora of young naked women knocking on young men's doors. They seem to have all dissipated at this point. However, my personal favorite was watching the rainbows and flowers that would on occasion pour out of your window. I must say, the glut of imagination seemed to have given you all some cheerful dreams. I'm glad; I don't know what we would have done if you two had started having nightmares while that high."

I blushed and swirled the goop in my cup around to have something to look at, rather than make eye contact; I was afraid she was going to ask who's dream all those nubile young women came from and I think it was mine, though the details were fuzzy. I took another sip before asking the one question I was afraid of. "Is Fred okay?"

"Fredderpillar is recovering and should be his old foul self by tomorrow. What you three tried was extremely foolish. We are not built to channel pure unadulterated imagination in that fashion. It's like mainlining life itself—it overloads our imaginative lattice and we start to come apart at the seams."

I was confused. "But we weren't pulling it through him, we were pulling it directly from his human."

"False. It may have felt like that, but unless you have a direct, solid connection to a human creator's imagination, you can only access that power through the characters that have been created by that mind. For poor Fred, you were pulling insane amounts of power through his young frame and it couldn't handle the load. Fred isn't that stable, you know. He is just an imaginary friend. He hasn't the thousands upon millions of people influencing and stabilizing his existence like you do. Also, you'll note, that you have no human you can pull from like that anymore since the humans that initially created you, and to whom you would be umbilically connected, have been long dead, so don't start getting ideas that you could tap into your own creators. And to draw that amount of pure creation before you'd learned to master it or to bend it to *your* will instead of letting it run rampant?" Kith shuddered and stood, turning to gaze out on her cliff-side daydream. "Suffice it to say, I'm very glad I'm not dealing with two dead characters, a dead imaginary friend, a dead human, and an island covered in glass and soot this morning."

Jack stopped nursing his drink and looked up, startled. "Wait, a dead human? How could we have killed the kid?"

Kith turned back to us and leaned against the window. "His name is Austin. He is an extremely bright and strong young lad. If you had succeeded in draining the entirety of the boy's imagination, you would have killed him, and both of you as well, though you were sharing the burden between you. Poor Fred would have been long dead from the channeling. A human being that is entirely without imagination has no will to live. He has no way to imagine his rewards and success and failures and future. He cannot see beyond the very immediate moment. He would have no reason to continue forward and so would stop. And die."

We were quiet a moment as we absorbed the enormity of our experiment the evening before. Though my physical symptoms of imagination overload were starting to fade, I was feeling worse, emotionally, with every word Kith said. I kept picturing Fred on the ground, his tongue lolling listlessly in the dirt as he panted.

"Wait. Wait a moment." I got up from the bed and started digging through my bags for my notes. I still had the journal I'd been taking notes in for the anniversary story and I pulled it out. "You said you need to have a living human creator at the other end of a fire in order for the imagination transference, right?"

"That's right," Kith said, wary.

"The theme of the ball is Spark Your Imagination, this whole fire theme, and, yes, here it is." I folded open my journal to the copy of the invitation I'd taped into it. "'We cordially invite our newest members to come mingle in the fires and meet their older counterparts.' Is this starting to sound suspicious to anyone else in here?"

Jack took my notebook from me and studied the bright orange invitation. "It's not a direct line of logic, but yes, yes it is."

Kith looked pale. "He'd have to be mad to try something like that. A large-scale imagination drain? What does he think he's going to do with all that power? Drawing on one human imagination could have leveled us and the island. How the hell does he think he'll be able to handle thousands without destroying all of us?"

Jack handed the book back to me. "All I can tell you is it felt mighty good when we absorbed even a fraction of what he's probably planning on tapping into. I could easily get addicted to that feeling."

"And we already know he must be using a massive amount of power to affect things across the land as he is. Maybe he's figured out some way to build a...a battery or something to store up the power." I closed the notebook and put it back in my bags.

"Whatever it is that he's doing, it looks like it's going to prove fatal for more than a few characters, and possibly even some humans as well, so we should probably get started for the day." I stood and started doing some limbering exercises, trying to work out the last stiffness in my muscles. "What was in that goop anyway? I almost feel like a real girl."

Shaking her head, Kith stood and started down the stairs. "Not telling. I don't want you to think you can just get over it every time you overextend yourself. Maybe when you're older."

"I'm already 600 years old, how much older do I have to get?" I hollered after her.

Jack drained the last of his glass and slouched to the floor to begin stretching. "By my calculations, we've got about two days here before we're going to have to start back to the mainland. I can't learn enough about shifting through space in that time to move us anywhere I can't see yet, so we'll have to take a boat and then ride."

I swept up from warrior one pose to reverse warrior and started trying to draw figments to my outstretched hand. "Two days it is."

👑

Kith returned shortly with Amund. After a brief group meditation to power up as much as possible, we split up, and Amund proceeded to give Jack a thorough drubbing, again. And again. For my part, the First Character and I spent the day on the porch drawing in progressively larger amounts of figments and carefully constructing items with the spooled power. By lunch, I had managed to create a small dagger and a dragonfly that was alive and fully functional. The pile of lifeless carcasses that it hovered over before taking off for the shore stood testimony to my previous, failed attempts to create something with actual life in it. The only other result was a splitting headache and my entire nervous system feeling like molten lead had been poured along it for the last two hours.

We broke for lunch and took a handful of sandwiches down to the beach. A group of imaginaries, hovering around our skiff, were startled by our appearance and vanished into the woods before we had a chance to ask them what they were up to. Jack stormed over to the boat to check and see if any of the food or water supplies had been broken into, and I followed him at a distance, drawn more to the ocean and what was coming on the other side of it.

"It looks like they weren't taking anything. They were leaving it." The admiration in Jack's voice was plain, so I went to join him at the skiff. The supplies had been rearranged to the middle of the boat and tied down under a tarpaulin while a large, shiny motor had been anchored to the back of the boat.

I paced around to get a better look at it. "Goodness, do they think it's big enough?"

Jack shrugged, already playing with the buttons and controls. "Certainly big enough to get us back to the mainland pretty darn quick, that's for sure."

"Then I guess we're set. We have today and tomorrow, that engine should take us back in half a day, then it's straight to the capital for an epic showdown that we have absolutely no chance of winning." I collapsed onto a fallen trunk at the edge of the forest and slumped with my arms braced on my knees. There wasn't a chance in hell I was learning fast enough to do any good in the upcoming confrontation; I was terrified. Kith's reaction this morning when we finally figured out what Charming was up to wasn't helping me any. He was going to be massively overpowered and he had the advantage of years of experience on both of us.

Jack sat next to me and offered me half of a corned beef sandwich. "Eat. You're always cranky when you haven't eaten enough."

I took the sandwich, but didn't bite into it. I toyed with the loose bits of beef around the edge, nibbling on them as they came off. "We're going to completely fail, aren't we?"

Jack took a bite of his half of the sandwich and thought about it for a moment before nodding. "Probably."

"Gah! I don't understand why Kith and the damn Storyteller don't swoop in there and take care of Charming themselves!" I stood and started pacing. "We aren't going to learn enough at all in the next couple days to even have the remotest possibility of taking him down."

"They did say they're a bit busy with other things, like keeping millions of characters alive and kicking, but, if you want my honest opinion? We're cannon fodder." Jack quirked his head and thought a moment. "Heh, canon fodder, that's pretty good. Get it, we're canonical characters?"

I made a face and swatted at him. "You are terrible."

He laughed and pretended to defend himself. "No, but seriously, think about it. They're kinda blind to what he does because he's all wrapped up in the fabric of the world; they have no idea how powerful he is or what he can do. What better option do they have than sending in someone else trained in imagination to sound out the extent of his control? And heck, we might even get lucky and take him out, which would mean less work for them."

I lost any appetite I may have had listening to Jack ramble and handed him back my half of the sandwich. "Do you really think Kith has that in her?"

"Sweetheart, these characters are older than the dirt we're standing on. There is no telling what sorts of stories have been layered into them or what traits they were born with. There sure as hell weren't anyone around that could have decided whether Kith should be locked up or not."

I frowned and went back to pacing. Movement helped me think. "But don't we to some extent determine their roles by our constant retelling of their stories?"

Jack took a huge bite out of my half of the sandwich and spoke around the mouthful. "If it all works like we think it does, yup, but also, remember, Kith and the Storyteller are an integral part of the fabric of the world. They probably have a *hell* of a lot more autonomy in that regard than we do."

I stopped pacing and leaned against a tree, ignoring the damp moss pressing into my back while I stared out at the sea. "I guess the only important question right now is whether we go through with Kith's plan, if we really are only meant to be a gauge for his power."

Jack finished chewing this time before he spoke. "I, for one, don't relish the thought of Charming gaining any more power than he already has, if only because he's a right tool and I've never liked him. So I'm game for honing my skills and taking a whack at him. Maybe we'll slow him down, maybe we'll take him out, maybe we'll get smited and retold. Hey, maybe we'd end up in the same adaptation class and start fresh without all the baggage we're carrying now, and I can't help but smile at the prospect of getting to know your body all over again from scratch."

"You're terrible!" I grabbed a handful of the trailing Spanish moss and flung it at him. He ducked, laughing. "But you're right. I don't know what he's planning to do with all that power, but it's probably best if someone cuts his legs out from under him, soon." I took a deep breath and sat back down, feeling more settled. "And I sure as hell can't do it on an empty stomach. Is there anything left of those sandwiches?"

♛

THE PEREMPTORY TARANTELLA

Jack and I finished our sandwiches in relative quiet, unwilling to keep talking about the potential death trap we were walking into. When we returned to the village, it was with a more subdued and determined aspect, because, damn it all, I was not going to go into this fight as a total patsy. I wanted to have a chance at knocking Charming from his high horse and at least get his clothes dirty. I almost confronted Kith about what we believed she was doing, then decided it wasn't worth the effort. One way or another, we were courting disaster and I'd rather do it purposefully—with full knowledge of what was going on—than from the sidelines at my castle, twiddling my thumbs while we waited to find out whether Charming managed to kill countless characters and humans.

Jack and I trained all that afternoon and well into the dinner hour. I wasn't doing too terribly by the end of it. I had managed to spindle enough figments to create an aggressive forest cat in under ten minutes, which was a vast improvement from where I had started that morning, though the effort left me exhausted. For Jack's part, he managed to part the woven strands of imagination long enough to pop out across the square from Amund. Right before we broke for dinner, Amund had to open up the strands and fish his wayward pupil out of the nothingness because Jack didn't have the strength to bend any more strands.

As we made our aching way to the dining hall, I slipped my arm into Jack's and asked, "What is on the other side of, uh..." I gestured to the forest at the edge of the clearing, "this. Our reality. When you got stuck, what was there?"

Jack shook his head, grimacing. "I don't know. It's like I don't even perceive anything over there. Not like it's black or something, more like there's...nothing there to observe. Rather creepy actually, but you don't feel time passing either. I didn't realize I'd been over there longer than a split second until Amund ripped reality back open to pull me out."

I tried to picture what that was like, but failed. "That sounds thoroughly odd."

"It would be if there was anything there but...there's nothing there to be odd. I can't figure out any better way to describe it."

"Fair enough." We were quiet the rest of the way to the hall, but I pulled Jack up short as we came into view of the doors. "Fred!"

The corgi mix was sitting patiently in front of the doors, and he stood, tail wagging, when he saw us. "There you two idiots are. I was about to give up and go find someone else to carry my food for me. Did the teacher keep you late 'cause you two dolts couldn't learn your lessons for today?"

"We're learning our lessons just fine, you foul dog." Jack knelt to ruffle Fredderpillar's ears. "How are you feeling?"

"I don't know what Kith puts in that atrocious green smoothie, but it does the trick." He came over to me and rolled over to have his belly rubbed. "All day in bed with a diet of that shit and I'm right as rain."

His tongue lolled out as I worked my fingernails along the lines of his exoskeleton. "I'm so glad you're okay, we were worried about you.

Well, we were worried this morning once we came down from the high. That was...needless to say, we're really sorry. We had no idea..." I stopped scratching at the thought of what might have happened and Fred rolled over, nudging at my inert hand.

"Stop it, you daft doll. If *I* had no idea that would happen, how could you have? There's never been anyone to try it with around here, so Kith never said nothing about not doing it, or the consequences. I say we all share the blame for being stupid gits and be done with it. We're all alive and we all know not to try that again. Though I might like to see what that high is like sometime..."

I laughed and swatted at his ear. "Don't you dare. Apparently we were leaking things all over the village."

"I know, I got a visit from one of the nubiles. Yours?" He asked Jack. Jack shook his head ruefully. "Not that I can remember."

I hoped neither of the men noticed my blush as I stood, brushing off my hands. "I could certainly use a hearty meal after the workout today. Let's go see if they've left anything for us."

I felt a knot I hadn't noticed in my chest loosen as I followed the boys into the cafeteria. I had been worried for the little monstrosity. I don't know what I would have done if he'd been permanently injured by our adventures last night. Regardless, it was a good cautionary tale about the problems one could encounter playing with imagination.

We ate a quiet meal and retired soon after, everyone needing to get extra rest. The next morning dawned cold and damp, just like every other day on the island. Kith woke us early and sent us to the dining hall before it opened to pick up a basket filled with snacks for the day, before leading us down to the beach.

"You're going to be playing with more power today than I'd like to have around the houses, and I have to accelerate your training, so I'd rather be down here where—if something goes wahooney-shaped—it won't hurt anyone." She set the picnic basket down in the shade of our dinghy and then made her way to the surf.

"We're going to be working together on this one, since you need to figure out how to fight an enemy as a unit." The First Character stood ankle deep in the mild surf and squared off against Amund. Her hands started to glow and, without a single twitch to give her away, projectiles started flinging out of the ocean at the old man.

His only response was to chortle, toss his cane to one side and then start ducking in and out of the fabric of our world to dodge the balls of seawater. He managed this for about two minutes, as the slugs of water came faster and harder, until he failed to notice that Kith had generated two balls and when he reappeared ten feet down the beach, the secondary missile took him full in the face.

"You cheated! You harpy, every time you promise, and then you cheat!" Amund sputtered, sitting on his backside in the sand and shaking water out of his ears.

"I did nothing of the sort, you old coot. *You* were running a pattern, thank you very much. Spontaneity and unpredictability, remember? But what should I come to expect from an aging imaginary?" Kith teased.

"I'll show you aging, you harridan." Amund popped out of sight and back into phase right behind Kith where he proceeded to use his cane to knock her on her ass in the surf. "How's that for predictable?"

Kith floated in the air, a comfortable few inches off the surface of the water, her head resting in her hand. "Better. You take the boy, I've got the girl. Let's see who's been training who better." She beckoned for me to join her in the surf and I slipped out of my boots and rolled up my hems before joining her. She didn't seem to mind that her robes were trailing in the water, but on closer inspection they didn't seem to be getting wet, either.

Before I could ask her about that, or any of the other handy tricks she'd shown us, she grabbed me by the nape of the neck and a hot flood of imagination began to spool itself at the back of my mind. "Okay," she murmured, staring over at the boys while they pow-wowed. "This is going to feel different than what we have been practicing. Instead of shaping the imagination into an object in and of itself, you're going to shape the figments into a tool to do what you want them to do. Make sense?"

"I think so." I started to unwind a bit of power in my head and tried to use it like a spoon to scoop up some of the seawater. It dribbled away halfheartedly, but I managed to raise it about a foot before it vanished.

At least Kith had the decency not to laugh at my attempt, but the amount of power coming in wavered a moment before tapering off and leaving me pleasantly charged, though nowhere near as buzzed as I had been the other night. "This'll be faster for today, but you do need to still be practicing spooling up the power on your own. As for the manipulation, have you seen one of those Chuck-it toys? Some of the dog-owning characters in the modern novels have been raving about them. I tend to think of that when I want to sling something at someone."

"Yeah, long-handled, gripper at the end to hold the tennis ball. Swing it like a whip, right?" I tried remolding the figments in my fingers into an abstract semblance of the toy made of raw power. It was much harder than trying to make them into something real. The figments *wanted* to be real. All of a sudden, I was holding a neon green molded plastic toy. I sighed and Kith did laugh this time.

"Now you see why we did the other things first. It's easier to let the power take the full form because it likes to be stable. Here, try again." She topped off my power level and stepped back.

This time I left the shape amorphous and, before I could slip and let it solidify again, swung it down into the water and lobbed it at the boys. "Oh, shit." My aim had been better than I anticipated and the ball of water splashed down squarely on Jack's head. Amund, spry devil, reappeared ten feet out of the way and started laughing hysterically.

Jack turned, murder in his eyes, and I backed away, waving my hands. "Truce, truce! Sorry, I didn't think it'd work. I'm sorry." I couldn't help but laugh at his sodden appearance. Slowly, Jack grinned, that troublesome quirk of the lips that meant I was going to pay for it in a very short while.

I leered in return and reached for another globule of salt water which I lobbed high, giving him plenty of time to react. Jack was slower than Amund, though not by much. When he reappeared behind me, Jack swept me off my feet, and then fell over backwards, dragging us both down into the surf, me shrieking the whole way down.

"Are you done, children?" Kith inquired, drily. She nudged me with her foot as I rose, spluttering and splashing halfheartedly at Jack. He grinned and splashed back. Then Amund appeared behind him and grabbed Jack by an ear to haul him upright.

"Ow, ow, lay off!" Jack managed to pull himself away by stepping through reality, but he wasn't fast enough and Amund followed on his heels, poking him with his cane until Jack managed to reappear behind the old man. "Alright, I'm ready to do this. I'm done horsing around, promise." He winked at me and I stuck my tongue out at him.

Kith waved a hand over me and I was dry, ruffled by a stiff breeze.

Jack pouted. "Hey, what about me?"

"You're going to be getting a lot wetter before you get dry, so what's the point?" Kith waved a hand at Amund and Jack and said to me, "They're both targets. On my mark, land as many water balls on them as you can. Jack and Amund, your safety buffer is about ten feet."

Jack shifted nervously. "I don't like the sound of that."

"You *should* be concerned. Concentrated imagination, when used as a tool like we are today, can sometimes...well. Here." She beckoned a coconut off the beach and it came to float in front of her. She held a hand out to her side a moment, and then clenched her hand as though griping a sword and swung it past the coconut, the imaginary blade passing through the coconut. It split in half, but its innards had turned into an explosion of oddly colored canaries that flapped about before scattering to the trees. Kith shook her head and grinned, relaxing her hand.

"I didn't manifest the birds, and I had shaped imagination into a rolling pin, so, obviously, it can be unpredictable when it's concentrated like this. The results of concentrated figments passing through material in our world can make some pretty odd things happen."

Jack's grin had frozen on his face and he took a couple giant steps backward. "Ten feet, got it."

"Well and good then. On your marks! Set...go!"

Kith and I started lobbing globes at the two men, first slowly and then with increasing intensity. Amund managed to avoid all of them until Kith threw multiples where she knew he would appear, and Jack managed a respectable showing. I managed to catch an arm or a leg here or there, but that was it. As we practiced, he got faster and faster and managed to avoid all of my projectiles. A few from Kith were still finding their mark, but I was hard-pressed to catch either man.

I paused, watching what Kith was doing for a moment. There was something subtly different about her stance and attention. In fact, it hardly looked like she was paying attention at all. She was landing shots mostly when she wasn't looking at the men, as if her attention was focused somewhere on the intervening space.

I looked back at my targets and let my attention wander, all while still lobbing water. That's when I felt this little niggling sensation at the corner of my attention and I threw hard at it, catching Amund full in the face as he stepped out of the blank space behind our reality.

He sat down hard, spluttering, and finally caught his breath enough to holler, "Cheating! What have you done? Teaching the lass to cheat, just like you!"

My inattention broken, I laughed, delighted that I'd caught the sprightly old man. "I felt him! I felt him coming through the curtain and I...how did I know?"

The First Character was looking at me thoughtfully. "Let's get out of the water and take a break for a moment."

As we waded out of the ocean, Kith waved at us, drying us off instantly. Jack sighed contentedly and flopped onto the beach, out of breath from the constant dodging.

"So?" I prompted Kith.

"So." She agreed. "You caught on faster than I expected." She settled herself against a rock, her robes carefully spread around her.

"And what, exactly, has she caught on to?" Jack asked, propping his head up enough to make eye contact.

"Sophia? Would you care to try and explain it?"

I frowned, trying to remember how it had felt to know where I should throw. "I wasn't hitting anything, so I watched you to see how you were catching them, and I noticed you weren't paying attention. Then I remembered how it's when we relax our minds that we can manipulate imagination in the first place, so I let my mind drift while I was throwing things at them and there was this—I guess the best way to describe it is that it felt like that spot was vibrating...or something." I stopped, trying to recapture the feeling.

"That's exactly right." Kith reached up in front of her and parted the strands of our reality and moved her hand in and out, letting it reappear a few yards ahead of her. "When I push on the strands like this, it can be felt along the lines—if you know what you're looking for. Kind of like a giant spiderweb. As you pull and push and bend and warp our space, echoes of it can be felt all along it."

Jack frowned. "Couldn't you have used those feelings to figure out that Charming was up to no good? Feel a disturbance in the force, as it were?"

Kith shook her head and we answered at the same time. "No."

"I don't think so." I looked at the First Character and she beckoned to me to continue. "The ripple Amund caused by moving behind the fabric of our world was so...slight. It was barely there. I don't think you could even feel it if you were too far away."

"Yes. Also, there is a lot of background noise as new stories layer onto existing characters. Don't even get me started about Central Hearth City. I get a headache whenever I go there because the vibrations of change are so strong. You need to be fairly close to an active manipulation of the figments before you can recognize it as such."

Jack rolled upright and started brushing himself off. "Does that apply just to predicting movement? Or does it apply to other manipulations as well?"

"Actually, I'm not sure. The Storyteller and I make such large ripples walking through the world because we have so much imagination spooled up at any given time that anyone else hardly registers. I can sense Amund parting our world because it's such a distinct and significant shifting in the very weave of the universe. But...Sophia, can we get a fresh melon to go with lunch please?"

"I can certainly try." I closed my eyes and let myself start daydreaming about a luscious, sweet cantaloupe. The kind that is so tender and flavorful it's almost like candy. I held out a hand and let the imagination unwind down my arm and coalesce into a ball. When I opened my eyes, a grapefruit sat in my hand. "That is almost the exact opposite of the fruit I was thinking of."

Jack snorted and Kith waved him silent. "It happens. I hardly felt a flicker though, so that should answer some of your question. You may be able to feel it more once you get away from the low-level vibration that this island and I give off. It's all so overcharged." She stood and dusted herself off. "Now, let's try something a little different."

We followed suit and paired off as she indicated, me with Jack and her with Amund. "We're going to try the same exercise, except we'll be working as teams. Amund, the swords please." The old man wandered up to the tree line and started inspecting fallen limbs while we trooped back down to the waterline. "Sophia and I will be lobbing water balls again, but the game is over if either swordsman can get a torso strike or Sophia and I manage to drench someone. Imagination can be used as a shield, a weapon, or a mode of transportation."

Amund handed a branch to Jack that was heavily weighted to one end. "To better represent the weight of your axe, young man."

We backed away from each other and made ourselves ready. Jack and I had a brief pow-wow where we decided the best way to go was for me to shield him while he tried to get in a strike. Meanwhile, I would wait for an opportune moment to lob a ball of water. Kith's command to begin almost got lost in the surf. I suspect her of doing that deliberately to get the jump on us as her first water ball came arcing down not a second later. I dove to the side as Jack slipped through a crack. What followed was utter chaos.

Needless to say, Jack and I failed miserably the first few rounds, and we were both panting heavily as he attempted to defend me from Amund while trying to get a strike in. I defended him from Kith, trying to divide my inattention between shields—which, being invisible, were damn hard to aim—and getting a ball in edgewise myself. We were both panting hard when I finally managed to dump water on Amund's head and Kith called a lunch break.

We trooped back onto the beach and Kith handed out sandwiches and apples while Jack and I struggled to regain our equilibrium. Both of us were exhausted by the exercises, but we were reluctant to show it. I, for one, felt like a wimp, especially since Amund and the First Character were reclining happily in the sun and acting as if they'd just been for a pleasant stroll.

"Does it really get as easy as you're making it look?" Jack grumbled, tearing a hunk off his sandwich.

"Well, for one, Amund was created to handle the stuff and I have had more years of practice than I care to count. The amount of imagination you can hold and how fast you can pass it through you definitely increases over time and with concentrated practice." She hesitated and turned an apple over and over in her hands, carefully inspecting it.

"But I'm afraid we're coming to the end of what I can do for you. You have the basic tools and we're running out of time. On your way back to the mainland, you'll have to practice. In every spare minute, I want you to daydream and spindle, to create small things. You'll get tired, but you'll also be increasing your capacity every time you even twitch a figment and you're going to need all the power you can get."

I hauled myself upright out of the sand. "What, now?"

She wouldn't quite meet my eyes. "You don't want to miss the daylight—it's hard to navigate the waters at night when you can't see through the mist."

"Can we at least say goodbye to Fred?"

"I would prefer you didn't. He's become quite enamored with you two and he wants to follow you to the mainland. It's dangerous for an imaginary where you're going, and he is too young to understand the dangers. I'll pass along your goodbyes and you can come back and visit this place anytime you want after you...well, when it's all over. When you want to come back, just head for the mists and then pull them aside as you would any other part of our reality. You'll find the island. Now, all of your things are in the boat already, so you don't need to come back up to the village." She put the apple back in her satchel and stood, having eaten nothing herself. "Good luck."

She disappeared back up the trail towards the village and I turned to Amund, a bit put out. That was all the goodbye we were going to get as we headed to our almost certain demise and re-creation? No last words of wisdom to hang on to and decipher on our trip back that might save our lives at the last moment? What use was it living in a story-written world if said world refused to obey the mechanics that created it?

"Don't look at me, young lass, that's the way of her. She can't stand goodbyes, normally she's just—pffft!" He waved his hands through the air, as if to dissipate smoke. "And I ain't got much more for you two. But I will help you haul the boat down to the line, if you don't object."

"That would be kind, thank you." Jack said, finishing off his sandwich and standing. "As long as you're done whipping my ass, that is. You've left it black and blue."

Amund cackled and grabbed hold of the gunwale. "If you were faster, you'd be able to dodge me, young man."

Jack crooked a half smile across the boat to me as he grabbed the bow and I the stern. "Maybe I will be. *When* we get back."

We hauled the boat down to the tideline in silence and then Amund patted Jack gently on the shoulder. "When," was all he said before disappearing up the trail behind Kith.

Jack perched on the rail a moment, holding it steady as I climbed in. "Well that was the oddest damn thing. Quite rude, don't you think? Here we are about to go to our certain deaths and off they go with nary a thank you."

"They can thank us when we get back." I settled in front of the mountain of supplies we likely wouldn't even touch on our way back to the mainland. I was sore and tired and I didn't want to think of the long afternoon of puttering ahead of us.

Jack shoved us into deeper water, leapt aboard and grabbed a pole that the imaginaries had thoughtfully provided to push us out far enough to lower the propeller into the water. After a few sputtering gurgles, the engine leapt to life and we were underway. I turned and propped my head on the pile of supplies for a moment to watch the island drift away from us, first slowly, and then more quickly.

Once the island was engulfed in the mists, I turned and sat back down, burrowing into the canvas to get comfortable. "Let me know if you want me to take a turn at the till. For now I think I'll practice not paying attention." Jack nodded, focused on keeping the massive engine under control.

I let my attention drift and lazily swept my hand through the air, playing with the figments, spooling them slowly. I didn't even notice it when I drifted off to sleep.

While I slept, I slid down the canvas until my head was cradled by something wonderfully soft and squishy. I woke when my pillow wriggled uncomfortably and let out a small grumble. I sat up, noticing by the sun that we had been underway for at least two hours, and turned my attention to the wriggling cloth.

Jack picked up his axe where it lay by his foot and I carefully drew back the fabric, the spooled figments in my head ready to do something drastic to whatever horror lay beneath. I grasped the edge of the cover and threw it back and a sleepy looking corgipillar blinked up at me.

"Damn it, that's bright. Warn a guy would you?" Fred stretched and shook his head. "Glad to see we're finally on our way." He clambered out of the pile of rope he had been nestling in and trotted up to the bow of the boat, lifting his nose full into the wind.

Jack placed his axe back by his foot and sat at the tiller again, making a small adjustment to our course. "How long have you been hiding here?"

"Since after dinner last night. I figured you had to leave today and I didn't want to miss the boat. And I knew if I asked the old biddy, she'd never let me go, so...." He gave as much of a shrug as his shell would allow and jumped back into the middle of the boat. "You're not going to turn around, are you?"

I grimaced, doing calculations in my head. We only had about four hours of sunlight remaining. It would take two to get back to the island, than another four or five to reach the mainland. "I don't think we can afford the time. Which I guess means you're stuck with us." He started dancing in place and yipping so I grabbed his snout and made him sit down. "On one condition. You stay safe and out of the way. The First Character will have our hide if anything happens to you."

He nodded as well as he was able with my hand still wrapped around his mouth and I let go. "Got any fruit in that sack of wonders? I'm plain starving. I didn't have breakfast *or* lunch and I have a hummingbird's metabolism."

From the sack, I withdrew the apple that Kith had placed there earlier and tossed it to him. He caught it easily and started to tear it apart with his teeth, using his paws to hold it steady. "Why are you here, anyway? I thought the life on the island looked pretty nice for all of you. Your needs are provided for and you get to do whatever you want."

Fred snorted and swallowed half the apple before responding. "If by nice, you mean boring as shit, you've got it in one. You try spending your days with nothing to do but talk to other imaginary friends and fading characters, who, if you don't mind my saying, are severely lacking in the brain pan. They're either too poorly constructed to be at all interesting, or they've totally given up on living and are happily fading into the denouement of their life, and all they want to talk about is how ready they are to go. Fuck that noise. I want to live my life while I have it, and the mainland is where I can do that. I plan to get to Central and hire out as a, a...well, I'll find something when I get there, but you can guarantee I won't be bored!"

I pulled a sandwich out of the bag, hummus and cucumbers, and settled back against the canvas to eat. "Do you have an ID card? It's pretty damn hard to get work without it, you know."

The antenna on his head wiggled as he frowned. "An ID card? Why would I have an ID card?"

Jack chimed in from the rear of the boat. "They're given to everyone once they've completed the rehabilitation training. Name, Title, Genre, date of writing, the usual."

"None of the imaginaries have anything like that. Do you think it'll be a problem?" It was odd seeing a distinct expression of worry in his canine eyes, with his antenna quivering.

I patted him reassuringly. "We'll figure that out when we come to it. Since we'll be heading into the city ourselves, we'll see that you aren't steamrolled anywhere."

"Thanks!" His whole attitude reversed and he went rifling through the sack of fresh foodstuffs that Kith had provided us. Jack and I traded looks while Fred's head was buried, mine plainly exasperated and his amused. It figures Jack would be happy to go along with Fred's seat-of-his-pants plan. I wondered what we were going to do with an inexperienced imaginary while we were getting our asses handed to us by Prince Charming. Hopefully something would come to me while I daydreamed.

"Want me to take the tiller for a spell?"

"Sure, it would be great to get a snack and practice." Jack slowed the motor to a putter and carefully swapped places with me in the boat. "Keep the sun on your left, that should bring us into the coast just fine." He wrestled the bag of food off of Fred's head, leaving the dog munching on a rind of melon.

For the rest of the afternoon, we drifted in and out of normal space as Jack opened holes in front of the boat for us to travel through. The motor didn't much like operating in absolute nothingness, though, and after one scary moment when we almost didn't have enough momentum to make it back to real space, Jack stuck to practicing *in* the boat rather than with it. Fred curled up in the bow where he was out of the way, and I spooled as much energy as I could while maintaining enough alertness to make sure I wasn't steering the boat in a circle.

It was almost sundown when we were close enough to the mainland to start picking out details on the coast.

Jack stopped fidgeting with the weave of our universe long enough to formulate a question. "Do we want to find a village to put in at? Or do you think something more discreet would be wise?"

"I'm thinking village. That way we can trade this boat for some horses. It's not like I have my credit cards to rent us transportation anywhere." I shuddered at the thought of the bill that had been racked up in my name. "I'd like to be able to pull out somewhere on the coast where we'd not be noticed, but we won't make it to the city in time if we don't get a ride."

"Sounds good. Let's find a suitably small town then, shall we?" Jack came back to take over the steering, as we agreed my skills were a little better for offense whilst we were still on the boat. I took Fred's place in the bow and kept a careful eye on the horizon. We passed on two villages that were too big or too small. We were all afraid of rumors running ahead of us to Prince Charming, but we still needed to acquire some horses.

Finally, just as full dark was closing in, we found one that suited our needs. After a quick trade with the dock manager, we found ourselves in possession of two passable horses and a saddlebag large enough to fit Fred. He grumbled quite loudly at the thought of having to ride, but quieted quickly at the ultimatum that it was either ride or run the whole way to the city. Corgis do not have very long legs.

We rode a few miles before straying off the main road onto a logging path to find someplace hidden to bed down for a few hours. We needed to wait until dawn so there was at least some light for the horses' sakes, but an inn was too dangerous, so we picked a clearing far enough from the road that we could safely set up a fire and roll out the blankets we had taken from the boat.

"Any fruit left?" Fred asked, already curled into the blanket nest we had made him.

"You ate it all on the boat before we even landed, or don't you remember?" I chided him.

"I was hoping that since Kith had given us the bag, it might be magical or something. Say, can't you create me a little something, doll? Just a strawberry or two? I know it won't last, but I'm *hungry*." He leveled his very best puppy eyes at me and I completely caved.

"Oh alright, but stop looking at me that way! Sheesh. Those eyes of yours should be classified as deadly weapons." I settled against the stump I had set my bedroll against and willed myself to relax. It was no mean feat, considering I was all keyed up about the impending confrontation. Convincing myself this was good practice, I started gathering all the figments I could sense in the clearing. I was already pretty well-stocked, but more energy could only be better for the next few days. I carefully blanked my mind and started daydreaming about fruit platters and fruit salad and my eldest sister's hideous fruit-laced gelatin "salad."

I held out my hand over the ground in front of me and let the wound-up power unspool through me and coalesce. In less than a minute I had a large pile of fruit, mostly berries of one sort or another. Fred yipped in happiness and dove into the pile so only his rear end could be seen, waving happily in time to his nonexistent tail.

I moved over to beside Jack, closer to the fire, and left Fred to his sugary delight. "He's only going to be hungry again in a few hours. Oh well. Do we have a plan for how we're going to tackle Charming? It seems like things have been moving so fast."

"We weren't given much time to prepare, were we?" Jack poked at the fire with a stick while he thought. "We've had less than a week to find out he's doing something dastardly, train up, and tackle him. We have two days hard riding before we get to the city, which should put us arriving barely in time to get to the ball. Not to mention I don't have anything in my packs suitable for getting us in the door."

"I think I can take care of that, fairy-godmother style." I paused as a thought struck me. "Damn, there are going to be a lot of jealous magic wielders when this all comes out, aren't there?" I shook my head; that was a discussion for another time. "Do we confront him? Try to take him out surreptitiously? I'd think getting him away from the fires would be the first point of order."

"Didn't the invite say it was a Fire theme? It's going to be awfully hard to find a single square foot without fire, knowing the Charmings. If he knows we're there, maybe he'll come talk to us. I think we're going to have to play this by ear, though. Unfortunately." He sighed and chucked his poking stick onto the fire proper.

I leaned into him and worked my way under his arm. "I don't like it either, but it's that or let him do...whatever it is he's trying to do, which will probably kill quite a few people."

Jack absentmindedly stroked my hair while he watched the fire. "You know, if this were a story concocted by those idiot simians on the other side of the Fire, we'd know exactly what his plan was, what the weaknesses were, how to attack it, and it would be threatening the very fabric of our existence." His hand paused. "You know, come to think of it, who knows what a charge of imagination like Charming is planning could do. It very well *could* be threatening our existence, we just don't know it yet."

"Like you said, this isn't a human fairy-tale. We'll have to make do."

Fred finished his pile of fruit and waddled over to the fire. "Do you two mind if I commandeer the fire for a moment? Have to make my nightly check-in, you know."

"Please, go right ahead." I hesitated, then decided asking was better than not. "Would you mind if I linked with you? I promise not to reach out to him, but I want to get a better feel for this kind of connection, so I understand what Charming is going to be reaching for."

Fred shrugged and settled in front of the fire. "Suit yourself. I'm going to be busy with the kid since I had to skip a couple linkings 'cause of our...mishap."

I felt guilty all over again, but did my best to push those feelings aside. I gave the dog a brief hug and then settled beside him, my hand on his back. Jack sat on the other with a, "May I?" and at Fred's nod, laid his hand beside mine.

I paid hardly any attention to what Fred was saying, nor did I let myself get lost in staring around at the human's world. Instead, I turned all my attention away, let it drift, and let my eyes go out of focus while looking back and forth between Fred and Austin.

I had trouble understanding what I was seeing at first, and struggled not to break my (lack of) concentration. I suppressed the urge to break the link prematurely and waited impatiently for Fred to be done with his human before turning to Jack. "Did you see it?"

He frowned, and rubbed his hand vigorously on his pants. "I felt it, I think. If it's that pushing-pulling thing?"

"Yes!" I got up and started pacing, trying to decide what it might mean.

"Will someone please tell me what you two are rattling on about?" Fred grumbled, curling up in his nest of blankets somewhat sleepily.

"Okay, while you were drawing a small stream of imagination from the kid, Austin, directly through the fire, it was nothing compared to what you were sending back."

Fred frowned. "What do you mean, I was sending something through to the kid? I was just talking to him."

"That may be all you *thought* you were doing," Jack started slowly, "but you said yourself that you are there as a support mechanism for these kids. Maybe...Soph, did the imagination he was streaming back look different to you? It sure felt...I don't know how to describe it. It was...different."

"Yeah, it did. What you were absorbing, Fred, was this messy, unsteady stream of filaments, but it was like you were returning a refined thread. It didn't feel so fuzzy and sparkly anymore. It felt... clean." I tried to bring back the image of it, but considering I'd been concentrating so hard on not concentrating on it, I was frustrated by the lack of clarity in the image.

"What, you're saying I'm like an imagination laundry? Like a money-launderer?" He scratched vigorously behind one ear. "I gotta say, I kinda like how badass that makes me sound."

I nodded, absently. "I'm not sure what it all means yet, but now I know what it feels like, that unique blending of a character connecting with its creator. I hope it holds true for all characters and not just imaginaries."

Jack grimaced. "I don't think any character has ever done it before."

"Then I guess we'll be the first to find out then, won't we? I wonder if when we siphoned figments through you, Fred, if it was pulling that refined stream as well."

He leapt upright. "No. You're not testing *that* theory."

"No, that wasn't at all what I was suggesting!" I hurried over to the distraught animal and cuddled him until his shaking started to subside. "I promise we'll never use you as a conduit again. It's too dangerous."

His shivers stopped and he nestled closer in to me as I held him on my lap. "You know, your tits make an excellent pillow."

"Fred!" I laughed and pushed the crude dog out of my lap.

Jack turned to him, "You know, I always thought so myself. There are just certain breasts that are made to be pillows and hers are of that category."

"You two are disgustingly male, you know that?" I huffed over to my bedroll, still smiling, and laid down. "I am going to go to sleep and pretend that you aren't discussing my chest. Wake me for my turn at sentry?"

"Of course. Sweet dreams."

◣◣◣

We passed a fairly uneventful night and were packed up and back on the road just as the sun started to crest the horizon. During the morning ride, Jack and I took turns spacing out for practice, while the other guided the horses.

As we crested a hill, Fred let out a whistle and sat up in his saddle-bag to get a better view. "Now *that* is what I call a castle."

I wrinkled my nose as I examined the sprawling grounds in front of us. "The Charming complex." It was massive, stretching a half mile in diameter, and had grown over the land like a fungus. The additions were all done in different styles, depending on what was in vogue when Charming decided he needed more room. Now I wondered if the different wings didn't house his different child brides from across the centuries. I looked closer at the central hall, the towers of which still stood taller than the surrounding buildings. "Hey Jack, take a look."

Jack squinted into the sun and then smiled. "Well, well. Looks like someone hasn't left for his party yet."

"What, what is it?" Fred demanded.

I gestured down at the valley. "See that flag, the one with the stag on it?"

"Yeah, what of it?"

"It means the prince is in residence. Maybe we won't have to confront him at the party after all."

Jack pulled his axe out of its sling on his back and hefted it. "I'm feeling game. Let's get this out of the way, shall we?"

I smiled at his eagerness, knowing full well his stomach was complaining just as loudly at our upcoming heroics as mine was. But I appreciated his attitude. "Let's try words first, yes? You never know, maybe all of this is some giant misunderstanding and he is still working for our good."

Fred snorted. "Sure, you think whatever you want, but while you're talking, make sure you're prepared to duck. I don't think he's going to appreciate you showing up. Particularly after he put you out to sea."

"I know, but a girl can hope, can't she?" I pulled off to the side of the road and dismounted, digging through my saddlebags. I pulled out a soft linen dress, or at least that's what it appeared to be. In actuality it had pant legs wide enough to appear like they were a skirt when I was moving slowly or standing still. I unspooled just enough of the imagination in my head to smooth out the wrinkles and stepped behind a convenient shrub to change.

"I know you're a princess and all, but do you think this is the right time to be primping?" Fred called out.

I stepped out of my travel leathers and smiled at the feel of the soft linen against my skin. I wished briefly that I had the time and place to shower before heading into the castle, but we couldn't waste the time. "How one presents oneself is extremely important. Now, this dress," I stepped out from behind the bush, doing up the last of my buttons, which fell low enough to display ample cleavage. "This is a dress designed to take people off the defensive. It's demure enough to look innocently feminine while still displaying enough of my womanly attributes to put men off a half step. At least, all those who have a working endocrine system." I tossed my leathers into the bag and remounted.

Jack did his best not to stare, but Fred made no such efforts. "Damn girl, that is one effective weapon you've got there. What on earth do you use such a dress for?"

"You'd be surprised the amount of information this dress can get for me." I winked at Fred before spurring my horse forward. "And drinks."

We left the main road and worked our way down into the valley. After a brief argument, we agreed to approach directly and ask for an audience. We stopped briefly beside an abandoned barn to leave Fred behind with a supply of fruit and a blanket to curl up on. Neither Jack nor I wanted to chance bringing him within range of a character that could use the corgi as a weapon, which would invariably mean killing him and his human. He complained, but when we reminded him how he felt on the island after we'd pulled imagination through him, he settled down.

We crossed under the first portcullis, and then the second, and then a drawbridge, and then a third portcullis. "Paranoid much?" Jack murmured, trying not to be overheard by the guards that were stationed liberally through the whole approach.

"The Charmings added a whole bunch of defensive structures during the Genre Wars. I guess he never bothered to take any of it down after the Dewey Accords." I looked closer at the glistening, rust-free chains that held up the fourth portcullis. "And he's kept it all in pretty good working condition, I must say."

We were quiet a bit longer until it was clear that we were the only ones entering or leaving the castle today and the guards just watched us go by. "How come no one is stopping us? I mean, you think they'd have orders or something."

"Maybe they don't know who we are." I tried for a hopeful tone, but felt pathetic. They knew exactly who we were and they were under orders to let us march straight into the lion's den.

We finally reached the main courtyard and dismounted in front of the steps to the large presentation door. A hostler appeared at our side and took our horses without a word. The doors opened and a footman stood there, staring down his nose at us.

I finally couldn't take the silence any longer, and made my way up and past the liveried man, into the entryway. "Please inform Prince Charming that Princess Sophia Saltare and Jack the Giantkiller are here and need to speak with him immediately."

He studied us for a moment longer, clearly unhappy with our travel-worn image, but finally said. "He is waiting for you in the throne room." He turned to lead us down the hall and I sighed, wishing we might have surprised him, just a little.

The throne room was as gaudy as I remembered from the last party I had attended. It was a huge room, floored in pale pink marble, with columns of the same spaced down its tournament field length. Swags of rich velvet swung dangerously close to myriad candelabras, which still housed traditional dip candles instead of being rewired for electricity. The dais at the end of the room was surrounded by windows placed and angled so as to concentrate any available sunlight on the throne in a sparkling array of colors.

And seated there, reclined with one leg over the arm of said throne, was Charming. He was playing with a quill and ignoring our entrance entirely. The footman cleared his throat, announced us, and left, closing the doors to the throne room behind himself with a loud thump. I told myself it only sounded so ominous because I was terrified.

Charming ignored us a moment more, examining the nib of his pen and cleaning it with a small penknife. "I am sure you are familiar with the phrase 'the pen is mightier than the sword.' And in our world, I would certainly agree. We are created and die by the stroke of a pen, and a sword only returns us to the Fire to try again." He put the knife away and spun in his chair till he was seated upright and studying us. "A little bird told me you had arrived yesterday, back from your little sailing trip. I would have assumed the currents had been kind, but then again, you came back plus one and with a snazzy-looking engine on your boat. I can only assume you found La Isla de la Perdida Historia. But where is your companion? You didn't leave him on the beach to fend for himself, did you?"

Charming's gaze was oddly intent and I felt a compulsion to tell him exactly where we had left Fred, but I resisted. Instead, I let my mind relax and could see the small tendril of imagination that reached from Charming to me, probing at my will. I reached out a hand and plucked at the strand of power, spooling it up as I would any other figment floating in the air. It felt different, though — slightly sour and slimy compared to what I normally picked up.

Charming frowned and Jack shifted into a more balanced stance. While he hadn't seen the exchange of figments, he could feel the difference in the tension in the air.

"It seems a friend was not all you found on the islands, now, was it?" He made a brief gesture and a different footman entered the throne room from behind the dais. "Our friends came in from the east road. Send out patrols to find the dog they left somewhere behind them. He's odd and distinctive-looking, you can't miss him." The footman bowed and left again. "Where have you been learning about the Power? Did you find yourselves a copy of *Emuq ina Awatum*? I thought I'd cleaned the Stacks out and caught you fast enough to prevent you from finding a copy anywhere else. Seems like I was wrong."

Jack and I stayed silent, me more from the fact I was afraid of what he might be able to make me say than anything else. From the frustration on Jack's face, I suspected that Charming was preventing Jack from snarking at him, which is a trick I was going to have to learn. I tried to spool more figments while Charming was talking at us, but the room seemed to be bone dry. There wasn't a stray glimmer anywhere and my fear rose just that little bit more. I don't know if it was a side effect of the mainland having less stray imagination floating about, or if Charming had managed to suck this area dry, but there was nothing for me to add to my supply of power, which was feeling mighty inadequate now that we were facing our target.

Charming put the quill behind his ear and stood abruptly, pacing the dais. "Don't you two have anything to say for yourselves? I mean, really now, silence is only becoming in a woman when she's also barefoot and in the kitchen. And we all know that's not the way you were written, Sophia."

I couldn't resist the compulsion to speak anymore, even while I was spindling all the fine tendrils that Charming was sending out. "Fine, you want me to say something? How can you even possibly think to do what you're going to be doing at the ball? You're going to injure all those characters and their humans, and for what? You could warp the very fabric of our world!"

"So you *do* know what's going on, how excellent." He returned to his throne and rubbed his hands together gleefully. "This means I can have more fun with you than if you were total innocents with a healthy curiosity for trouble. Now let's see, should I turn you into horses to pull my carriage? No, I don't know that I'd ever be able to break you. How about cats? Hmm, I'd rather you didn't savage me in my sleep. A piece of furniture might do, but I'm out of room in the storage hall..."

As the prince continued his musing, I could feel the swell of power begin to fill the room and coalesce around him. It was more power than I'd felt Kith pull at any one time; it was even more than Jack and I had managed to pull down straight from Austin's imagination. Jack already had his axe out and was trying to break the binding Charming had cast over him when we'd entered the room, while I carefully constructed a shield of pure imagination around the two of us. Just as I got it up, Charming abruptly stopped talking.

"Now, that's not fair. Where did you learn that? That's not in the book." And he took the quill, sent it flying through the air where it lodged itself in my shield. He sent a surge of power after it and my imagined wall came shattering down. The backlash of my figments flying apart sent me to the floor, gasping.

As I hit the ground, Jack took off, flickering out of our reality and back again behind the prince. He attempted an overhead swing of his axe, but as he was about to bring it down, the prince turned faster than the eye could follow, the quill rushing back to his hand, and he buried the steel-tipped feather in Jack's abdomen.

To Jack's credit, he barely grunted in surprise and still tried to bring the axe down, but he couldn't handle the weight of it. It barely brushed Charming's shoulder as it fell from his hands. The prince yanked his pen from Jack as he toppled over, and I could see that fully half the length was reddened with blood.

I still had a fair amount of imagination spooled up, but I didn't know what I was going to be able to do with it. I gouged a chunk of marble from the floor and flung it at the prince, but he deflected it easily.

"You are as children to me." Charming's face was made ugly by a condescending sneer as he worked his way closer and closer to me, brushing off the marble chunks I was throwing as if they were flies. "And *you* must be put in your place." He was less than three feet from me and I didn't have enough power to throw anything else at him. There was barely enough to forge a small knife that I hid from his sight behind my back. As soon as he was close enough, I struck for his heart, but he easily deflected me, a wash of power cloaking his arm so that my blade went flying across the room and embedded itself in the wall, before dissolving into a black slime.

His hand was around my throat before I could recover and the last of my spindled power fled, sucked out by Charming, before he tossed me to the floor beside Jack. It took me a moment to recover myself enough to crawl over and check on him. Jack was still breathing, barely.

The prince straightened his cuffs and gestured to the door where four footmen entered. "If you two will excuse me, I have a party to attend to." Two of the men grabbed me. I fought them, as hard as I could in my drained state, exhaustion deadening my limbs. The other two grabbed Jack, grunting with the effort, then the four of them dragged us from the throne room. Charming smiled and waved as the door slammed shut behind us.

♛

The Prince's Pasodoble

I cussed out the footmen as they dropped me into a pit and lowered Jack none-too-gently after me. I cursed their heritage and their author and their morals, and, just for good measure, I leveled a curse at their manhood. As a grate clanged shut above us, I knelt beside Jack. It was hard to find the source of his bleeding in the murk and mud but I was shortly rewarded with a pained grunt when my fingers found the center of the cold, damp patch on his shirt.

His voice was faint, but cheerful when he spoke. "Careful, Sophie, I've got a papercut."

"Papercut, my ass. This is more like a butter knife cut. Those always bleed more." He tried to laugh but ended up coughing. I worried at how wet it sounded, but forced a laugh myself. "Oh, how cliché Jack, failing to laugh at the joke and bubbling up blood. You always were one for ridiculous tropes."

I may not have been able to see it, but I could hear the smile in his voice when he replied. "Only for you, Sophie... Soph. I save all my clichés for you."

"Well then, that means you're going to recover and lead the charge on the castle!" I couldn't keep myself from tearing up, though I blamed the smoke from the crappy torches Charming kept in his dungeon. "Some miraculous, ingenious plot device is going to save your life any minute now."

He cupped my face. "You, lover, it's you. You're going to save my life with that wonderful twiddly magic-type stuff and we'll be out of here before Fredderpillar even has a chance to piss on the guards."

"But there's no power here, can't you tell? Charming's sucked this place completely dry. I have nothing." I tried not to let him hear the tears in my voice, but he was already wiping them away.

"If you don't want me to know you're crying, don't drip tears on my face, Soph."

That dragged a waterlogged chuckle out of me, then his hand fell away. "Jack? Jack!" I patted at his face, but he didn't respond. "Oh no, you don't. Those were shitty last words!" My fingers searched desperately for a pulse, but I could hardly feel anything through the damp mud clinging to everything. Finally, I found it, weak and uneven.

I gently dislodged myself from Jack and began working my way around the edge of the pit, following every small crack with my fingers. I didn't need much, just a few rough edges and I'd be able to haul myself out of the pit and go get help. There had to be a way to get out from under Charming's power drain to get enough energy and come back and save my ex-boyfriend's life. Because, damn it, I wasn't going to go through all the trouble of training the next Jack. There wouldn't be any of the history, none of the memories and it would be too damn painful to love someone as much as I loved Jack if his new version had no idea who I was. Who we were.

Between the darkness in the pit and the tears in my eyes, I didn't see the steps until I kicked the bottom of them, hard. The splitting pain in my foot combined with the panic I was already feeling ignited a sobbing string of curses that would have made any deity within earshot blush. Kith and the Storyteller were my particular targets, for leading me to this shithole and nearly killing Jack and putting the insane pressure on us to do what they damn well should have done in the first place. I was so wrapped up in cursing the pantheon as a whole that I didn't even hear someone enter the dungeon.

"Damn, girl, you got a mouth on you. You better hope Kith didn't hear that. She's got one hell of a magical bar of soap."

The relief was so overpowering I almost couldn't breathe. "Fred! Oh, god, Fred, it's Jack, he's hurt, you have to get us out of here."

Fred started sniffing around the grate. "Can't you magic your way out?"

"No, this place is completely dry. Charming is like this vortex, just sucks it all in. I managed to catch a piece of something he threw at me and it felt all weird. Contaminated almost. Then he emptied my reserves, too."

Fred found the latch and tried to pry it open with his teeth, then his teeth and his paws. "Damnit, I need hands. Can you reach this?"

I strained through the grate but my arm was a full foot short of the mark. "It's hopeless. Jack's going to die and Charming is going to win."

"What did Jack say before you started freaking out on me?"

I was thrown by his non sequitur. "What does that matter?"

The dog returned to pacing around the grating. "Humor me."

"He said to not drip tears on his face if I didn't want him to know I was crying."

Fred snorted. "Those are terrible last words. I don't think our universe will *allow* someone to die with those words on his lips. Okay, I have an idea. Don't yell at me, promise?"

Hope warred with caution. If Fred thought it was worth getting yelled at, it was probably pretty dangerous. "What are you going to do?" I heard him jump a couple times and then the clatter of a torch falling to the ground. Fred carried the torch to the grating and wedged it in one of the cracks.

"Can you reach a hand up through to grab my leg?"

"Yes, but...no Fred, that's not right. You're not reaching through to Austin, are you? You can't! I *know* you remember what happened last time." I started to panic all over again, sure the dog had lost his mind.

"Damn it, woman, Jack is *your* man and *my* friend and he's down there dying and Charming is about to rip apart our world as we know it. I trust you to moderate yourself, so grab onto my damn leg!"

It was with no small amount of trepidation that I reached up and wrapped my hand around his hind leg.

"Whew! Cold hands—watch your fingers, missy. Alright. Here we go." He let out a soft croon and I watched the torch change color and the portal into the human world open. Fred started whispering, though it sounded more urgent than usual.

Keeping in mind the need for restraint, I reached through the fire to the supply of imagination known as Austin. I found myself whispering as I did. "Hi Austin, it's me, Sophia, back again. I'm sorry about last time, but I'm in a bind here and I hope you don't mind if I borrow a part of you to fix things on this side of the Fire. Jack is dying and Charming has gone completely crazy. We need your help."

This time it felt like the imagination reached out and enveloped me. I wasn't tapping into the fountain so much as the warmth of his imagination flowed through me, investigating, and, seemingly satisfied, started spooling itself into the deepest recesses of my brain. It was too fast at first, but it slowed down to an even pace that I could spindle before tapering off.

"Thank you." I whispered into the fire. I broke the link with Fred, gave him a glance to make sure he was okay and not writhing on the floor, then I stepped down from the steps and knelt beside Jack.

Everything seemed to shimmer. I could see the warp and weft of reality, the delicate structure of figments that gave everything life. I could see how they swirled up and around Jack's muscular frame, and I could see where they had broken, where the weave was stretched and where it had torn. I grasped the ends of the broken figments and wove them back together, using a sparkling droplet of the glittering power in my head to mend each snapped fiber.

I don't know how long I was working, but when I looked up, Fred had finished his conversation with Austin and Jack was sitting upright, staring at me. "I thought you said this place was dry as a bone?"

"Apparently more like a good stock bone than a finger bone from a hundred-year-old skeleton. Come on, let's get out of here." I still felt like I was looking at the world through a snow globe, but the actual weave had faded into the background. I let my mind drift through the room until I had a fairly good idea where the latch was on the grate and then turned it into Swiss chard. I was aiming for "full of holes" like Swiss cheese, but the imagination coursing through my thoughts bumped my metaphorical elbow. The grate swung open at a push and we clambered out of the pit. I closed the grate behind us so that, at first glance, it would still appear occupied.

Before we could plan our next move, Jack caught me up in his arms and kissed me, hard and long. After a startled moment, I returned it. "And that was for?"

"For being enough of a cliché to save my ass." He let go of me only to the point that we were still holding hands, and turned to Fred. "Alright, how'd you get in with all the guards?"

"There's a drainage chute between here and the kitchen. A nice tabby showed me how to trip the latch." Fred trotted out of the dungeon. Jack and I paused long enough to pick up our packs from the corner before following him.

Though we could hear voices coming from the kitchen, it didn't seem like anyone else was around. I guess when the cat was away, the mice didn't care about proper security. Or they'd never put anyone in the dungeon before, so the guards didn't know they should be keeping watch over the prisoners. When I thought of it, the rarity of prisoners would explain the pleasant smell of dirt and moss rather than putrefaction and piss in our pit.

Fred took a quick left into a cold storage room and came up against a half-circle grate in the floor. He pawed at a stone, which turned out to be a latch, and popped it open with a soft clank. It was too small for us to go down carrying our saddlebags. Jack went first, sliding the ten feet or so down to the sewer floor and then turning to catch first Fred, then our supplies. I climbed in and wedged myself at the top of the chute long enough to close the grate behind me, then slid down to Jack's waiting arms.

He held on a moment longer than he needed to, then picked up our packs. Jack rummaged through my bag until he found the emergency hand-crank lantern that I had packed. With a twist of his wrist, he got it up and running. When the light finally came up, I looked down at my once sage green dress and sighed at the large streaks of dirt and other unidentifiable brown smears that I didn't want to think about. I wondered if the maids at my father's castle would be able get the stains out, then I wondered if they would even get the chance to scold me.

I took my pack from Jack and shouldered it. Together we followed the gently sloping tunnels through the castle's drainage system, keeping quiet for the most part. All of us feared that if we made too much noise, it would bring all the guards down on us. As soon as the tunnel started to brighten ahead of us, we doused the lantern and stowed it. The tunnel terminated at the backside of the castle, which was in our favor, since it was away from the myriad guards and footmen near the main gate. Fred jumped on another rock to open the unattended gate and he exited first, blending quite nicely with the surrounding foliage.

He yipped an all clear and Jack and I exited, carefully latching the gate again behind us. The sun was still well above the horizon and it took me a moment to realize that it was still the same day as when we entered the castle. Events had been moving much faster than they seemed. Though, to be fair, when a good portion of them are happening deep under a castle, you tend to lose your sense of time.

Jack stretched hard, straightening out all of the kinks from the cramped march through the tunnels. "Alright, we have about 24 hours till the start of the festivities. We have a lot of ground to cover between here and the city. Do you think it's worth it to find horses, or should we try something a little faster and less unobtrusive?"

I set down the packs and started rummaging for something that looked relatively clean. The only thing left in the bag—in any state of cleanliness—were my travel leathers. I pulled them out with a sigh. I ducked back through the bushes to the clear space in front of the grate and started changing.

"Charming has himself a train station, though how he convinced the town council to...oh, yeah, now I remember. He probably magicked them into submission. Anyhow, we've got access to wheels." I came back out to find Jack changing as well, the outfit he was removing being liberally stained with his own blood. When he took off his shirt, there was an impressive scar where Charming's pen had entered, and I couldn't keep myself from reaching out to touch it.

"I thought if I rewove your matrix, it would heal you entirely." Jack held still while I took a closer look. "It almost looks like there are stitches here."

"That's basically what you did, wasn't it? Stitched me up with a thread of figment?" He pulled a fresh shirt over his head and started stuffing the ruined outfit into his bag before changing his mind and chucking it back into the bushes. I raised my eyebrow at him. "What? They'd just get blood all over everything and it's not like I'd ever want to wear them again anyway."

"Fair enough. Let's go catch a train. Wait, do we have any gold left? Charming didn't bother to return my charge card." I began digging through my pack again.

Fred snorted. "You're fair sparkling with enough power to manifest something from nothing and you are digging through your purse for change? Come on, honey."

I blushed a little and closed the flap on my bag. "I'm not used to thinking that way. Besides, it's a crime to counterfeit money."

"So make us a few gold nuggets then and we'll sell 'em for coin. Or something." Jack held up my packs so I could balance them on my shoulder, and I started down the hill. He then held out the empty pack Fred had been traveling in previously. "In you go, doggy."

"That is insulting. I'm not *just* a dog, I'm a caterpillar-dog or a dog-caterpillar or...or a corgipillar or something. And why?"

"There aren't many of you around on the mainland. You stand out." Jack shook the bag invitingly.

"Fine, fine." Fred hopped in and curled up so Jack could easily close the flap. Jack groaned as he picked it up. Though Fred complained, the leather adequately muffled his grumbling, so we could ignore whatever invective he leveled at us.

"Soph, gonna make us something shiny? You know how I like shiny things."

"Alright. Make sure I don't fall down any holes and I'll work on it." I slipped my arm into Jack's and let him lead me down the hill toward the village proper. I let my mind drift through my favorite jewelry but decided against any of my designer pieces. I left my mind to think of simple gold chains instead, something with links large enough to barter with. I wrapped a few strands of power around my neck and imagined them solidifying into a satisfying weight. After a moment, it was no longer imaginary.

I opened my eyes and fingered the chain now resting on my blouse. It was cruder than I would have liked, but it wasn't supposed to be a fashion statement. I slipped it under my jacket so it wasn't as obvious, and we quickened our pace.

We were in luck when we reached the station. The next train leaving for Central Hearth City was arriving in ten minutes. I negotiated with the station master and handed over half the chain to ensure a private cabin for the six-hour ride into the city.

It was a tense few moments on the platform as we waited for the train. Jack and I spent the time keeping an eye out for any soldiers or guards, while Fred kept his head down in the satchel. The last thing we needed right now was a curious character wandering over to investigate our odd little doggy. But the train arrived without incident, and we boarded and settled into our cabin without any trouble.

After our tickets were punched, we closed and locked the cabin door. Finally, I was able to relax as the rocking of the train reassured me that we were indeed on our way into the city. My stomach grumbled and I was surprised at how hungry I was, but then I remembered I hadn't eaten since breakfast. As Jack unpacked Fred, I dug around for whatever travel rations remained in our packs. I was loathe to use any more of my spindled power to create vanishing food, since I was going to need that once we got to our destination, so we settled for the packages of nuts and jerky at the bottom of my satchel.

While I was digging, however, I stumbled across the little chapbook we had taken from the Stacks, those long days ago. "Hey, Jack, look at this. Kith must have slipped it back in our bags before we left."

Jack reached for the small book while Fred trotted up and down the length of the cabin for a moment before engaging in what appeared to be a canine version of yoga. I was impressed with the flexibility of his shell.

"Charming assumed we had found this book and that's how we knew how to do things, ergo he was never taught like we were, he's following the rules of the book." Jack opened it and started skimming through before sitting back and rubbing his eyes. "I can't make heads or tails of most of this, even after what Kith taught us." "Here, let me see." I took the book back and Fred jumped up onto the seat beside him. Jack gave him a pat and then started scratching the dog's floppy ears.

I studied the first diagram and the accompanying caption: "Thy manipulations of thine power require of thee a vessel to direct thine intentions." It showed a diagram of a man holding a stick in various positions beside a pond of water that was reacting in unnatural fashions. "I think...this is saying that you need something to channel the figments through, to actually do something. That must be why he was using that quill! I just thought he liked the symbolism of it because he's like that, but he must have thought he was dependent on it for manipulating the figments. Though he managed to drain me without it." I started flipping through the book, trying to see where else the rules as laid out in the book would handicap Charming in a fight.

Jack stole the nuts from beside me and put out a small pile for Fred before taking a handful for himself. "If we get the quill from Charming, that might throw him off his game."

I nodded absently, but most of my attention was on another diagram towards the back of the book. It seemed to be illustrating the relationship between character and creator through the Fire, though it was not labeled legibly. The lack of proper distinction in the diagram was probably what had kept Charming from attempting this a long time ago. He had to have tested it on someone before now, though. I wondered how he was planning on reaching through the fire; I'd seen how the imaginaries did it, but the book didn't have anything to say on the matter.

"You know, I don't see any warnings in here about how much power you can channel at once. I wonder if he's ever tapped into a human's raw imagination before. He could be completely unprepared for that sort of influx. He'll be off balance, and probably not paying attention to anything else. He probably assumes it's like a mega dose of figments." I reached for the bag of nuts and tried to hand the notebook to Fred. "You want a go at this thing?"

He swallowed before answering, "I can't turn the pages."

"Fair enough. I guess it's up to me to decipher what's here then." I curled up against the window and turned to another page in the book.

Jack got up and wandered over to the door to peek outside. "You know, this travel food has gotten gross. I think we'll be safe enough if I make a trek down to the dining car. Any requests?"

I shook my head, but Fred bounded up. "Fruit? Lots and lots of fruit?"

"Sure thing. Soph, could I have a few links of our chain?"

I took it off and handed it to him without breaking my concentration on the book.

Jack took it with a bow, and started to leave before turning back. "You know, you should probably spend this trip spooling up."

"You're probably right. You can study this when you get back and I'll zone out for a while."

He left the car and I tried to block out Fred's humming while he sat on the opposite seat with his nose pressed against the glass.

I read while Fred whined about not being able to put his head outside. About half the book was still indecipherable, though I did come across a diagram explaining how Charming had managed to compel us to speak. I wondered briefly if Kith had used such a compulsion on Jack and me to make us that much more likely to play along with her plans. If she had, I hadn't been able to feel it — not like the tentacle of power Charming had been using.

Jack returned to the cabin and locked the door behind him. I closed the manual and looked up. "Any trouble?"

"Nope, the car was empty. Guess it's late enough in the day that no one wants any food." He handed over a steaming cup of coffee and a sandwich. I was starting to get tired of sandwiches. When this was all said and done, I was going home and making an enormous salad and the biggest plate of pasta anyone had ever seen.

Jack opened another container filled with a slightly wilted fruit salad and set it in front of Fred. "I hope this will suffice, everything else looked like it'd been sitting there too long." The dog had already dived into the fruit facefirst. He tried to answer around his mouthful of melon chunks and grapes and I shook my head at the mumbling, glad that at least someone was enjoying himself.

Jack settled in beside me with his own coffee and sandwich. "Got anything new?"

"Nothing that'll help us. From what I can tell right now, he probably doesn't know the dangers of powering directly off of human imagination and he thinks power has to travel through an object, a talisman of sorts. Your turn to read, I'm going to charge up as much as I can."

Handing Jack the book, I curled into a corner with my coffee and stared at the steadily darkening countryside outside the window. The sunset this evening wasn't even pretty, which I thought was unfair. The least our universe could offer, as we sped off to defend it, was something pretty to look at.

For a couple hours, the cabin remained relatively quiet. Fred finished his fruit, fell asleep on his back, and started snoring. Jack read, occasionally frowning and turning back a page. I let my mind drift, eyes closed, as I attempted to snag as many figments as possible while we sped along the track. It took me a moment to get the hang of catching them as we were racing past, but eventually I figured out how to spread my consciousness like a net to either side of the train and use it to draw the figments to me.

I hadn't even noticed I had fallen asleep until there was a sharp rap on our cabin door. I bolted awake, the power boiling inside, ready at any moment to leap to the imagined threat on the other side of the door. Jack held his axe in his hand behind the cabin door. Fred stood, and...well, he would have raised hackles if he'd had any. He was doing a great job of conveying the *idea* of hackles without the actual fur at hand. But "Central Station, next stop," followed the knock. We then heard the porter moving down to the next cabin and repeating his warning.

"I can't believe you let me sleep this long!" I scrambled to start packing up our things and Jack slowed me down by grabbing my hands.

"We've got twenty minutes before we pull into the station. And you looked exhausted, so of course I let you sleep. Whatever you did to me in the pit, I'm still bright-eyed and bushy-tailed, so I was more than capable of watching over us for a few hours. But you need to be on your A-game today." He laid a soft kiss on my forehead. "Now, where do you want to lay low in the city? I was thinking Gustav's would be nice."

Jack let go of my hands and I went back to packing, more slowly this time. "I think he'd harbor us, even if Charming had warned him off. He has more than a few Underground Railroad characters layered on him. We should be able to plan our attack from there. And the ballroom Charming's using is less than a half mile away, so we could walk there."

"Saves us having to find a pumpkin to make into a coach then!" Jack laughed at his own joke. I rolled my eyes; I wasn't awake enough yet for his humor. Nor was I feeling at all humorous. The time was quickly approaching when I would have to confront a man who vastly overpowered us, *again*. And our plan was to take away his favorite toy. Yeah, this was going to go great.

After the train pulled into the station, we made our way through the terminal, Fred once again secured into a saddlebag. We found a taxi and gave him directions to the Boar and Unicorn. I tried to relax. Terror of being stopped by the City Watch, or Charming's henchmen, kept my eyes wide. I didn't want to use the power I'd spooled against anyone other than Charming if I could help it, but I was afraid I wouldn't have a choice in the matter if I was startled into action. I could feel the heat of the figments pulsing and pushing for a way to come pouring out. It was more power than I'd ever spindled on my own, though it didn't come near the overabundance of imagination that Austin had provided on two separate occasions. A surprising amount of that power had been required to stitch Jack back together. But the remainder of Austin's gift, together with the strands that I'd netted on the rail journey, were eager to escape back into the world.

The taxi pulled up in front of the inn and Jack and I got out, tipping the driver with the last of the gold chain we carried. The driver hardly blinked at the gold in front of him, testing its softness briefly with the time-honored bite test, then grunted his approval and drove off.

Jack frowned as the cab turned the corner. "Care to whip us up some more gold? Otherwise I doubt the old goat who runs this place will let us hang around."

"Gustav is a dear. And he will definitely start a tab for me." I strode through the front door, leaving Jack to pick up all the bags on the sidewalk and bring them in himself.

"Gustav!" I greeted the portly gentleman behind the counter, as Jack entered the lobby behind me, staggering under his burden.

The innkeeper turned with a courteous smile, processed my face, and frowned. "Girl, git your head down." He hurried out from behind the counter and ushered us quickly through a service door on the other side of the lobby. "Did you know that you two are fugitives? There's a crier in town and posters every other block. They're saying you two were written bad in a recent reinterpretation of the fairy tales, cast as truly vile villains, and that you've gone on a crime spree."

The bottom dropped out of my stomach and the power I'd been carefully keeping in check surged against my will. The air around the corners of my vision started to sparkle. "Gustav, they're lying! I promise. If anything, Charming is the one that's been corrupted, not us. You know a single telling couldn't have that kind of effect on us anymore, not unless it was some summer blockbuster movie. We're too established.'"

Gustav glanced at me and Jack, came to a decision, then continued, sotto voce, "I know, chickie, that's why I didn't start hollering for the guards right off the bat. I figured you'd gotten on the wrong side of someone powerful." He went quiet as a maid passed us, paying no attention to anything but the bundle of laundry she was carrying. "Let's get you someplace you won't be bothered."

He led us around a few corners and opened the door to his office. It was more spacious than I'd envisioned, more the corporate corner office than the old-world cubicle. There was a couch and a table with chairs along with his desk, computer, phone with multiple lines, and two separate television set-ups.

Jack wandered over to check out the bigger of the two TVs. "This is quite the swanky technological retreat you've got here."

"Since all the unnamed inn and motel keepers still get layered onto me, even the modern tellings, I find that I can't stand to spend all my time cut off from the convenience of this stuff. At least while you're here, you can keep track of the news and everything. I'd ask *why* you're here, but I don't think I want the answer to that. Just promise me, you're not here to kill anyone, are you? I don't think my old heart could stand to see you involved in something so dark."

"Of course not, Gustav. We're here to stop someone from doing something that would do a hell of a lot more damage than straight-up murder. And we'll be out of your hair by dusk tomorrow night. Promise."

"Fair enough. Keep your head down in here, there's a toilet through that door there, shower too if you need it. Feel free to raid my fridge and pantry behind the desk. When you're ready to leave, continue down this hallway, it'll take you out through the alley instead of the front, where I'm sure someone would recognize you. Your faces are all over the news." Gustav wrung his hands for a moment before enveloping me in an enormous hug. He turned and did the same to Jack, who endured it for a moment, before slapping him heartily on the back and disengaging himself from the florid man. "Be careful, you two. Promise me that."

"We will. And thank you, Gustav. I will make it up to you." I was worried that the innkeeper was taking too big a risk letting us stay here, but I was seriously thankful for the opportunity to clean up and prepare for tomorrow's confrontation.

"Oh pish-tosh. I have too many rum-runners and smugglers in me to do anything different. Now relax, Gustav has this one handled." He left his office, and we locked the door behind him.

Jack flopped onto the couch and picked up a remote. "I think I'm going to see what they're saying about us." Fred struggled out of his carry case and jumped up beside Jack.

"Can we check out the Food Channel next? It's like porn for foodies."

Jack started flipping through the channels until he found the news. "You got the Food Channel out on the island?"

Fred barked in amusement. "We got everything, man. Kith rigged it up somehow. Otherwise, it gets real boring out there, real fast."

I shook my head and started toward the door to the bathroom. "I am going to clean up. While I'm in there, I'll dream up some clothes that'll get us into the party. I wish it were a masquerade, but I guess you can't have everything." In the cramped little bathroom, I started stripping.

"Awww, you're no fun." Fred hollered.

Jack poked his head in and I chucked my vest at him. He ducked and grinned. "I was thinking, maybe we should change the cut and color of our hair while we're at it, you know, for as much of a disguise as we can manage."

"Fine, I've always wanted to be dark and curly. Here's my chance. Now get out. Please." I wouldn't have objected at this point if he had decided to join me, if there hadn't been a vulgar dog with an unnerving sex drive in the next room.

The feeling of hot water cascading over my sore and tired muscles was euphoric. I wasn't all that dirty, per se, but there is nothing like the feeling of hot water on your skin to make you relax. It feels simply divine, and it does wonders to wash away whatever anxiety you're currently harboring.

After my initial blissing out, I turned my inattention to my hair. I pictured the kinds of locks I'd always envied, long flowing tresses of dark curly hair, masses trailing down the back and pooling on the shoulders. Not tight crinkled curls, but the soft, natural ringlets that take hours to put into straight hair like mine. I invited the overabundance of figments in my mind to work their magic along my scalp. They flowed over my mid-length blonde cut and I felt a sudden weight change as it solidified into the hair of my dreams. I then turned my attention to Jack's short-cropped brunette style in the outer room and he yelped as it turned into a cascade of blonde fit to rival a romance novel hero.

"Really, Soph, *really*?" He called out. I could hear Fred laughing hysterically at the change.

I snickered to myself at the look I was imagining on his face. "You can put it in a ponytail if you want, but you said you wanted different!"

I couldn't quite make out his answer, but it made Fred laugh all the harder, so I decided I didn't want to know. Instead, I turned my thoughts inward again and contemplated the dress code. The ball was themed after the spark of inspiration, so I was trying to decide whether to go with red or white in our ensembles. White would be striking, but with my new black hair, the red would be drop dead gorgeous. And what kind of girl would go to her almost-certain death looking any-thing but her best?

There would be people there in every era of formal wear, which gave me plenty of room for a modern look that would allow me more flexibility and agility. My heart longed for the full skirts and corseted bodices of the Victorian ball gown, but those were only suitable for slow dancing or standing still. I couldn't even sit in them, much less take down a madman.

Still, I let those be my inspiration and started constructing an A-line ball gown in a rich red—none of that orangey-red nonsense—with a sweetheart neckline, the better to accentuate my "character traits." I let the figments spool out of my head and gather at the back of the door, first creating a hanger, and then weaving the dress out of thin air. Opening my eyes when the gown felt finished, I studied it while soaping up in the shower. It was gorgeous... but dreadfully plain. After so much travelling and fighting, I longed to wear some sparkle. As I rinsed off, I added a judicious beading around the neck and hemlines, flames done in clear and white crystals, to better emphasize the theme. And oh how that gown sparkled when I opened my eyes! It was like I was back in my bedroom with all of the sisters, sneaking out to our magnificent nightly party all over again. I couldn't help loving pretty things; it was written into the very fabric of my being.

Satisfied with my dress, I spent a moment and a touch of power to create matching shoes, a low square heel for stability and plenty of comfort, and a ruby-studded comb for my hair. I was going to have to bind up this new mass of hair to make sure it didn't get in my way.

Next, time to turn my thoughts to Jack. I thought tails would be a bit much for him, particularly with his new hairstyle, so I spun him a tidy white suit and a crimson shirt to match my dress, with a white silk tie and white patent shoes.

At this point, the hot water was running out, so I got out, dried off, and wrapped myself in an extra towel. We had a few hours before the event and I didn't want to muss the dress. I carried our outfits into the outer room and Fred let out a low whistle.

"Damn girl, you work fast."

"The shower helped get my juices flowing. Remind me of that the next time I need to make something." I hung the clothes from the bookshelf on one wall and went to the saddlebag to pull out a pair of leggings and a shirt. I went back to the bathroom to dress, then came out to curl up on the couch. "Your turn."

Jack made a big show of smelling himself, then sighed and traipsed off to the bathroom. I took over the remote and flipped through news broadcast after news broadcast, all of them proclaiming that Jack and I had gone bad. Apparently the rest of the characters who were affected by this recent reinterpretation had already reported for adjustment, but we had taken off on a killing spree.

According to the news agencies' elegant fictions, we were running a black widow con. I was amused at their ability to make up such outrageous stories; it wasn't easy for characters to manage.

Jack didn't take long in the shower. Emerging wrapped in a towel, he headed directly to the fridge, where he rummaged for protein and carbs. After toweling off, he impersonated a waiter, balancing a tray laden with sodas and sandwiches.

I sighed. "More sandwiches?"

He shrugged as he popped the cap off a soda. "I promise you a fantastic five-star dinner tomorrow night, how's that?"

"You're just saying that because you don't think you'll actually have to pay up." I pretended to pout and he put the soda down and pulled me over onto his lap.

"I'm saying that because I think we have a solid plan. Well, outline of a plan. Get his focus, beat him at his own game, and get the hell out."

I laughed and slid off his lap, but stayed curled up against him, under his arm. "Get the focus, beat him, get out. That might be hard to remember."

"Well then, leave the remembering up to me and you relax. Spindle as much power as you possibly can between now and then. In case, you know, plan A doesn't work." He gave me a squeeze and a quick kiss on the top of my head.

"Now that I can do." I relaxed into his hold and closed my eyes, happy to ignore the looming ball, and let his smell and warmth and feel combine to help me drift away.

We stayed in that quiet suite all evening and the next day, though that required a few moments of clever work by Jack, who figured out how to rig the toilet to help the corgipillar balance. Otherwise, we switched back and forth between news coverage and the Food Channel. About midday, the news coverage switched from general stories to coverage of the upcoming opening of the festivities. The ball tonight was to launch a full week of festivals and parties for the anniversary. The who's who of our world were going to be in attendance; so was the entirety of our media personnel.

We paid attention when they started talking about which characters were scheduled to be in attendance. All the big names were going to be there, Charming of course at the forefront. Luke and Leia were expected to make an appearance, as well as Baba Yaga and Mbeku, who promised to be on his best behavior. The newscasters were universally impressed with Charming's generosity in inviting a slew of new arrivals such as the Cullen family and Professor Dumbledore. It usually took a century or two before a character wielded much power in our society, and events like this had previously been restricted to characters of canonical standing. From the list that was given and what we could remember about the status of authors—living or dead—Jack and I figured Charming would have roughly 300 humans he could access to drain tonight. I couldn't begin to understand how he could hold that much imagination without bursting the strands of his own weave; hopefully we wouldn't have to find out.

As our departure time loomed, the tension in the room ratcheted up. Jack and I began dressing, and I had to use a smidge more of my power to create the appropriate makeup for myself, more than I normally would have worn, to give my eyes a different cast and change the shape of my cheekbones. Anything I could do to escape notice during our quick dash outside.

After a brief and vicious argument with Fred, in which he insulted our lineage, human and character, he agreed it was safer for him to stay behind. He couldn't add much to the fight and his direct linkage to such a vulnerable and powerful human would make him a liability at best and an outright danger at worst.

Finally, the red carpet walk at the Spark of Inspiration Ball started on TV, and we got going. Jack offered his axe to me and I concentrated to shrink it sufficiently to fit in his pocket. I'd re-enlarge it after we were in the ball and ready to take action. I pulled the invitation out of my journal and stepped out into the hallway.

We locked Fred into the room and headed for the alley, working up our courage to brave the crowded streets. Jack carefully pushed the door open and peered out, then nodded to me when it was all clear. At the head of the alley, I paused to adjust my dress one last time, Jack offered me his arm, and we entered the flow of foot traffic. We didn't sneak and we didn't hurry, as either would have drawn attention. Even from a few blocks away, we could see the glow of lights over the massive ballroom the Charming family had built centuries ago for just this kind of event. The prince was not penny-pinching on his electricity bill for this party.

We weren't challenged, or even noticed, on our walk to the ball. It felt almost like an insult, considering how proud I was of our new looks. Of course, we were just one of many stunners headed towards the ball, so we hardly stood out.

Reaching the streets outside the venue, we approached the lavishly decorated building with the stream of other attendees. The big names were all chauffeured in gleaming black limos and dropped off where the red carpet met the curb. The lesser-known characters, organizers, or characters who didn't want a fuss were all heading toward the side portico, where Jack and I joined them.

There were two guards at the door, one with a clipboard, the other with arms crossed, scanning the crowds. "Invitation please."

Jack handed the engraved card to the overly muscled man who scanned it, placed it in the box beside him and scratched a tally on his clipboard. "Thank you, enjoy your evening."

Once we were through the door and onto the crowded dance floor, I exhaled a huge breath that I hadn't realized I'd been holding. "This is too easy, all of it."

Jack snorted. "Just remember, James Bond could get in anywhere. It was the getting out that required him to blow shit up."

"I think I could handle that right now. I feel like all this power is going to boil out of me." I clutched his arm as we circulated around the floor, trying to find Charming while at the same time avoid the obvious security stationed along the walls.

"Keep it bottled up for now." He took a closer look at me. "You know, when you're carrying this much power you *actually* glow. I think if it was dark in here you'd stand out like a nightlight."

Any other time, I might have thought he was being cute, but I could feel the truth of his words as the power bubbled inside. "Gee, thanks, that's terrifically comforting. Let's find Charming, I'd rather get this over with before the evening gets into full swing."

The ballroom was stunning, I had to admit. Somehow, the decorators had managed to arrange ice sculptures strategically throughout the room—and had placed flames *in* each sculpture—but managed it so that the ice remained frozen. I suspected that Charming had been at work with artful use of figments. But, if so, it certainly wasn't obvious. At the front of the main dance floor, there was a small dais and microphone in front of the biggest sculpture in the building. It was an enormous faceted sphere that reflected the bonfire at the center of the dance floor, casting shards of surreal light across the room.

Double-checking to make sure no one was paying us any attention, I guided Jack near it for a closer look. The light coming off the ball didn't look right. As we got closer, I could feel an absence of figments near the ball, almost as if it were sucking them in. "I think...Close your eyes, do you feel it?"

Jack closed his eyes and took a deep breath before frowning. "It's like the center is hollow. But not just hollow, there's nothing there, the same nothing that's waiting when I step through the fabric of our reality and outside for a moment. Do you think this is some sort of, I don't know, a capacitor, like the book talked about?"

"I think that's exactly what it is. Come on, we have to get to Charming before he starts filling it."

We continued on our mission to locate the prince. Ten minutes later we had successfully ducked various people who might recognize us, while failing entirely to find any trace of Charming. That's when we heard a spoon on a glass and turned to the dais in unison with everyone else in the room.

There was our target, on the dais with a glass of champagne, the quill pinned where a boutonniere should be.

"Welcome, welcome one and all. I am so happy to be hosting this magnificent occasion, with friends new and old. I don't know of any better way to inaugurate the celebrations of the Hearth's anniversary than to bring together those who founded it and those who have most recently benefited. In fact, we have the two newest characters in the whole city with us! Wave hello over there to Mary Fairbrother and her husband: their book is going live in three months! Good to see you, Mary. Now, I am going to keep this short so all you characters can get to partying, but I do have a treat for all of you here." He pulled the microphone off the stand and started to pace with it. "As most of you know. I love the history of our little world and educating characters about the beginnings of our time here. Imagine my surprise when I came across a prayer that we haven't used in a few thousand years, and imagine my even greater surprise when I discovered what this prayer could do. I have little William Halloway here with me tonight—say hello to everyone, Will...."

He tilted the microphone down to a sandy-haired youth who then waved, giving us a sheepish "Hi."

Charming put his arm around the boy and turned back to the audience. "As most of you here know, Will comes from the mind of Ray Bradbury, an industrious fellow on the other side of the Fire." The prince leaned conspiratorially down to the boy, winking at the audience. "Will, would you like to meet Ray? After a fashion, I mean."

"That would be awesome." The joy on the character's face was unmistakable. The ability to meet, maybe talk with the mind that had created us was a dream most of us harbored, some to thank the author, others to curse him. When you know, definitively, that you were deliberately designed and created, how could you not want to know why? Charming was going to tap into that desire to make these little lemmings leap off his cliff.

"Absolutely. Step up to the fire here. Alright, now repeat after me." Charming arranged Will at the fire and kept his hand on the boy's shoulder. "Awil awatum, semu annu nagiru; Abi awatum, nisme annu damu; Mina ankida ina mudutu."

William repeated the Sumerian words haltingly, staring hungrily into the fire. The fuel popped, sending up a cascade of sparks almost to the art-deco ceiling. We couldn't see what the fire was showing him, since we weren't in contact, but everyone clearly heard him gasp. He leaned into the fire and started murmuring to it. Charming stiffened and recovered himself quickly enough, but I could see he'd started a power drain through the boy. A thick thread of imagination streamed out of the fire, through William, and had started gathering in Charming. Characters all over the dance floor started shifting uncomfortably, but the prince didn't give them time to think.

By this point, Jack and I were struggling to get close enough to him to grab his quill before he had a chance to start the larger power drain, but the characters around us were also pushing in closer to the fire, trying to see what was going on, and we weren't quite ready to draw the attention of the guards yet.

"If your author is still alive, join us around the fire! Join hands in a circle, and speak these words after me." He waited until everyone was arranged and then spoke the words of power again and characters all over the room cried out, or sobbed, or laughed, depending on their natures. Slowly at first, and then more quickly, a stream of imagination poured out of the fire, into the characters connected to their creators, then around the circle to Charming. He'd stopped pretending to pay any attention to the party and reached up to his lapel for his quill. He pulled it out and pointed it behind him at the sphere, his other hand convulsively grasping at William's shoulder. Charming was pulling too much energy too fast and the bolt of imagination erupted out of his quill and shot into the crystalline structure behind him.

The channel of imagination shot through an unfortunate Dumbledore, who happened to be standing behind Charming, turning the old wizard into a pile of steaming kittens, all sporting long beards and a patch of hair that stood up like a hat on each head. One of the characters at the fire screamed, another collapsed, and as the kittens scattered into the crowd, characters not connected to the fire started to realize that something very wrong was happening. Whatever was going on, it was *not* the party they'd been promised. In fact, characters all around the room were beginning to realize they would probably be much safer if they made a strategic exit at this point. As one they all started pushing and screaming for a way off the dance floor.

Jack abandoned all pretense of composure and started shoving his way through the crowd. He reached into his pocket and retrieved his miniaturized axe, which I helpfully enlarged as he held it above his head so he wouldn't hurt anyone fleeing Charming's insanity. Jack tried to weave in and out of our reality to get closer to Charming and failed once, then twice as screaming characters bowled into him and knocked him back from the gaps he'd created. Finally, Jack managed to get a clear enough spot where he could phase and in a blink he was standing behind the prince. I saw Jack's axe descending in a glittering arc towards the quill, and the hand holding it.

For a moment, the axe seemed poised in mid-air. When it struck, the axe shattered.

Jack was left gaping at the shattered end of the handle while I finally managed to work my way through the last of the crowd to reach his side. Charming didn't even seem to be aware of our presence. He was caught up in the bliss of the power transference and couldn't see beyond the golden nimbus that surrounded him. William was convulsing, held upright only by the prince's hand on his shoulder. The circle of connected characters were flaring out with equal rapidity, collapsing against their neighbors, but held in place by their clasped hands.

"Grab the quill!" I hollered into Jack's ear—over the noise of the spontaneous evacuation and the hissing and spitting stream of imagination pouring out of Charming.

"You get it!" Jack bawled, trying to shake the shock of the impact out of his arm. "I've already given it my best!"

I started to reach for the pen, then thought better of sticking an unprotected hand anywhere near that stream of unshaped power.

Instead, I created a chainmail glove and coated it in a sheath of imagination, just to be on the safe side. Then I reached out again. As

I neared Charming's hand, the air felt progressively thicker until my hand came to a full stop just inches from the quill. Concentrating, I pushed even harder, feeling the seconds tick by as the crystal—clearly reaching its capacity for power—reverberated unsteadily, pounding against its restraints and screaming for a form.

At last I had my hand within grasping distance, but as my fingers came in contact with the edges of the feather, the pen exploded into dust. I felt a surge of joy as I watched the quill fragments swirl away, as I felt sure it would mean a weakening of Charming's power, but the stream of power continued unbroken. We obviously needed a new strategy, so I decided to disengage. As soon as I let up my pressure on the nimbus of power around Charming, I was thrown backwards and thankfully found myself encircled in Jack's strong arms instead of smeared across the back wall of the ballroom.

We stared into each other's eyes, dumbstruck. "Now what?!" It was a struggle to be heard above the steadily climbing whine and churn of the power beginning to overload its new crystalline matrix.

A shrill bark made us turn to the door. "My turn!"

"Fred!" I screamed as the corgi streaked past me, having launched himself at the hand connecting Charming to the boy. He didn't even slow down as he reached the edge of the cloud of figments surrounding the prince. Upon impact, Fred latched his jaws around Charming's hand and bore down like a pneumatic vice. A tearing sound filled the air as Fred managed to rip the hand from Charming's arm, disconnecting him from the circle.

A massive feedback explosion confirmed that the stream of power was cut off prematurely, and I could see the undirected power wash back along the circle and through the fire. Charming and Fred were propelled backwards a good twenty feet, landing to either side of the dais. The circle of characters collapsed like marionettes with their strings cut, breaking their links with their authors as they crashed to the dance floor. The lights flickered briefly, then went out, leaving us illuminated solely by the fire flickering through the ice sculptures and the constantly shifting, atomic glow of Charming's giant capacitor. Silently, I sent a brief prayer to the Storyteller in the hopes that we were in time to save both the characters and their authors. Then I ran to Fred's side.

"You stupid dog! Are you alright?"

"Man, he tasted *terrible!*" Fred climbed to his feet, wobbling, but panting happily at me. His eyes uncrossed and refocused. One antenna had been snapped, left hanging on by a thread. "Hey, did you create some doppelgangers or something, how come there are three of you?"

"Very funny. Go find a corner to hide in, okay?"

He started staggering away. "You don't have to tell me twice."

Charming, who had been motionless since his circle snapped, now emitted an anguished moan and attempted to sit up. "Goddamn it, my hand! Where's my hand! Dog, that dog, that bastard cur *took my hand!*"

Jack appeared at my side and helped me to my feet. "I think you're going to want to be upright for what happens next."

"Here." I let my mind go blank for a moment and re-created his axe from memory, only this time I made the whole thing out of platinum with an iron core for heft and a coating of pure imagination to ensure its stability. As I handed it over to him, Jack's eyebrows rose and he let out a low whistle of appreciation. "You always did know how to accessorize."

"It's a knack." I gave him a brief smile before starting to creep around the dais toward the sound of Charming spitting out curses, the majority of them aimed at Fred's mother, but with plenty to spare for the rest of characterkind. Beyond, sparkles of light and occasional cascades of sparks from the swirling figments were starting fires in the drapery and linens around the room. When we rounded the corner to face the prince, he was kneeling on the floor, rocking back and forth, and cradling his abbreviated arm. He seemed to be trying to re-create his hand, but he was so over-full of imagination that he couldn't control it. We watched the missing limb flicker in and out of existence, first as a tentacle, then a can opener, then a lobster claw, then a hammer, until he noticed us standing and staring at him.

"You miserable, interfering, meddling whores!" he shrieked, springing to his feet. All pretense at civility had fled and he seethed, the power in him swirling visibly under his skin, creating rippling patterns of light. The capillaries of light broke through his skin occasionally, creating miniature cascades of sparks—and small explosions of potpourri, of all things. He finally managed to rein in his concentration and his rage fashioned two poorly constructed— but massive—direwolves.

"Kill them!" the prince howled, glaring at his new constructions and pointing with his remaining hand toward us. Jack leapt in front of me and met the animals with two strikes of his gleaming new axe. While Jack kept them at bay, I stumbled back and to the side, keeping as far out of his way as I could manage while still following Charming. I coated Jack in a shield of raw energy, then turned my attention to the base structure of the animals, but they were too full of barely restrained energy for me to even attempt to break them down. Praying Jack could handle them, I turned to deal with Charming instead.

I had no idea how to fight a character so charged with imagination, so I opted instead to try and distract him from Jack's fight long enough to give Jack the chance to kill the wolves and come help me. "Why, Charming? The only thing I don't understand is, why give up every-thing, your status, your influence, for *this*?"

"Why?" As the prince turned to me, I could see that the power was eating him alive from inside. His skin had started to slough from his face and his hair had become patchy. "Do you know how old I am, truly? I was first told long before the name Prince Charming was imagined. I was powerful and I was mighty and I could have anyone and anything

I wanted. And then, for some reason, my stories became tempered, and weak. I was a smarmy pretty boy destined to ride in at the end of the episode and sweep the girl off her feet. There wasn't any fight left to it, no challenge, no power. Society weakened and needed weaker heroes, faceless morons who looked good on a horse. The shame and drudgery of it destroyed my strength. I have constant stories piling on top of me, little girls creating fantasies of their perfect prince to rescue them from naptime and dish drying. Old spinsters who have failed to find a man who could tolerate their nasal breathing and hordes of filthy cats. And now, all the gay men...do you know what it's like to be perfectly straight for three thousand years and now to be obsessed with the bodies of men? Then there are these...these *infants* that demand and demand, louder and louder, layering obsession and story and fantasy and pure stupid want! I can't take it anymore! I want to go back to what I was, the strongest man in the land, undefeatable in battle, bedding any wench I pleased, and ruling by right everything I saw! I want to be *me*!"

I glanced back at Jack to make sure he was faring alright against the wolves before pushing Charming a little further. Finally, I had figured out how I might bring him down.

But it was going to take some fast talking on my part. "You were, what, going to cut yourself off from the Fire and strike out on your own? No character can do that. You'd die! You may hate them, but you need all those lonely women and men to keep you alive. They are the reason you exist! You have to deal with their demands, like we all do. What are you so afraid of, anyway? This isn't some nightmare to wake up from!"

The prince was shaking now as the imagination ate away at the threads that made him real. He convulsed, grimaced, and then straightened again. "I am not afraid, you blithering trollop. I have no nightmares." His eyes changed as the overabundance of imagination ricocheting through him latched onto the idea of a nightmare. "No nightmares about being eaten alive by these women who want nothing more than a stick figure to act as a buffer between them and the real world. No nightmares about losing my soul to the demands of a fickle and tawdry child." And there it was. I could see the imagination in him tighten and condense. It had a bead on his dreams now and it wasn't going to let go easily. As Kith had said back on the island, it was a damn good thing Jack and I hadn't had any nightmares the night we overdosed.

I pushed him even harder. "These hordes of women, you've seen them even today, outside, straining against ropes and bodyguards, eager to get just one taste of their idol, the paragon of man that they've forced up onto a pedestal. The crowds of women who would trample characters to their death on their way to get to you. Screaming and crying to touch you. Desperate to have you just how *they* want you."

"No, no, no, NO!" Charming screamed, collapsing into himself, clutching at the explosion of imagination that ripped out of him, forming girl after boy after girl in white pinafores, medieval night-gowns, Justin Bieber t-shirts, blonde, brunette, raven-haired, and a sprinkling of redheads for good measure.

The room was rapidly filling with little girls, teen beauties, even adults and a few elderly individuals who still pined for the perfect man. Their numbers forced me further back from Charming. Jack startled me when he grabbed my arm. "What did you start there, Sophie?" He was out of breath and blood was streaming from a gash on his scalp, but he was in one piece.

"I don't think we're going to like what happens." I murmured and turned away as the first little girl called out.

"Prince Charming? Strong and true and loves puppies and kitties and will buy me my own horsie?" She was immediately drowned by a chorus of demands from others.

"Prince Charming? Quiet man, not like daddy, never hits, wants to take me shopping?"

"Prince Charming? He's my handsome prince, come to take me away!"

"No, he's *mine!*"

"Back off, he's *mine!*"

The little girls—and the not-so-little—kept multiplying. Prince Charming had built up an awful lot of imagination, more than he could ever have hoped to control properly. Twelve, then sixty-four, then two hundred fifty-six demanding monsters crushing in on Charming, and pushing Jack and me farther and farther back. Their cries of admiration and desire filled the air, and even I could feel the pulse of their demands pulling at me, commanding me to change, to be exactly what they wanted.

Those sweet voices turned jealous, then tense, and finally erupted into fury as they fought over whose Prince Charming he was and what he should be. What he *had* to be.

Charming tried to get to the edge of the crowd, to run, but their grasping, sticky hands were dragging him under. He surged up once, back on his feet, and forced himself the other way through the crowd of pinafores, crop-tops and sweaters, through the mass of sweet-smelling curls, until he had his back pressed up against his capacitor.

"I'll show you!" He screamed. "I'll show you all, I'm not yours! You can't have me, never again!" The whole room started to shudder as he tapped into the insane amount of power he had stored up earlier. Like lightning, jet-fire, and paintball guns, the power lashed out of him without control, and the horde only multiplied faster. Screaming, Charming tried cutting swaths through their ranks with raw beams of power, but each time the pure imagination swept through a child, ten more took her place. They were crawling over top of each other, grasping and pulling the tails off his coat, the cuffs from his sleeves, screaming with perverse glee as they came away with handfuls of cloth or hair or skin.

I turned away from the gruesome sight and called for Fred. We had to get out of here before Charming brought the whole building down on top of us. His erratic aiming was starting to damage the marble support columns as he swung wide of his mark.

Fred came galloping up, wide-eyed. "Jeez, Sophia, what did you do to him? Did you make those?"

I had to swallow bile before I could answer him. "Nope, all his. That's his nightmare." I refused to even look at what I had started. "Here, Jack, check and see if any of these characters are still alive. We have to get them out of here."

Most of the characters that had fallen around the fire were still alive, but they were sluggish and unresponsive. I turned a spray of water on them, tapping into my dwindling reserves of power to conjure a fire hose out of my palm. That got most of them up, moving, and helping each other out of the exit. William, however, hadn't even twitched at the deluge. Jack went over and took his pulse, then bowed his head. He picked up the lifeless body of the young hero and joined Fred and me to bring up the rear of the train of frightened characters. The building was starting to shake and I was worried it could collapse at any moment. We had just reached the hallway that led out to the back of the building when I heard Charming laughing behind us.

Surprised that I could hear it over the crowds of young girls clamoring for his blood, I looked back. He had somehow managed to get on top of the crystal sphere, and there was a pulsing mass of screaming fans slamming against it, using each other for unwilling ladders, trying to reach their prince.

"You can't have me! I am my own! Mine! I belong to no one, I will answer to no one! And that is final!" He raised his arms slowly to the ceiling, urging the mass of power beneath his feet to grow and expand, seriously compromising the capacitor's matrix and causing spiderwebbing cracks to explode over its surface.

"*Not good. This is so not good!*" Fred muttered and picked up the pace toward the door, nipping the heels of the characters in front of him when they didn't move fast enough for him.

"Sophia, let's go!" Jack grabbed my arm and hauled me through the doorway. Behind me, over the tapestry of demanding voices, I could hear Charming screaming with laughter and the steadily increasing whine of power confined to a too-small space. I took the last of the power I was carrying and threw all of it into a bubble-shaped shield behind and around us, just in time.

There was a moment of absolute silence and then the sound of a shattering glass. Not loud at all, more like the sound of a hollow glass bird being dropped on the flagstones outside my father's library. And then a roaring tidal wave of power slammed against the shield around us and I ricocheted off the stone wall of the hallway.

My vision flickered, like a dim bulb, and I could see marble dust swirling around outside the dome I'd created, along with fragments of decoration, shards of the dance floor, and building bricks raining out of the sky: a demented hailstorm bouncing and tumbling around us. Jack was unconscious beside me and I couldn't see Fred, but as I looked for him, I saw a figure standing in the rubble, staring back at me, and I managed to think, *that's not right, no one should be standing after an explosion like that*, before I lost consciousness and gratefully faded to black.

♕

THE DENUE-MINUET

"**S**he's awake!" A rough and vigorous tongue slobbered over my cheek. I batted it away, wiping at the slime it had left behind. I had hoped I'd be waking on a soft bed of linen, maybe at home, maybe at Gustav's, but no, I was definitely lying amid rubble. Rubble is never a good thing.

I groaned and refused to open my eyes, knowing that if I did, I'd have to start dealing with the world, which, when I last looked, had been going distinctly wahooney-shaped. Besides, I probably had a concussion. You're supposed to rest when you have one of those, right?

The rubble to my left shifted and Jack knelt down beside me. "Sophie, are you okay?" Briefly, he checked my pulse and then tried to open an eyelid to look at my pupil. I knocked his hand away with extremely poor coordination.

"Fine, fine, fug-off," I managed to mumble, giving in and opening my eyes, blinking a few times to make sure the drifting lights I saw weren't a side effect of my abused brain but were actually things floating in the air.

Jack followed my gaze. "Yeah, stray figments. They're lighting up the night something pretty. Charming let loose, but not all the power blew away in the explosion." Jack helped me sit upright and that's when I noticed that his left arm was caught up in a crude sling. Fred was sitting a ways back, shifting back and forth. When I extended a hand to him, he bounded forward, happily starting to wash the grit from my face again.

"Enough, enough!" I laughed, but immediately started coughing. That made my ribs hurt. I struggled to catch my breath and looked around for the rest of the characters. They were scattered through the remains of the hallway, and from what I could tell, not too much the worse for wear than they had been a few moments ago. But there seemed to be no sign of the shadowy man I had seen right before passing out. I frowned at that, but decided now was not the proper time to bring up visual hallucinations.

Finally, the welcome sound of sirens sounded in the distance and I prayed they'd get here fast. I didn't want to be responsible for anyone anymore. I wanted nurturing Red Cross characters to give me a blanket and a bottle of water. I hoped the authorities would wait to ask inconvenient questions until our heads were clearer and our wounds were at least bandaged, if not healed.

"Charming?" I asked, pretty sure I already knew the answer.

"Basically disintegrated by that explosion. We'll know in a few hours if he comes through the Fire as a fresh young spark. You should be proud of yourself, though. Between your shielding and my first-aid skills I think we only lost the one character." Jack turned on his heel to sit beside me and wait for the sirens. "Do you think the First Assholes will be happy with this outcome?"

I looked around the disaster area, four square city blocks reduced to gravel, and started giggling. "They better, I don't think we could have eradicated the problem any more thoroughly."

Jack started laughing, which made me laugh again, even through the coughing and pain, and we couldn't stop until tears were streaming down our faces.

♛

All of us were shuffled off to the hospital. In the ER, we were poked and prodded by a succession of well-meaning medicos telling us we were lucky to be alive. After a brief tour as curiosities, everyone stopped talking to us. Then they sequestered me and Jack in separate rooms.

My injuries totaled a concussion, a sprained wrist, bruised ribs, and several lacerations. Apparently flying debris wasn't much hindered by my dome shield, even if it did protect us from the wave of raw imagination. I was given a whole day to contemplate how badly everything hurt before anyone came to start asking their uncomfortable questions. I tried to meditate during that time, to open myself up to imagination, and build up a little reserve, just in case, but I was so tired and there was so much pain that I had trouble holding onto enough power to make a grain of rice, let alone start mending my injuries. Therefore, my only distraction was what I could see out of my sixth-floor window, since the orderlies had taken the TV out of my room.

Finally, an investigator came knocking at my door. "Princess Sophia Saltare?"

"That would be me." I waved the portly gentleman in and curled up on the bed, bringing my knees up to my chest. "How is everyone?"

"With the exception of Prince Charming and young William, they're all going to pull through just fine. Bruised, confused, but fine. Your boy there," he made an elaborate show of consulting his notes, "Jack? Yes, Jack, he's more banged up, seems like he got in a fight with a pack of wolves, though where he came across those, and where the bodies went..." He shrugged and gestured to the seat beside my bed. "Do you mind?"

I shook my head and he sat. "I'm sorry, I never introduced myself, I'm Detective Colombo." He paused to clear his throat, then continued, apologetically. "Are you feeling up to talking about the incident?"

I couldn't help but smile at the awkward man. "I'll answer any questions you want, Detective, though I'm not sure you're going to like all the answers."

"Whether I like them or not, that's an entirely different matter. Just make sure they're honest. First things first: I know that fugitive story is complete bunk. It was proven to be false yesterday, but with the coverage of the ball and all of the distractions..." He shrugged again and made a what-can-you-do gesture. "Apparently people like talking about pretty dresses more than they do vindicated characters. How about you tell me what's actually been happening?" He sat back in his chair and pulled out a cigar to chew on, though, in deference to the hospital's staff and guests, he didn't light it.

"It starts about a week ago and it'll take some telling, so please be patient." I tightened my arms around my legs and started the story at the inn on my way into town, where I initially ran into the First Character. I rambled through the whole story and, to his credit, he didn't interrupt me once, but made copious notes. When I wrapped up at the point where we were picked up by the ambulances and brought in, he closed his notebook and capped his pen.

"Thank you, Ms. Saltare. Your story seems to mesh with everyone else's renditions. I wish I could get my hands on that First Character, but for now, this'll have to do. Charming was re-sparked within minutes of the explosion, just so you know, though there's still no sign of William."

I almost didn't want to ask, but I had to. "Has there been any news about Ray Bradbury? William's author? I'm afraid the strain of being drained might have been too much."

Columbo shook his mop of unruly hair and frowned around his cigar. "We're not sure yet. It usually takes a while before news like that makes it through to us. We'll keep you updated. For now, young lady, you concentrate on getting better."

I thanked him and he left me to my solitude. The only company I had were the silent nurses who came in to change my bandages and record my temperature and pulse. I fell into a restless sleep early that evening, but was woken sometime past midnight by the soft sigh of raw silk as someone settled into the chair beside my bed.

I opened my eyes to see Kith sitting there, smiling with all the pride of a mother watching her child accepting first prize at the spelling bee. I groaned and turned over, leaving her to smile at my back. "What do you want? We could have used your help there, you know. Or now, clearing all this up. They probably think we blew up the whole place ourselves. And plotted to assassinate Charming."

"I think you did quite well. To start with, neither of you died."

I turned to look her in the eye. "William did." I wanted her to sense how pissed off I was about that fact. He had been a sweet character whose only crime was a desire to lay eyes on the one who had created him.

The damnable woman hardly blinked. "He's alright. He's about to...ah, yes, there's his spark now. They've just caught it. He won't remember anything from his previous run, as usual, but he's as alive now as he was then."

"But he's not the same," I said, bitterness warring with relief in my voice.

"No, and neither is Charming, you'll be happy to hear. No human remembers the old gory stories anymore and The Storyteller has judiciously removed them from his own repertoire. Charming'll be a golden retriever of a prince, genuinely dedicated to the good of his own people now." She wrinkled her nose. "Boring, really."

"I'll take boring, I like boring. Boring is good right now. Kinda done with your brand of excitement." I lay back down, hoping she'd get the hint and leave.

"For the moment." Kith agreed. She hesitated before continuing. "They're clearing you and Jack of any charges this evening. The authorities think there was a massive explosion triggered by the fire effects, and they're painting Charming as the hero who stayed behind to make sure everyone was safe. People are saying that the author connection in the fire was just a gag." She frowned, preoccupied with the thought.

I didn't like the look she was giving me. "But Jack and I are done, aren't we?"

"For the moment," she repeated. "Once you two are feeling rested and repaired, I would very much like you to return to the island to continue your training. As it stands, you two are only half-trained and could end up doing more damage than you realize."

"We'll have to visit Fred, won't we? I assume you'll be carting him back off to his island prison, whether he will or no."

Kith laughed. "Not in the slightest. First, it's not a prison. I simply didn't think he was prepared for dealing with this world. Secondly, he's a full-fledged character now. That stunt he pulled while Charming was connected to the authors? It implanted his matrix into the minds of an awful lot of authors. I'm not quite sure what he's capable of now, but he's been reinforced quite strongly as authors have woken this morning and started writing down the strange dreams they had the night before. I should expect that he will live a very long and healthy life past Austin's need."

"That's something then." My eyelids felt very heavy all of a sudden. I suspected Kith had something to do with that, but I was in no condition to fight back. "Wait, stop that, I'm not done with my questions yet. What about the man?" I felt the sleepiness recede a little bit.

"What man?"

I could hear the frown in her voice, though I was too tired to open my eyes again. "The man, in the building, after Charming blew it up.

Shadowy man standing in rubble. He shouldn't have been there." I yawned and curled up tighter in the bed as the sleepiness came back full force.

"I'll look into it. For now, good night, Sophia. May your story end well." I was too far gone to return the blessing.

♛

The next morning Jack burst into my room before I had managed to choke down the awful hospital breakfast. "Discharge papers! They're letting us out of here, and we're going before they change their mind."

He waved a sheaf of papers at me with his good arm, the other bound into a cast and anchored to his body. The gash at his hairline had more stitches than I thought was probably necessary, but, overall, he looked well enough. I took the papers from him before he wrinkled them in his enthusiasm and flipped through them. Beyond the doctor's recommendation of discharge and instructions for check-in visits, there was also a note from Colombo informing Jack and me that we were no longer under suspicion for the explosion.

I pushed aside the tasteless egg-like blob before me and struggled into the sweats the overly-sympathetic nurse had provided for me. Jack had to help with the t-shirt since my bruised ribs made lifting my arms painful, but within a few minutes I was ready to walk out the door.

I was distracted momentarily by the scar still on my wrist, the delicate quill burned into my skin. I had hoped after our brief conversation last night that Kith would have removed it, but I guess she truly wasn't done with me yet.

I shook off my anger at that. Right now, I didn't care what the Firsts wanted, I needed rest and recuperation. "Where are we off to?" I asked Jack, threading my arm through his good one. He guided me out of the ward and into the sunshine.

"I figured first stop would be that little diner run by Mrs.

Butterworth, then head over to Gustav's for a good solid romp and rest. And then we'll take it from there."

I laughed and pulled him off the pathway to give him a kiss full of as much slink and sensuality as I could muster, which wasn't a whole lot, but seemed to be enough for him. "Sounds perfect, lover. As long as there are no stories, no movies, nothing I need to use my imagination for, I'm good. I don't think I ever want to imagine anything ever again."

He gathered me as close as he could with his cast in the way and murmured into my hair, "But that's where all the fun is."

THE FAIRY TALE FARANDOLE

The Twelve Dancing Princesses
Or, The Shoes That Were Danced to Pieces

Once upon a time, in a land far away, there was a king who had twelve daughters, each more lovely than the last. Every night, the king locked the princesses into their room to protect them, and each morning their shoes had been danced straight through. They refused to answer his questions about where they were going every night, and so the king offered a reward to anyone who could find out where his twelve daughters wore out their shoes. If the young man managed to figure out the riddle, he was to be given his choice of daughters to marry. However, if after three nights, he had failed, then he was to be killed.

Many young princes and knights heard of the challenge and came to test their mettle, and one by one they all died. Eventually, the stream of potential heroes dried up, and the princesses continued to wear out their shoes every night.

A retired soldier, on his way home from battle, heard of the challenge, and thought to himself, *I have nothing to lose but my life, and I am used to risking that for less reward every day.* So he started to make his way to the castle of the king with the many daughters.

Along the way, he met an old woman whose cart had overturned in the road, spilling her harvest of root vegetables across the path. The old soldier stopped to help the woman right the barrow and retrieve her crop, then sat beside her at the side of the road to share his waterskin with her.

"You are a very kind man," the old woman said, "and so I shall offer you some advice. The princesses you are going to watch are tricky ones. Do not drink the wine they offer you at night, for it is drugged. And take this." She removed her cloak and handed it to him. "Put this on when you go to follow them, and you will be invisible to their prying eyes."

The soldier thanked the old woman and continued on his way to the castle. He presented himself to the king while the twelve princesses twittered from the balcony. The youngest princess didn't like how shrewd the soldier looked and said as much, but her oldest sister hushed her. She knew how soldiers liked their wine and believed this one would be no different.

That evening, when the eldest princess offered the soldier a cup of wine before bed, the soldier made a great show of drinking it, but instead poured it out into a potted plant. He then feigned sleep, with deep, even snoring. The princesses, satisfied that he was drugged, began their preparations for their evening adventure. When they were ready, they went to the eldest princess's bed and she rapped three times on the bedframe, which descended through the floor to reveal a steep staircase.

As the princesses began to walk down the stairs, the soldier carefully rose and donned the old woman's cloak, then queued up behind the youngest princess at the end of the line. As he descended the stairs after her, he accidentally trod on her skirt, and she let out a cry, calling, "Someone is behind me on the stairs!" Her sister replied, "It is nothing, you caught your skirt on a nail is all."

At the bottom of the stairs, they came to a forest where the trees were all made of emeralds. The soldier left the path to break a branch off of one of the trees as evidence, and the youngest princess again cried out in alarm at the crack. Her eldest sibling again hushed her, saying, "The princes are simply letting off fireworks to welcome us back."

After the forest of emeralds, they came to trees made entirely of silver, and then another forest where the trees were made entirely of gold. The soldier broke branches from each forest, before continuing behind the princesses. Finally, they reached a lake with an island in the middle, on which rested a glowing palace. On the shore were twelve boats with twelve princes waiting to row their dance partners across the water. The soldier got into the boat with the youngest princess and as the prince began rowing, he said, "My, the boat seems heavier this evening and we're going much slower than usual." The youngest princess peered about herself suspiciously, but her eldest sister simply called for the prince to put his back into it.

Once they landed at the palace, the princesses and princes danced, drank wine, and made merry for the entirety of the evening. The soldier entertained himself by picking up their wine cups and draining them, then laughing at the expression on their faces. He made sure to never drink from the cup of the youngest princess, for she was too observant.

When the princesses began to take leave of their princes, the soldier ran ahead to the boats and climbed into the bow of the eldest princess's boat. When they reached the opposite shore, the soldier ran ahead through the three forests and up the stairs to the princesses' bedroom, took off the cloak, wrapped the three tree branches in the cloak, and pretended to go back to sleep.

When the princesses arrived at the top of the stairs, they checked on the soldier and found him sleeping soundly. "There, you see?" said the eldest princess, "There is nothing to worry about, he is as clueless as the rest." The youngest princess frowned, but said nothing.

The next two nights, the soldier once more followed the princesses down to their princes beyond the three forests and on the other side of the lake. On the final night, the soldier stole one of the golden goblets at the conclusion of the evening. The next morning, when the king called for the soldier to present himself, the twelve princesses congratulated themselves on having fooled yet another man.

"Your majesty," the soldier began, "I must tell you that for the three nights that I slept in the room adjoining the princesses' bedroom, I followed them down a secret stair below the bed of the eldest princess. They went first through a forest of emerald trees, and then through a forest of silver trees, and then a forest of gold trees. We then came to a lake where they were met by twelve princes who rowed them across to a palace on an island where they proceeded to dance the entire night."

The princesses began to argue that the old soldier was foolish and imagining things, but he calmly unwrapped the bundled cloak that he carried and produced the branch of emerald, the branch of silver, and the branch of gold, along with the gilded cup from the palace. The princesses then began to beg their father for mercy for their twelve princes, who were enchanted and trapped in the world below.

The king was gracious in the face of knowledge, and spared the twelve enchanted princes, and allowed the soldier to choose which of his daughters he wished to marry, as he had promised. The soldier chose the eldest daughter, for he was no longer a young man. And they were married that very day, and he was chosen to be the king's heir.

♛

Jack and the Beanstalk

Once upon a time, there was a poor widow who had a son named Jack, and a cow named Milky-White. All they had to survive on was the milk the cow produced, which they took to market to sell. One morning, Milky-White gave no milk, and they were at a loss as to what to do.

First the widow bemoaned their fate, but then Jack offered to find work. "We've tried that before," said the widow, "and nobody would hire you. We must sell the cow and use the money to start a shop or buy crops."

So Jack took the cow to market, but not far out of the gate, he met a funny-looking old man.

"Good morning, Jack," said the old man. "Good morning," Jack replied, wondering how the man knew his name.

"Where are you off to?" inquired the old man.

"Off to market to sell our cow," Jack replied.

"You look the proper sort to sell a cow," the old man opined. "Tell me, do you know how many beans make five?"

Jack, never slow of wit, replied, "Two in each hand and on in the mouth."

"Absolutely right," replied the old man, "and here they are!" He pulled out a handful of strange-looking beans from his pocket and offered them to Jack. "Here, I'll trade you these beans for the cow."

"You have to be kidding," replied Jack.

"Ah, but these are magic beans," the man admonished. "Plant them, and overnight they will be as tall as the sky!"

"Pull the other," said Jack.

"I tell nothing but the truth!" said the old man. "If I tell a lie, you can have your cow back."

"Alright," said Jack, thinking this a fair deal. So he handed over Milky-White's harness, took the beans, and returned home.

"Back already?" asked the widow. "And without Milky-White. How much did you get for her?"

"Beans, mother! Magical beans—" Jack began.

"What?" the widow exclaimed. "You fool, you dolt, you idiot, to give away my Milky-White for a paltry five beans?" The widow proceeded to give Jack a solid drubbing, threw the beans out the window, and sent Jack to bed with nary a thing to eat or drink.

When they woke, the light in the house was dark and shady, and when they looked out the window, they saw the beans had grown into a giant beanstalk that went up and up until it reached the sky.

The beanstalk grew quite close to Jack's window, so he opened up his shutters and started to climb it, just like a ladder. He climbed, and he climbed, and he climbed, and he climbed until at last he reached the sky. When he got above the clouds, he found a road, straight as an arrow, leading to a great big house, and on the doorstep there was a great tall woman.

"Good morning, madam." Jack called, "Would you perhaps have a bit of breakfast for a hungry traveler?"

"It's food you want?" the giant woman admonished, "It's food you'll be if you don't leave now. My husband is a giant and there's nothing he likes better than boys broiled on toast."

"Oh, please, madam," Jack entreated, "I have had nothing to eat for supper and nothing to eat for breakfast, and I may as well be broiled as die of hunger."

The giant's wife was not a bad sort, so she took Jack into the kitchen and gave him some bread, cheese, and milk. But Jack had barely begun to eat when the whole house was shaken by the thump! thump! thump! of something coming.

"Quick, hide!" cried the giantess, and bundled Jack into the oven just as the giant came in.

When he came in, the giant cried:

Fee-fi-fo-fum,
I smell the blood of an Englishman,
Be he alive, or be he dead,
I'll have his bones to grind my bread.

"Nonsense," said the giantess, "you only smell the scraps of that boy you had for yesterday's dinner. Go have a wash and I'll make your breakfast."

Off the giant went and Jack jumped out of the oven, but the giantess whispered, "No, wait till he's asleep, he always has a nap after breakfast."

Sure enough, after he had finished eating, the giant took out his bags of coins to count until he fell asleep and his snore shook the house.

Jack snuck out of the oven, grabbed a bag of coins, tucked it under his arm, and ran for the beanstalk. He threw the gold down, which of course landed in his mother's garden, then climbed down after it. When he reached the earth once again, Jack took the gold to his mother to prove to her that the beanstalk was magic after all.

They lived well on the bag of gold for quite some time, but when they came to the end of it, Jack made up his mind to try his luck again at the top of the beanstalk. Up he climbed until he was once more on the road in front of the great giant house. Same as before, the giantess was standing on the doorstep waiting for her giant husband.

Once more, Jack inquired as to whether there might be a bite of food to have.

"Go away," the giantess exclaimed. "The last time you were here, a bag of gold went missing."

"How strange," said Jack. "I might be able to tell you something about that if you should happen to have a bite to eat on you."

The giantess was curious as to what Jack might say, so she let him in and gave him some bread, cheese, and milk, as she had before. And, as before, he had barely begun to eat when the house began to shake with the thump! thump! thump! of the approaching giant.

All happened as it had before, but after breakfast, the giant asked his wife to bring him the hen that lays the golden eggs. She brought it and the giant commanded it to lay, which it did, after which the giant nodded off.

Jack crept out of the oven, again, and before you could say *Jack Robinson*, he was gone with the hen. As Jack ran to the stalk, he heard the giant asking his wife what she had done with his hen.

When he got home, he showed the widow the wonderful hen, who laid a golden egg every time it was commanded to do so.

Before long, Jack decided to try his luck once more at the top of the beanstalk. This time, he knew better than to go straight to the giant's house. Instead, he hid by the house until he saw the giantess leave to get water and snuck inside and hid straight away in the cabinet beneath the wash basin.

Before long, the thump! thump! thump! of the giant approaching rattled the house, and as he came inside he exclaimed, "Fee-fi-fo-fum, I smell the blood of an Englishman, I swear I do!"

"If you do, it's sure to be the thief who stole your gold and your hen and he'll be hiding in the oven!" the giantess replied. They rushed to the offending appliance, but as Jack was not there, they once more attributed the stench of an Englishman to have come from the giant's leftovers of the night before.

So the giant sat down to breakfast and afterwards commanded his wife to bring him his golden harp, which he commanded to sing. It sang most beautifully until the giant fell asleep and started to snore.

Jack opened the cabinet very carefully and crept to the harp, whereupon he snatched it up and dashed for the door.

But the harp cried out, "Master, master!" and the giant woke in time to see Jack exit the house with his harp in tow. Jack ran as fast as he was able, and by luck and a head start, reached the beanstalk before the giant. The giant was wary of trusting his weight to such an unnatural ladder and so he hesitated until the harp once more cried out, "Master, master!" at which point he began a slow and arduous climb down.

By now, Jack was nearly at the bottom and called out, "Mother, mother! Bring me an axe!"

The widow came rushing out of the house with an axe in hand. Jack took the axe from her and swung with all his might at the beanstalk, which started to shudder. The giant stopped to look down to see what was the matter and let out a great shout. Two more chops of the axe, the giant fell down and broke his crown, and the beanstalk came toppling after.

Jack then showed his mother the magic harp, and between concerts with the harp and selling the golden eggs, Jack and his mother became very rich, Jack married a great princess, and they all lived happily ever after.

THE ROYAL CHARMING FAMILY TREE

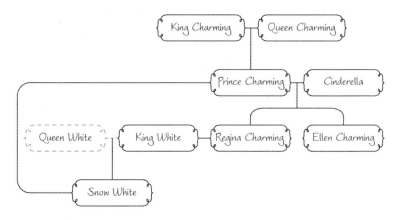

ACKNOWLEDGMENTS

There are many people whose efforts go into building a book, and it's hard to give them all their due. First, my husband, who started reading drafts with these characters in them before we were even dating, and proceeded to marry me even though I asked him to read the novel four times. Next is my family, without whom I would never have had the courage to pursue being a writer, or have met my wonderful editor...which leads me to everyone at Parkhurst Brothers. They were kind enough to entertain my vision for this novel, in both the writing and design, and I can't thank them enough for that. The next round of thanks goes to my friends and their tireless ability to listen to me go on and on about this world and these characters while I was working things out, especially Kristen Brown who proofread it enough to make it passable. Lastly, I want to thank every author I've ever read since a little part of you is in these stories, even if you can't see it right away. Trust me, your stories — and your characters — are very much here and alive.

AUTHOR ESSAY

When I was a young child, my family moved quite a bit because of my father's work. If we lived in a house longer than two years, it was a minor miracle. It was hard to make friends at school because I knew we'd be leaving at some point—so I made friends with books instead. You could take books with you from state to state, and books never stopped writing letters. I spent most of my free time with authors like Tamora Pierce, Bruce Coville, Ray Bradbury, Isaac Asimov, and Robert A. Heinlein. I read their books so many times that the spines were broken and lay flat on the lunchroom tables; pages had been so repeatedly dog-eared that some of the words were coming off. I loved my books and the characters within them, and I learned most of my life lessons from them, rather than through interactions with my peers. I knew all about handling bullies from Tamora Pierce, and scary moments from Ray Bradbury, and well, if the robot revolution came, Asimov had me covered.

It didn't take me long to try writing stories of my own. I believe the first one I wrote was sometime before I turned 10, closer to 5 if the handwriting is any indication (yes, I still have it — my mother saves everything). It was about how the butterfly got its colors. Can you tell I'd read a few Just So stories that year? That was the first in a long line of stories, written for fun or for class, and two journals worth of horrific poetry. There are a few not-so-bad pieces, but most of it is pre-pubescent angst and should never again see the light of day, trust me. By the time I got to high school and our final culminating project, I managed to sweet-talk my teachers into letting me work on a novel while researching the publishing industry. It almost didn't seem fair how fun my project was. While my friends were griping and groaning, I was gleefully going home to my computer every night to explore a new scene with my characters. This partial novel (they only required 40 pages) is sitting at the bottom of a drawer until I can read it without laughing quite so hard at how poorly it's written.

When I was accepted to Willamette University after high school, I actually thought I wanted to be an anthropologist, specializing in ancient and bizarre religions. I reasoned that no one actually made money at writing, and I loved Indiana Jones and his ilk, so why not join the ranks of those studying the long-dead? However, I took my first anthro course, finished it with an A, and promptly applied to be a psychology major instead. I learned rather quickly that the cinematic version of studying antiques was way more entertaining than real life, as with most things. But the Intro to Psych course I took my first semester fascinated me. I couldn't get enough of learning how people's heads worked, mine included. I've struggled with anxiety most of my life (coping with books, writing, and crafts of all kinds) and learning the hows and whys of the human brain was a whole new experience. Then in my sophomore year, I took a creative writing class because I needed the art credit and I missed writing. I told myself it would be a one-time thing. I was going to be a psychologist now, earn a decent living, and make a difference. Then I entered Michael Strelow's classroom.

I really should have known better. There's no such thing as dabbling in writing. It's all or nothing; at the end of the semester, I was a declared double major in Psychology and English. I loved them both, and figured I could work out some way to make them complement each other. And I did really well in both areas, even earning some awards from the Psychology department, but when it came time for theses, my true passion became clear. For psychology, I orchestrated a study of domestic abuse survivors and the relationship between Stockholm Syndrome and PTSD. For English, I took a seminar on Grimm's Fairy Tales, which allowed me to do a creative reinterpretation of the tales for my thesis. I'll let you decide which one had me screaming at a computer and throwing my phone against the wall when the statistics program wouldn't work, and which one I finished early, longer than was strictly necessary, and beautifully bound. (Hint: it involved wicked stepmother queens and big bad wolves.)

At that point, I decided that no matter how slim the chances of actually making a living at writing were, I had to give it a try. I applied for a few creative writing masters programs, and was accepted at Emerson College in Boston. It was my dream writing school, one of the best outside of New York or L.A., two cities I just don't get along with. I immediately accepted, and spent the next two years honing both my writing skills in class, and my book design skills in publishing courses while working on the graduate-student-run journal, *The Redivider*. Because Emerson's faculty are primarily realistic fiction folks, I tucked my undergrad English thesis away and buckled down to start work on what became my debut novel, *Undeliverable*. It was a fiction novel about a father whose son went missing a year prior to the novel's start, and it chronicles his obsession with the search, how it comes to destroy his life, and, finally, the beginnings of his recovery. I spent years both on the writing and editing of it, and finally published it independently in March 2014, to excellent reviews from Kirkus and others. Many people ask me why I chose to publish *Undeliverable* independently—it's because I was determined that part of the proceeds would go to the National Center for Missing and Exploited Children. My family raised me to give back whenever possible, and this felt particularly appropriate. Independent publishing allowed me to make good on this decision, and give more of the profits away than if I were splitting the proceeds with a publisher and agent.

While I was getting *Undeliverable* ready for publication, I was already hard at work on two other projects: *The Ozite Cycle* and *Mark of the Storyteller*. The former is a series of five illustrated novellas following the journey of Thea through the land of Oz, well after Dorothy's time. It's noir-ish in its flavor, and the illustrations by Jason Morgado are simply beautiful. The first one was released in August 2014, and the second is slated for November 2015. During this time, I also had several short stories published or scheduled to be published, including in an anthology of space operas and on NPR's *To The Best of our Knowledge*.

And then we come round to *Mark of the Storyteller*. A few years ago, I decided I wanted to see what this NaNoWriMo nonsense was all about, so I pulled out that old English thesis (originally titled "Interviews with Evil") and started developing it into a full-fledged novel. I had a ton of work to do to set up the world's rules and physical laws, as well as figuring out just what this Charming fellow was really up to. It took several months of planning and self-imposed writing prompts to get to the core of what I wanted the story to become, and then November hit. I made it to the 50k words without too much trouble, and then promptly set the story aside for three months. The one thing the NaNoWriMo folks fail to mention is just how draining writing that much in a single month can be. Once I had paused long enough to catch my breath, I picked the story up and finished it off, giving it the title *Less Than Charming*.

While I was working on this story, I came to realize that what I had was not just an individual novel, but the beginning of a series, an exploration into what it truly means to be human and what role imagination plays in that. As of right now, I'm not sure how many books will be in the *Mark of the Storyteller* series, but I can tell you that I have the second planned out, and I know the precise character arc for Sophia across the series. All I have to do is figure out how long it's going to take us to get there.

♔

For more information on Rebecca's writing,
please visit her website at http://rebeccademarest.com

Author Q&A

Q: Was there a point in your life that prompted your desire to write, or have you always wanted to be an author?

A: I wrote my first story pretty much as soon as I learned to write. (Its called "How the Butterfly got its Colors," and I still have it. Thanks, Mom.) So you could say I always had the bug. Get it, bug, butterfly? But I went through periods in my childhood where I was determined to have a range of careers, including sculptress (verbatim), veterinarian, anthropologist, and forensic psychologist. However, in college, as I was taking my psychology courses, I slipped in a creative writing course and it really showed me that I didn't want to do anything but write, and hang the monetary consequences. The satisfaction of getting the words on the paper just right and then getting to share them with others was far better than the thought of spending the rest of my life in unending meetings or dealing with other people's problems. If I was going to deal with problems, I'd rather it be my characters' problems, where I had the benefit of both causing them and knowing exactly how to solve them.

Q: How do you come up with the names of characters in your books?

A: The naming of characters is actually rather difficult for me. My go-to website is *http://www.behindthename.com,* where I will spend hours going back and forth between names, looking at their meaning and their prevalence during the era and area in which the story takes place. I take into account their role in the story, the various possible meanings of the names, and so on. You'll find that if you look up most of the names I use in my stories, they have additional meaning in relationship to the plot.

Q: Where do you go for inspiration when you're feeling blocked?

A: News sites, actually. Articles about bleeding glaciers, people hijacking barrels of maple syrup, or the fact that the ancient Egyptians made jewelry out of meteorites can all give my imagination a boost. Also, turning off your music and actually paying attention to the world around you while you walk, including eavesdropping on your fellow commuters, can provide some outlandish leads.

Q: What's the strangest thing that has ever inspired you?

A: The absolute strangest thing was an article about a lithopedion, or stone baby. A lithopedion is the result of an ectopic pregnancy that self-terminates after the 14th week. The mother's body can't reabsorb the tissues, so it calcifies the fetus to prevent it from causing harm to the mother. I couldn't help it, the idea just grabbed hold of my brain and I couldn't shake it, and it produced the short story "Rock-a-bye Baby."

Q: Tell us about an inspirational figure in your life.

A: While I have found many of my writing instructors and friends inspirational, the woman who is the most inspirational would have to be my mother. She has not led the easiest of lives and has dealt with a series of genetic and environmentally-induced health problems, many of which required surgery and extensive recoveries. But through all of this, she has never lost her sense of adventure, determination, or love. In fact, she started her first business just a couple years ago as a professional storyteller, and has reached her five-year goals four years early. If she can deal with all of the health issues, two kids, and a husband who traveled extensively for work, and come out the other side with enough energy to devote to a whole new career, then I can do anything.

Q: What are some books in your genre that have inspired you?

A: This is a really hard question to answer because I read a lot of books each year. In the literary genre, I find the work of George Saunders, Scott Nadelson, Steve Yarbrough, Tom Perotta, and a handful of others to be greatly inspiring; mostly modern literary authors. In the speculative fiction genre, I draw a lot of inspiration from Tamora Pierce, Robert A. Heinlein, Patricia C. Wrede, Jasper Fforde, and Terry Pratchett.

Q: What are some words that you live by?

A: Be and not seem. This is one of Emerson's philosophies, and I've had it on my wall as long as I can remember. In my life and in my writing, I try to stay true to myself and my ideals. Do not pretend you are a good person, let your work speak for itself. Do not pretend you are competent, actually go out and do the hard work to make it true.

Q: Tell us about a typical day in your world.

A: My day job is a basic 9-5, working as a technical illustrator for O'Reilly Media, drawing flowcharts of programming and networking. Its actually rather fun and not only provides a steady paycheck and benefits, but it is also a fairly creative endeavor. But before and after work, my life belongs to the written word. I'm constantly reading, on breaks at work, before work, before bed, and the rest of my time is filled with my writing, book designing, and crafting. Right now, this rotates between the sequel to *Undeliverable*, the sequel to *Thea of Oz*, the next *Mark of the Storyteller* book, or a series of sci-fi novellas called *Ask Corporate*. Basically, I work on whatever either grabs me that evening, or has a deadline looming.

Q: When you start a writing project, do you outline first or do you allow the story to progress organically?

A: I can't write without an outline, though outline is a bit of a strong word. I have a scaffolding, a set course of benchmarks I know my characters need to hit, and essentially how I'm going to get them there, and what emotional depths I need to drive them to, to get them to take the actions I want them to take, but I don't map out all the small details of each section before I start writing. Those I let come naturally, and I'm happy to adjust my outline or character concept if something fun comes up. For instance, I was writing along in a scene in my first novel, *Undeliverable,* when all of a sudden Sylvia starts getting really angry at Ben for something he said and I had to sit back and ask my subconscious what in heck it thought it was doing. It turns out I had been working on an even stronger backstory for Sylvia than I had even realized, so I made a few adjustments to the plot to account for it and it made her character even stronger.

Q: What is your view on ebooks versus paper books? Do you have a personal preference?

A: I am a fan of getting a book into just about every format possible. I am of the firm opinion that a book should be available in every possible format — regular print, digital, large-print, audio, braille, etc. — to allow maximum accessibility. With the advances of technology today, there is no reason that any person should be unable to obtain or read a story because of a lack of bookstores or Internet access, or physical disability. For me, the priority is to share my story with as many people as possible, and help my community with my writing.

As for my personal preference, it totally depends on the kind of book I am sitting down to read. If it is a book that I suspect will have a fun design (*Mr. Penumbra's 24 Hour Bookstore* actually glows in the dark) or that I want to cherish and share, I'll buy a hard copy. Books that I suspect I will only read once, or are only available in digital editions, I'm happy to read electronically. Actually, my body prefers it. For years I suffered from carpal tunnel, which I attributed to all the typing, designing, and percussion playing that I did. It turns out that I read so much that holding up books on a near-constant basis was actually the bigger problem! A digital reader really helps take the strain off of my wrists.

♛

COLOPHON

The display fonts are SEASIDE RESORT by Nick Curtis and
GLOBE GOTHIC by Morris Fuller Benton & Joseph Warren Phinney

The body font is *Athelas* by TypeTogether.

WEBSITES OF INTEREST

www.rebeccademarest.com
www.parkhurstbrothers.com
www.storynet.org